Praise for Courtney Walsh

Is It Any Wonder
"[A] pleasing tale of lost love, forgiveness, and rekindled romance. . .Walsh's wholesome plot weaves faith elements nicely as Louisa relies on her faith to make sure all is finally made well. Walsh will please her fans and surely gain new ones with this excellent inspirational."
~ PUBLISHERS WEEKLY

"A story of forgiveness, hope, and enduring ties that proves it's never too late for a second chance. . . Courtney Walsh once again shines as a master storyteller." ~ KRISTY WOODSON HARVEY, *USA TODAY* BESTSELLING AUTHOR OF *FEELS LIKE FALLING*

If For Any Reason
"Second chances and new discoveries abound in this lovely tale from Walsh, featuring a nostalgic romance set against the backdrop of Nantucket. Readers of Irene Hannon will love this."
~ PUBLISHERS WEEKLY

Just Let Go
"Walsh's charming narrative is an enjoyable blend of slice-of-life and small-town Americana that will please Christian readers looking for a sweet stc
~ PUBLISHERS W

"Original, romantic, and emotional.

the typical romance novel. . . . She makes you feel for all the characters, sometimes laughing and sometimes crying along with them."
~ ROMANTIC TIMES

Just Look Up

"[A] sweet, well-paced story. . . Likable characters and the strong message of discovering what truly matters carry the story to a satisfying conclusion."~ PUBLISHERS WEEKLY

"Just Look Up by Courtney Walsh is a compelling and consistently entertaining romance novel by a master of the genre."
~ MIDWEST BOOK REVIEW

"This novel features a deeply emotional journey, packaged in a sweet romance with a gentle faith thread that adds an organic richness to the story and its characters." ~ SERENA CHASE, USA TODAY HAPPY EVER AFTER BLOG

Also by Courtney Walsh

MERRY EX-MAS

a novel

COURTNEY WALSH

Sweethaven
Press

For everyone who has ever wanted a second chance.
And for everyone who didn't but got one anyway.

Visit Courtney Walsh's website at www.courtneywalshwrites.com

Merry Ex-Mas

Cover designed by Courtney Walsh

The author is represented by Natasha Kern of Natasha Kern Literary, Inc.

PO Box 1069, White Salmon, WA 98672

Merry Ex-Mas is a work of fiction. Where real people, events, establishments, organizations, or locales appear, they are used fictitiously. All other elements of the novel are drawn from the author's imagination.

For information about special discounts for bulk purchases, please contact Sweethaven Press at: courtney@courtneywalsh.com

Library of Congress Cataloging-in-Publication Data

Printed in the United States of America

Chapter One

Marin

"**M**arin, you ready?"

I glance up at my producer Steph, who looks completely out of place standing in my parents' front yard. Steph grew up in New York, and is exactly what I imagine a New Yorker should look like. Her long, dark hair falls in waves to her shoulders, and a neatly tailored gray wool coat covers a black and white striped shirt and a pair of form-fitting black ankle pants. She's added a camel-colored scarf and boots to complete her look.

She's decidedly "big city" and not "small town." For her, Pleasant Valley is like visiting a foreign land.

The big white farmhouse behind her is glowing with white twinkle lights ("classier than colored lights," my mother, The Queen of Christmas, has declared), and a lit-up wreath hangs from every window.

If I'm honest, I also feel out of place standing in my parents' yard. I glance down at my own sleek outfit—a black blazer layered over a loose blouse and dress pants. I'm wearing an extra skin of make-up, which I've mostly gotten used to. Mostly.

"And you're sure your parents won't mind us barging in?" My cameraman, Danny, hoists the camera up onto his shoulder and begins fiddling with the focus, adjusting a few knobs.

I turn and glance at the front door, which is flanked by two small, twinkling evergreen trees. A real evergreen wreath with a big, red bow is fixed to the center of the black door. It looks like something out of *Country Living* magazine.

"Not a chance," I say to Danny. "She's going to eat this up." Plus, she's been asking me to come home for eight years.

"Okay, because some people don't love being on camera."

Danny obviously doesn't know Lydia McGrath. How many people test out combinations of scented candles to get the right mix of pine tree and cinnamon? How many people clear the whole month of December to dedicate every free minute to preserving their town's Christmas traditions? How many people have an ornately decorated Christmas tree in every room of the house?

Truth be told, she could probably have her own HGTV show. "You Can't Spell LYDIA without DIY" or something. This whole thing is right up her alley.

Steph claps her hands. "Let's get this filmed so we can go find something to eat."

I chuckle. "It's cute you think my mother is going to let you go somewhere else for dinner."

I start toward the door, shutting away uncomfortable memories in a box with a tight lid on a shelf in the back of my mind.

"Are you nervous?" Steph's brows draw together in confusion. "All you've done for as long as I've known you is talk about," she holds her hands up like addressing a marquee, "*Christmas in Pleasant Valley.*" She pauses to tuck the microphone wire in my coat. "It's nauseating, really."

"Christmas is nauseating? What are you, the Grinch?"

She looks at me, humorless. "No. I'm cold." After a moment, a smile finds its way to her face. She gives me a slight push and says, "This is why the viewers love you. And this is why we're here. And also so you can show Tim you're the right person to take over *Good Day Denver*...right?"

I wince and give her an "ooh, ya caught me" gesture. It was true. I *did* glamorize Christmas in Pleasant Valley. I talked about it every year. At my desk. In the break room. Behind the scenes.

And eventually, on the air.

People listened. Viewers began asking questions about my Christmas traditions. About my parents and their big farmhouse. People took a genuine interest in my life.

I was connecting.

That's probably why Tim, our producer back in Denver, gave me this shot in the first place. If viewers are interested just from me talking about it on air, imagine what kind of response I'd get if I actually *went* there. *At Christmas.*

A live, two-week-long, behind-the-scenes deep dive into my favorite Christmas traditions. I could prove that I know how to find and tell really good stories, and in turn?

I could be the new host of *Good Day Denver*.

Me.

The host of my own show.

I'll admit, I've already designed the posters. I've got files and files of story ideas and ways to make the show better. It's a huge opportunity, and I can't afford to blow it.

But women like me tend to operate our lives like we've got a browser running with twenty-seven tabs open. There's a lot of processing going on in the background.

Now that I'm here, standing outside the door of my childhood home, there's a twinge of *Oh, no, what am I doing?!* I'm not so sure I want to share. Family, traditions, relationships, any of it.

Home for me, or for anyone, really, is not without its complications.

This whole "Home for the Holidays" series was Steph's brainchild, but I was the one who ran my mouth like I was an integral part of Pleasant Valley's Christmas festivities. I touted myself as the Princess of Plum Pudding when, really, I'm more of a prodigal daughter.

What did I actually know about Christmas in Pleasant Valley anymore?

"Marin." Steph is wearing the face of a petulant child who doesn't want to be dragged to another store.

"I'm ready," I half-lie. "It'll be good."

Focus on the good things, Marin. My mind spins. *Good things. Good things.*

1. I am going to make my mom's whole December by showing up to surprise her.
2. I'm about to eat better than I have in eight years. I can practically taste the maple-apple upside-down breakfast cake right now.
3. Nowhere else on earth makes me feel more relaxed than sitting in the living room at my parents' house.
4. I won't be alone.

I pause at that thought. It feels so morbid.

It's not like I've spent the last eight Christmases eating Cinnamon Life and mindlessly playing Solitaire while Hallmark movies play in the background.

I do have friends—I just haven't spent Christmas with a single one of them.

Through the window, I catch a glimpse of a fire glowing in

the fireplace. The tree isn't up yet, which is odd, actually. Maybe that means I'll get to unearth all my old ornaments, a memory attached to every single one.

At that, my stomach sinks. Some memories are better left wrapped up in a box in the basement.

Danny shifts. "All right, let's do this, before someone hears us sneaking around out here and ruins the surprise."

I nod as Steph checks my microphone—again—and my hair and makeup.

This is good for you, Marin. You're tearing off the Band-aid. You've been away long enough.

When everything is good to go, Danny flips the switch on the light attached to his camera and gives me the thumbs-up.

I also flip a switch. I'm on camera. And we're going live.

Steph counts me down, giving me the signal when we've connected to the station's social media livestream.

I flash my best smile. "For years now, you've heard me talk about Christmas in my hometown, Pleasant Valley, Illinois, and I'm excited to tell you that this year, I'm home for the holidays. The warmth of the fireplace, the smell of my mother's kitchen, and the best part of all," I lean in toward the camera and whisper, "*you all get to come with me.*"

I feel tension in my shoulders. I need to relax or I'll come off looking like I'm hiding a poison apple in my cloak.

I start toward the door, talking over my shoulder to the camera. "I'm excited to introduce you all to The Queen of Christmas—otherwise known as my mom." I stop and turn, full on, talking with my hands. "She has no idea I'm home, and while we're here, I'm going to introduce you to some of my favorite Pleasant Valley Christmas traditions. And believe me, there are many. . .and they are *marvelous*." I smile wide at the camera, hoping it doesn't look as forced as it feels. "But first, let's surprise my family, shall we?"

I rub my gloved hands together for effect, even though it has to be about fifty degrees outside. "It's two weeks before Christmas, but in the McGrath family, the holiday season officially begins the day after Thanksgiving. It's like the changeover at Disney World, where we go to sleep Thanksgiving night and wake up to a house decked out in twinkle lights and holly sprigs. I haven't been home in a few years," I pause slightly, surprised at my honesty, and quickly recover. "But my family's love of Christmas is one thing I can always count on."

I glance over at Steph, whose expression seems to say, *"Yeah, yeah, Christmas cheer, blah, blah."*

I love Steph. I love her candidness in a profession that is predicated on looking good and pretending everything's fine on camera. And I know her well enough to know that she's not being mean.

At the same time, I refuse to entertain her seasonal grumpiness. I grew up loving Christmas and being away all these years hadn't dulled my appreciation for the holidays.

It's just. . .more complicated now.

For instance, if I poke my head around to the other side of the house, I'll see the gazebo. And beyond the yard, the dock of our lake and the boathouse, hazed in the soft light of the moon. I'll remember chilly nights ice skating when it finally got cold enough for the water to freeze. I'll hear the echoes of laughter carried on the wind. I'll see my dad's Wishing Tree at the center of the lake and think about all the wishes that came true over the years.

And all the ones that didn't.

So, I don't poke my head around the side of the house.

Instead, I will focus on one task at a time.

The task at present is to ring the doorbell, which for some

reason my poised hand is unable to do. I can practically feel the angst radiating off of Steph from behind me.

I turn toward Danny, who is leaned to one side from behind the camera, eyebrows raised as if to check that I'm okay.

Am I?

I could try and convince myself this is just another assignment—but I know better. This is so much more than that.

I'm being dramatic. I'm a professional. I've got this. Without giving it another thought, I ring the bell.

No turning back now.

I breathe deep, paste on my TV smile, and prepare myself for whatever chaos is about to ensue.

I imagine my mother's shouts of joy. I can almost feel the warmth of my father's tight hugs. I picture myself right back in their living room, surrounded by laughter, and for a fleeting moment, I'm angry that I ever gave this up.

There's the sound of footsteps approaching the door.

"I can hear them coming," I say to my invisible audience.

This is it—there's only going to be one genuine take of my mom's reaction, and this is my chance to shine. I raise my shoulders and eyebrows in anticipation at the camera and turn back toward the door, bubbling with expectancy.

But when the door opens, the world comes to a screeching halt.

It's not my sweet little mother in her flour-decked Christmas apron standing on the other side.

"Mom, what is my ex-boyfriend doing at your house for Christmas?!"

Chapter Two

Marin

I stare at the grown-up version of the boy who broke my heart eight years ago.

"Mare? What. . .?" I see his eyes dart to the camera, then back to me. He breathes out a chuckle that's a third embarrassed, a third shocked, and a third terrified.

It's the same look that a mom would give a checkout lady when her toddler repeats the swear word he heard on the car ride there.

"Max?" I say his name, but it comes out in a whisper.

My mind races. What is he doing here?

And why is he answering the door?

"Marin? What. . .what are you doing here?" His eyes, gray in the twinkle lights poking through the evergreen garland, are fixed on me, and I almost—almost—have to look away.

A half-laugh escapes like someone sat on a Whoopie cushion, and I do nothing to gather myself. "What am *I* doing here?" I search for some kind of coherent thought. "This is *my* house!"

I tilt my head at him. "What are *you* doing here?"

He looks both confused and amused for a moment, like watching a middle school version of *It's A Wonderful Life.* "I'm. . .here for Christmas." His eyes dart to the camera behind me again, but I ignore it. I am too busy focusing on how nonchalantly he said he was here—in *my* childhood home— with *my* parents—for *Christmas.* "Are you filming this?"

"Duh," I say, without thinking.

Behind me, Steph clears her throat—a reminder that I am still live on camera and need to maintain my on-air persona.

"Hello? Max? Did you get the door? Who is it?" My mom calls out again.

Oh. I've missed her. A lot, it seems.

Seconds later, she's standing in the entryway, staring at me. It's like her eyes have gone out of focus, and she's not sure what she's looking at.

And then, as if she's just put on a pair of reading glasses and can finally see clearly, her entire face lights up. "Marin!" She shouts my name, then pushes past Max and draws me into a tight, warm, familiar hug.

In other circumstances, I would've relished this moment. After all, it has been too long since I've been properly hugged. But as it is, I can't even enjoy it because there is a single question racing through my mind—and it needs an answer.

I pull from my mother's embrace. Without thinking about the camera, Danny, Steph, or the potentially thousands of viewers, I say, exasperated, "Um. . .*Mom?*"

She looks at me, then at Max, then back at me, eyes wide. Her smile fades, as if she'd only just that moment realized this could be a problem. "Oh. Oh!"

I turn to the camera, which is still blinking the red light on the top, indicating a live feed. "Never a dull moment at my house at Christmas! We are just full of surprises!"

"Wait. Is this live?" my mom practically shouts. "People

can see us right now?" She immediately starts fussing with her hair and her apron.

"Maybe we could turn the camera off?" Max suggests.

On some level, I agree—there is no reason to film this. However, I hear myself say, "You can keep filming, Danny," and I think it's more out of a sheer need to disagree with Max than anything else.

"Max," I say, half turning to him and half turning to the camera, "maybe you should go back inside?" I try not to glare at him.

"Oh, Marin," Mom says, her tone radiating disappointment. "Max is—"

"Not staying?" I cut in, secretly thankful for the college improv classes that have helped me be quick on my feet.

My mom looks bemused. "You and Max are ancient history. Surely, we can all be civil by now?" She turns full-on to the camera, and to my horror, says, "They were friends long before they dated, just inseparable, these two." She waves. "Hello everyone! I'm Lydia, welcome to our home!"

I'm dying. I'm literally dying in front of a live audience.

"What's all the commotion? Lyddie, who's at the door?" My father hollers this before appearing in the entryway. Danny swings the camera toward my Dad and as the light hits him in the face, he holds up a hand to block it. "What the. . .! Who in the. . ."

I cut him off before he can bless my viewers with a few colorful adjectives.

"Dad! Hey, it's. . ." I hold out my arms to the side, as if to say, "*here I am!*"

"Marin? We didn't know you were coming!" He steps out onto the porch and messes up my hair with all the gentility of a WWE wrestler. "There's a Star Trek marathon on, you're just in time!"

I quickly try to tame my nest, hotly aware that this is still live.

"We're having cheesy potato soup for dinner tonight, Marin," Mom says, as if I care about food when Max is standing in her entryway. "You're just in time! And of course, your friends will join." She turns to Danny. "Are you hungry? You look like you like to eat."

"Mom!" I am properly horrified.

Her eyes go wide. "What? It's a compliment. Food is one of life's simplest pleasures."

Danny chuckles, clearly not offended. "I do like to eat, Mrs. McGrath. And Marin says you're the best cook."

She points at him, which means she is essentially pointing directly into the camera. "You call me Lydia, young man, or you'll be out on your backside."

I stand and watch the scene as it starts to unravel before me, the comments overlapping like we're in an episode of *Parenthood*.

Dad: "Will you stop threatening the guy? You don't even know him!"

Max: "Maybe we should move this inside?"

Mom: "Oh, I'm just teasing. He looks like he appreciates a good meal, that's all I'm saying."

I now understand why animals gnaw their own limbs off.

Steph gives me the ten second sign, and it's like finally feeling the Tilt-a-Whirl slow down at the carnival.

I face the camera, and with my best effort, try to close it out.

"What a beginning to this amazing season, and more surprises are, for sure, on their way—even ones more shocking than my boyfr. . ."

I stop mid-word I mentally take a sledgehammer to my brain for slipping *that* one up.

". . .EX. . .boyfriend. . .helping kick things off!" I clap my hands together. "It's all leading up to our big Home for the Holidays special on Christmas Eve, so mark your calendars—you don't want to miss it! I'm Marin McGrath, signing off and wishing you all a wonderful night."

I can feel the three people behind me in the doorway give a little wave and a smile.

"And. . .we're clear." Steph says, giving a thumbs-up. I turn around, ready for a frank discussion, when Steph steps into the light. "Hi Lydia, I'm Steph, Marin's producer." She sticks her hand out toward my mother. All business, that one.

"So, you're the one keeping our daughter from coming home at Christmas. . ." Dad crosses his arms as he says this, and I shoot Steph a look that begs her not to tattle.

Steph gets the hint, but judging by the knowing expression on his face, so does Max.

I try to breathe. It's hard knowing that Max—my first (and only) love—is standing only inches away. On my porch.

It was hard not remembering all the other times we'd stood or sat on this porch. That porch swing. Those steps. That railing. Every single one held a memory of us.

Those pesky unwanted memories I've been trying to forget assault me now, like a bully in a middle school bathroom.

I try not to look at Max, but a single glance is enough to tell me what I wish I didn't know. Age had certainly been kind to my once-thin, slightly scrawny ex-boyfriend. Now, Max looks taller. Broader. More rugged. Like he'd lived more life and he'd lived it well. And he's tan. Who is tan in December?

Inwardly, I sigh. Max looks good. Really good. And now that I'm aware of it, how do I make myself forget?

Darn him.

"Maybe we should go inside," Max says again.

"We? There's a we?" I snap. It's the only way I can see

12

getting through this unscathed—to shield myself behind anger. And despite the years and the distance, the anger is still there.

I'd balled it up, bagged it, and buried it, but shocker—it's easy to unearth.

"Marin Josephine McGrath!" If my mother had been wearing pearls, she would've been clutching them.

"It's okay, Lydia," Max says. "I'll go get the bread bowls out of the oven."

Now he's helping with dinner? My mother has some explaining to do.

I force myself not to watch him walk away, even though I really, really want to. Part of me is enthralled—even now, after all we'd been through, after he broke my heart and I vowed to never, ever forgive him.

Once he's gone, my mother's expression turns slightly sheepish.

Oh, so she does realize this is a horrible surprise.

"I told you this would catch up to you eventually, Lyddie," Dad says with the shake of his head.

Eventually? What did that mean?

"Oh, shush, James. Marin is an adult." She turns to me and rubs my arms, talking about me in the third person. "She will be perfectly fine once she understands."

I tilt my head. "I will be what when I what?" I look at my dad, begging for some kind of mental life preserver.

My father tosses me a dubiously raised eyebrow and shakes his head again. "Come on in, Marin's friends," he says, waving for Danny and Steph to follow him.

They do, which leaves me standing on the porch alone with The Queen of Christmas. Who, at the moment, I am working very hard not to strangle with the pre-lit pinecone and berry-flocked garland affixed to the window.

"Marin. . ." Mom pulls the door closed as she says this.

"Mom?! What in the world!"

She puts up her hands. "To be fair, I didn't know you were coming."

I look at her, incredulous. "That's what you're going with?"

She shrugs. "I mean, it's not like you've been here in eight years, so you know. . ."

Low blow, Mom. True. But low.

She sits on the top porch steps. "He really didn't have anywhere else to go. What did you expect me to do?"

"Oh, I don't know, Mom," I sit next to her. "Maybe not host my ex-boyfriend for Christmas?"

"He was my best friend's son long before he was your boyfriend," Mom says pointedly.

I stare out across the dark yard. It was true. My mother and Jenny Shaw-Weber were the kind of best friends who didn't just talk about growing up and having houses next door to each other—they actually did it. Which meant that my brother Teddy and I had grown up with Max. We might as well have been triplets.

Never mind that once we turned fifteen, everything shifted between "M + M," as we were so affectionately called by our parents. That was the year I started to notice boys.

That was the year I started to notice Max.

He would catch me watching him sometimes, and I'd play it off and call him "weird-looking" or a "goof," or something. In reality, I was admiring his looks, his humor, his kindness, his smile.

And then I started noticing him watching me, too, like I was a puzzle he was trying to solve.

Max could read me better than anyone. He knew what I was thinking before I did half the time. Our little kid relationship shifted, and when it did, I was a goner. I fell hard. And fast. And with my whole heart.

Six years we'd been together. We were supposed to get married. Have kids. Our moms were supposed to be grandmas together.

But life had other plans. It was cruel that way.

"Marin," my mother puts an arm around me and pulls me close. "You're home."

I cross my arms over my chest and lean into her, drawing in a deep breath. "Surprised?"

Mom squeezes again. "Yes! It's the best surprise! I'm going to make all of your favorite foods. I'll start the cinnamon rolls tonight. You're never going to want to leave."

That's what I'm afraid of.

"I'm going to gain twenty pounds in the next two weeks, aren't I?" I say, attempting levity.

"I hope so. You're too thin." I look at her, and see that she's absolutely serious. "Now, can we go eat dinner?" She stands.

"Is he. . .Mom, is Max staying?" I chew the inside of my bottom lip, a nervous habit I'd picked up from the woman standing before me on the dimly lit porch.

Mom stills, then straightens her apron. "Yes."

"Until Christmas?"

"Yes." Mom watches me. "I know it's a little awkward, but isn't it time to put the past in the past?"

If only "the past" wasn't so heart-breaking.

I stand. "Is there any way you can just make him go?" I feel like I'm fifteen all over again, already knowing the answer.

"Marin." Mom's voice is stern. "You know I'm not going to ask him to leave. Same way I won't ask you to leave."

I frown. "It's a little different. I haven't been here in a while." I try humor. "Plus. I'm your daughter. And I'm your favorite."

She smiles, gently saying, "Max is part of this family too."

I look down. That stings a little.

"Come on in, the soup is my best batch yet." Mom says that about everything she makes. Every cake or souffle was "the best one yet" and oddly, it was always true. "Are you coming?"

I smile. It's genuine. I've missed this, and her, and the food, and the lights, all of it.

"Sure, Mom," I say. But my head is spinning. How am I going to survive two weeks with Max?

A whole holiday season.

With Max.

Mom puts her hand on the doorknob, but stops. "Max is. . ." She sighs. "He's a good boy, Marin. And he feels terrible about what happened between you two. But it was a long time ago. Maybe you can find a way to be friends again?"

"Oh, I don't think so, Mom," I say, quickly. "I'm not in the habit of forgiving people who rip my heart out, throw it on the road, and then run over it with their car," and then I add, "and then back up just to run over it again."

Mom rolls her eyes. "Oh, daughter, you are so dramatic. No wonder you went into television." She walks inside, leaving me standing on the porch contemplating spending the night at the hotel with Steph.

But then I hear my dad's laugh coming from inside.

And for whatever reason, that sound is enough to realize. . .I'm home.

With Max.

Chapter Three

Max

I should've known better.

I mean, I *really* should've known better. I'm the kind of guy that mentally kicks himself when doing something stupid—which is often—but this one requires a proper beat-down.

Did I actually believe that I wouldn't run into her, staying here?

Come on, man.

The day after Marin and I broke up, a full three months after the accident, Lydia called me. She was the one crying even though I knew I was the one who'd ruined everything. I expected her and James to chew me out, but she surprised me.

"Max, you know that you will always have a place to come home to. Especially during the holidays—you never have to be alone. This will always be your home."

I've never been the sentimental type, but for some reason it was the *always* that stuck with me.

And it didn't shock me that my mother's best friend knew that this particular holiday would be especially hard.

I should've taken it like any other empty, meaningless promise people make in the middle of a tragedy. Like when people tell you, "Let us know if there's anything we can do to help," as if there's any way you could actually find the words to tell someone else what you need.

Lydia didn't just lose her best friend. Because of me, she also lost the dream the two women had carried—not-so-secretly—ever since the year Marin and I were born.

We were practically betrothed. It was the kind of thing where they'd coordinate our outfits for birthday parties and holiday gatherings. When we were young, it was adorable and funny, but I turned thirteen, then fourteen then fifteen, and we began to understand our mothers' plan—and we vowed to just be friends no matter what our matchmaking moms wanted.

If I'd just kept that promise instead of letting my feelings get in the way, everything would be fine right now.

I would've opened the door and found her standing there, and we would've hugged and laughed and simply caught up like old times. Like the *friends* we were supposed to be.

Instead, I opened the door and all of a sudden, I was sixteen and in love again.

Marin.

The one I pushed away.

I can't change the past, and I can't pretend I'm sorry to be here over the holidays. In a lot of ways, I sometimes think Lydia and James saved my life.

They were family. They *are* family.

It just so happens they are also my ex-girlfriend's parents.

Who am I kidding? Marin is so much more than just an ex-girlfriend.

I stand in the kitchen, impatiently waiting for the last five seconds of the timer on the bread bowls. The look on Marin's face when I opened the door replays in my mind. She'd looked stunned. Shocked.

Beautiful.

Hurt.

I should've known better.

The timer beeps, getting me out of my own head. I pull the hot, golden-browned bread bowls out of the oven and place them on a wire rack Lydia had set out on the counter.

Marin's mom always made too much food. Not that Lydia would ever mind extra company for dinner. I mean, she'd certainly welcomed me whenever I'd shown up.

And I had shown up. More than a few times.

I grab the color-coordinated bowls for the spread of bacon bits, cheese, and green onions when Lydia returns to the kitchen, a smile working overtime to cover up a crease of concern etched on her forehead.

"Hey, I can go," I say quietly.

She waves me off. "Don't be ridiculous." She grabs some bacon bits and pops them in her mouth. "This was bound to happen sometime."

"What does *that* mean?"

We both turn to find Marin standing in the doorway.

Good grief, she's gorgeous. I pray that she doesn't catch me staring. She used to do that all the time when we were kids.

"That means. . ." Lydia says, grabbing more bacon bits, "you and Max were bound to bump into each other sometime." Her tone drips with guilt disguised as phony innocence.

"Yes, but here? At my parents' house?" She turns her gaze on me. "How are you even here?"

"Marin, he is totally welcome."

I put my head down, knowing that neither of these women will ever know how much that means to me.

"And we didn't expect you, Marin, let's not forget that." Lydia has kept her tone light, as if she's simply stating a fact.

"How long has it been? Like, five or six years?" I trail off as the smile fades from Marin's face.

Smooth.

I'm making it worse and I know it.

Marin's eyes dart from me to her mother and back to me. Then, they narrow as if she's just realized something. "This isn't your first Christmas here, is it?"

I start to speak, but shut my mouth and look at Lydia, like I'm on the stand and she's my lawyer.

Lying is just not an option. The half-truth of eight years ago *still* haunts me. I don't lie, especially not to Marin.

I'd hoped Lydia had explained the entire story to her on the porch, but obviously she hadn't.

After a brief pause, Marin turns her glare on her mother. "Mom?"

"Marin." Lydia draws in a breath and walks over to me, placing a hand on my shoulder. "Like I said, Max is part of the family too."

"You're avoiding the question."

"Let's eat," Lydia says quickly. "I'll go get a bottle of wine."

She hurries off, and Marin takes a step toward me. I force myself not to break eye contact. Truthfully, I've always loved sparring with Marin. I'm not intimidated by her fire.

Her beauty? Well, that's another story.

I study her face—a face I know so well it shows up in my dreams. She's so beautiful and feisty, and. . .

"I'll give you ten seconds to tell me why you're here and after that I'm calling 911 because there's going to be a homicide at the McGrath house."

Oh. And quick. I forgot how quick her wit is.

This is going to be fun.

Behind the furrowed brow and underneath all that makeup, she's still Marin.

My Marin.

"You've been here before, haven't you?" Her eyes stay trained on me like a cheetah in the tall grass locked on to a gazelle.

I try to be nonchalant. "I grew up next door, Marin, so yes, I have been here before."

She squints at me. "You know what I mean. How many times have you been here for Christmas?" She stares at me, as if the answer were written in invisible ink on my forehead.

"How many times have you *not* been here for Christmas?" I counter.

"Don't change the subject."

"Don't make this into a thing."

"How many times?" Her gaze is still holding steady.

Dang it.

". . .five," I tell her.

"What?!"

I say this next part as if I'm moving a fully decorated three-tier cake from a tray to a cake stand in front of the judges. "Six times if you. . .um. . .count this week."

She plants her hands squarely on her hips, and tilts her head.

"Starting when?"

I drag a hand down my face, aware that Marin was not going to let this go. "I don't know, Marin, like, five or six years ago?"

"Five or six years ago?" A look of disbelief washes over her face. "You've come every year for five or. . ." She doesn't finish. "Why didn't my mother ever tell me?"

"She was probably afraid you were going to freak out," I

21

say, and then indicate to her with both hands as if to say she's doing exactly that.

"Well, gee, Max, why in the world would I do that?" She crosses her arms over her chest and watches me. I find myself intrigued by this older version of the girl I'd loved. She's got some experience on her now, maybe toughened up by her job.

Or her heartbreak.

"Why did you come here?" she asks.

I wince. "Well. That's the million-dollar question, isn't it?"

There is no way I'm getting into the specifics with her. The past is in the past. "Can we just move on? We're both here, let's try and act like adults."

"Act like ad. . ." She cuts herself off with a scoff. "Are you saying I'm not acting like an adult?" She takes a step even closer to me, and I don't look away. Heat flushes my skin. I can feel it on my face.

"I don't believe for a second that work has been keeping you away every single holiday for eight years," I say.

She straightens. "We're not talking about me, Max."

"Well, maybe we should be."

We're standing mere inches apart from each other, each of us having dug in our heels.

I feel like my observation is valid. Why would someone with parents like James and Lydia choose to stay away on the biggest holiday of the year?

Unfortunately, her question is valid too. Why would someone with a history like mine and Marin's choose to drop in on her parents during the biggest holiday of the year?

It's not a question I'm interested in answering.

A gasp behind us pulls our attention. Lydia has returned with the wine, and now she's standing in the doorway, hand to chest in dramatic fashion.

"Mom?" Marin frowns. "What's wrong?"

"Look at you two," Lydia says. "It's just like old times. Both of you huddled up together in the kitchen, all secretive."

"Mom. We aren't huddled up." Marin takes a step back.

"Well, we were kind of huddled up," I say.

"Can we eat?" Marin asks sharply, then she looks at her mom and says, "I'm not done with you."

She glares at me as she walks into the living room.

"She asked," I say. "I couldn't lie."

"No," Lydia says. "It's my fault. I should've told her after that first Christmas, but I thought, what was the harm? She wasn't here, and it was just one year."

"But then I came back," I say.

"Yes. Yes, you did." Lydia smiles. "And we are so glad you did. You are our godson, after all."

"The last thing I had ever wanted was to cause trouble for you guys," I say. "I just...I didn't want..." I can't finish.

Lydia smiles again, and places a warm hand on my arm. "I know," she says. "I know."

I take a deep breath, hoping that will prepare me for the rest of the evening.

"I can try to smooth it over with her," I say.

"Let me handle her," Lydia says. "Between the two of us, I think she's less angry with me."

Fair point.

I glance toward the living room and find Marin chatting casually with the others. It had always been so easy for her to talk to people, so her job choice made perfect sense. She'd always been the person who wanted to know the whole story. I've never met anyone who listened as well as Marin.

The cameraman says something and Marin laughs.

Man, I've missed her.

"You okay?" Lydia stands at my side, eyes trained on me as if reading my innermost thoughts.

I pick up the pot of soup and "cheer" it in the air. "Never better. Let's eat."

I walk toward the table, noticing that three more Christmas place settings have appeared. I swear, Lydia is magic. How many times had she done the same for me over the years? I never once felt like an imposition at their house—not until now, and not because of Lydia.

"Dinner is ready, kids," Lydia says, bustling in from the kitchen carrying the bread bowls. "James, turn that off."

He grunts as he stands up from his recliner, pausing the television on Captain Picard's face—frozen on one eye closed, one eye open, one hand in the air and looking like he's had a few too many.

"Pause face!" Marin and I say in unison.

She looks at me, almost mad that we dare connect, and I stifle the smile playing at the corner of my mouth.

I'm not sure when or why we started doing it, but pausing movies to try and get the worst "pause face" on the actors had become something of a game for Marin, Teddy and I. It was stupid kid stuff, but I still do it to this day. Apparently, Marin does too.

"Well, that's a blast from the past," Lydia says. She smiles awkwardly, but no amount of social grace can eliminate the tension in the room. "Shall we sit?"

I already know how this meal will go. We'll sit. We'll be polite. Lydia will pepper Marin's co-workers with a million questions. And I'll probably eat too much potato soup.

I brace myself as I take my seat—right across from Marin.

I look at her, determined not to cower to the grudge she's holding. Maybe I shouldn't be so bold given the fact that she has absolutely every right to be mad at me, but it's not in my nature to back down from a fight. Even one I have no business trying to win.

24

Lydia serves up the soup in the bread bowls, and we begin passing the bacon, cheese, and green onions around the table, everyone murmuring about how good it all looks and thanking Lydia for feeding them.

I'm quiet, content to eat and listen.

Marin catches me staring, and I quickly look away. I can see out of the corner of my eye that she smiles, politely, and continues her conversation.

I have a feeling it's only a matter of time before she stops being polite.

Chapter Four

Marin

"**S**o. You finally come home for Christmas after eight years and you bring a camera crew," my mother says pointedly, handing me a bowl of bacon bits.

Only then do I realize that my parents have no idea what I'm doing here—and immediately feel self-conscious about it.

I catch Max watching me. Silently chewing and silently watching. I assume he's judging me for not being home before now, but he really has no right. After all, if it weren't for him, Christmas would still be my favorite holiday.

That's not exactly fair. I still love Christmas, more than anything. It's just difficult to celebrate something that has heart-wrenching emotions attached to it.

As it was, I'd taken to celebrating less complicated holidays, like Arbor Day or Boxing Day, even though I'm not Canadian. Or October 25th, which is National Cartoonists against Crime Day—that one doesn't have a single painful memory attached to it.

"So?" Mom's waiting for an explanation, and I know whatever I say is going to come out wrong.

"I wanted it to be a surprise," I manage to say. "But now I guess maybe I should've called first."

My mother frowns. "Called first? Honey, you never need to do that! There's plenty of food. You know you're always welcome here."

For a moment, I wonder if she even remembers the night Max broke up with me.

I wonder if she has a clue why I've made all those excuses for all these years.

I've tried to fool myself into thinking I've moved on, but there's a reason none of my relationships have lasted longer than three months.

And that reason is sitting across from me, still watching me.

Time to go on offense for a minute.

"I'm sorry," I say. "I still don't really understand how this—" I wave my hands around the table in the general direction of my parents and Max—"happened." I set my spoon down and wait for one of them to respond. Nobody says a word.

"I'd like to hear more about your show," my mom says, deftly knocking the ball back on my side of the net. "Do we get to be on television?"

"You do," I respond, hitting it back, "but I thought it was going to be just our family."

I notice Max stop looking at me for a brief moment. I hate that it makes me feel bad.

Lydia beams. "Well, it's a good thing that Max is here then," she says, putting a hand on his shoulder. "What better time than Christmas to bury hatchets and start new traditions?"

Oh, she's good.

I want to pack it all up and go back to Denver. Back to my quiet little apartment. Back to my solitary life. It's easier and less messy.

Now it's my turn not to respond.

"The idea to come back here came up because Marin speaks so highly of Christmases back home," Steph says.

Across from me, Max chokes and coughs a mouthful of water over the top of his glass onto the table. "*Sorry.*" He coughs again, then takes another drink. "*Wrong pipe,*" he sputters.

I glare at him.

"It's true," Steph continues. "Every year, we'd sit around the station and trade old Christmas stories and Marin's," she turns and looks at me, smiling, "were always the best."

I make a face.

"It sounded like a real-life Hallmark movie," Steph says. "Sometimes, she'd talk about it on-air, and the viewers started asking questions."

"About us?" My mother is beaming. *Darn it.* I wanted to be the one to tell her this. I knew it would make her whole year. But I'm far too surly to be cheerful.

"Yes, and about Pleasant Valley," Steph says. "It's a segment we're calling 'Home for the Holidays.'"

"Huh," Max says. "Catchy."

I don't miss the sarcasm in his tone. He looks over at me, and his smirk transports me back to high school and the first time I ever felt a ridiculous flutter of butterflies over Max Weber.

Practically my brother Max Weber.

Boy-next-door Max Weber.

Butterflies.

I read somewhere that the feeling you get when you get "butterflies in your stomach" is actually similar to your fight or flight response kicking in because you see a potential mate. Your emotions go into overdrive, almost like panic mode, and it mimics the same brain activity and physical response as craving water when you're dehydrating in a desert.

It was the first day of our junior year of high school. We'd spent the entire summer together at the lake. I swear, we'd both practically grown gills we were in the water so often. There was a boy—Hayden Stone—who, for reasons I didn't understand, started paying attention to me.

Every class period that first day, Hayden stopped by my locker. I wasn't great at recognizing when a boy was flirting with me—I'm still not—but my best friend CeCe made it clear that's what was happening.

"He's just being nice," I protested.

"No, he's *definitely* not just being nice." CeCe said as Max walked up to my locker. "You're a guy, Max. You see it, right?"

"See what?"

"That Hayden is into Marin."

Max stiffened and made a face. "Hayden Stone?"

"Duh," CeCe says.

Max turned to me. "You like that guy?"

"No," I said quickly. "I mean, I don't know. I don't even know him."

Max shook his head.

"What's wrong, Max?" CeCe closed her locker and said, sing-songy. "You jealous?"

I scoffed, but when I looked at Max, I noticed his eyes were serious.

CeCe saw it too, and took that as a cue. "On that note. . ." She waved as she walked away, leaving me standing there with a boy I know better than anyone but couldn't read at all.

"What's the big deal?" I asked.

"Don't go out with that guy, Mare," he said.

I turned away and pulled my history textbook from my locker. "Why?" My tone was playful, but when I turned back around to look at Max, I realized his gaze is anything but. "What? What's wrong?"

29

He didn't respond. Instead, he took a step toward me. Even at sixteen, he was about a foot taller than me. To anyone else, that might have been a little intimidating—but I felt nothing but safe.

I remember the way he looked at me—it was different. Not like I was his friend. And certainly not like I was his sister.

I said his name, barely a whisper. "Max?"

But he silenced me with a kiss—*right there in the hallway.* He kissed me like he'd been thinking about kissing me for a very long time. I dropped my history book and instinctively wrapped my arms around his neck.

Until that moment I had only kissed one other boy—barely a peck on a dare and nothing like this.

This was—electrifying. If I think about it, I can feel now how I felt then, like my whole body was plugged in, firing.

Call it nerves, thirst, butterflies, or hormones, whatever. . .I felt it all.

When he finally pulled away (probably ten seconds but it seemed like a half hour and even then, not nearly long enough), he smirked down at me.

"Because I want you to go out with me."

I linger on his face in my mind for a moment, then shake the memory away, hating that it came back so vividly my toes are tingling. That smirk no longer has any effect on me. At least that's what I'm telling myself.

So far, *myself* isn't believing it.

I glance at Max, fearing that he can read my mind. He always did seem to have a sixth sense about me. He's still watching with a quiet intensity that makes my insides spin.

"This is all so exciting," my mom says, and for a moment, I can't remember what we were talking about.

"So, you'll be filming all our little traditions?" Mom is smiling so brightly she's practically incandescent.

"That's right," Steph says. "It was mostly Marin's idea. She felt like you all had something really special here growing up, and she wanted to share it with her fans." She turns to me. "She's really generous that way."

I look back at Steph, who, for maybe the second time since I've known her, lets on that she has a heart. Because it was absolutely not my idea. I've been thinking I needed to come home for Christmas, sure, but on my own terms—and not with a cameraman.

"Generous with her fans," Max says. "Hmm."

I volley. "What do you mean, 'hmm'?"

He half smiles. "So, you've got time for them?" He quirks a brow so slightly I almost don't see it.

"As opposed to. . .?" I ask.

He holds up both hands and gestures to the whole room, the house, the food, then picks up his glass of water and takes a sip, never breaking eye contact with me.

"Some people do work for a living, Max," I say, taking his point.

"Oh, Max works," my mother chimes in. "He's been *all* over the world!" She pats his arm twice. "Tell her, Max."

He sets his drink down, still holding my gaze, and I will myself not to blink or look away. He's too handsome (*unfair*) and the tension is too strong. And I'm instantly enraged because as much as I want to hate him, there is a tiny piece of me that imagines staying up all night, cuddled under a blanket finding out what he's been doing the last eight years.

And another part of me that wants to scream—*you traveled the world? We were supposed to do that together!*

He looks away, as if he's just remembered his broken vow at the same time I did.

A small victory, but I'll take it.

"Well, we should get going." Steph stands, and motions to

Danny to do the same. He frowns, looks back at his bowl, and then up at Steph. It's clear he wants to stay and finish his third serving of soup.

"I've taken the liberty of packing up leftovers for the both of you," my mother says.

Steph starts to ask, "When did you have time to. . ." but Mom brushes her question off with a wave of her hand.

Danny shovels two more spoonfuls in his mouth. "It's so good, Mrs. McGrath. . . and thanks!"

My mom beams at the compliment.

"We'll be back in the morning," Steph says. "Marin, I'll text you."

And after a brief stop at the front door, several bags filled with food in tow, they're gone.

But Max is wonderfully, horribly still here.

Chapter Five

Marin

After dinner, Mom shoos Dad back to his recliner, and Max off to who-knows-where, leaving the two of us to clean up the dishes.

She chatters on about the ladies at church, and the Christmas Stroll, and the kickoff parade, and the *Twelve Shops of Christmas*—and while I should probably be taking notes for my show, I'm mostly just waiting for her to take a breath so I can bring up the topic she really doesn't want me to bring up.

"Helen Steele has been smack-talking about the chili cookoff for three months straight," Mom says. "That woman is insufferable. She's so intent on 'de-throning' me, which, let's be clear, is not going to happen. Not with my secret ingredient."

She glances at me, then out the doorway that leads into the living room. I look, too, wondering what the heck she is looking at.

"Are we. . .are there spies in the house, Mom? What are we doing?"

"Oh hush up, you just never know who's listening."

I hold up my phone. "Should I turn this off, too? They say it listens to you. . ." I pick it up say loudly into it, "to the FBI listening in on this call, my mom's secret ingredient is. . ." I then hold out my phone to her, with an expectant look.

"Go ahead, Mom. Jeff in Cyber Services is waiting."

She laughs and throws a dish towel at me. "The secret is Coca-Cola." She bustles into the kitchen, carrying a pile of dishes, which she places into the sink. "Barb thinks maybe it's time to let someone else win, but I don't think I can do it. I like being the best—what can I say?"

I smile as I set a stack of bowls on the counter by the sink. It's all so familiar, and I love it.

"I can do this, Marin, I'm sure you're exhausted."

"You're exhausted too, Mom, what with all the *entertaining* you've been doing."

She flips on the water and fills the sink. She has a perfectly good dishwasher, but she still insists on hand-washing the plates and glasses. "No machine is a substitute for good, old-fashioned elbow grease," she always says.

"Not so much entertaining," Mom says innocently. "Just simple dinners and a few desserts. You know how your dad likes his sweets. But now that you're here, I'll step up my game."

"Mom."

She turns off the faucet. "Yes?"

"Could we stop pretending that this is normal?"

She frowns. "That what is normal?"

"Max! Here! In the house!" I hiss.

Mom starts scrubbing a dish, avoiding my eyes. "I realize I probably should've mentioned it."

"Mother," I say, trying to remain calm. "He said he's been here five times. *Five.* Typically, when a boy breaks a girl's heart, the girl's family doesn't invite him over for the holidays."

"It wasn't like that, Marin," she says with pleading eyes.

"Then what was it like?"

Mom nods to the spot next to her at the sink. "If you're going to interrogate me, at least dry."

I sigh, then walk around to the opposite side of the counter and pick up a dish towel.

"I was devasted when the two of you broke up," Mom said. "Especially because it was so soon after. . .you know."

Max's parents, Jenny and Steve, had been killed in a tragic car accident. To say we were all shocked is a gross understatement. That accident carved all our lives into two pieces—before and after.

Sometimes, even now, I forget they're gone and have to relive that day all over again.

"I was pretty shattered too," I tell her.

"I know, Marin. We all were. And then you called it quits and I just thought. . ."

"You thought we'd be together forever, and get married, and live down the block?"

She smiles, almost to herself. "Well, maybe not the house part, but we all thought you two would end up together. Jenny and I thought it was your destiny—even when you were little."

"Yeah, you didn't hide that very well." I open the cupboard to my left and stack three clean bowls on the shelf inside.

"So, I reached out to Max. I knew he was hurting too."

"*He* was hurting?"

My heart squeezes at this.

Max breaking up with me felt like the worst kind of betrayal. There I was, just a few weeks before Christmas during my senior year of college, and he dumps me and flies to North Carolina to spend the holidays with a friend from school. I thought maybe he just needed space—it was hard being here after his parents died.

I waited around, knowing he was going through so much pain. But he made it clear it wasn't Pleasant Valley he needed space from—it was me.

And eventually, I realized he hadn't broken up with me because of his grief. He'd broken up with me because he didn't want to be with me anymore.

"Marin, I couldn't just toss him aside so easily. He's Jenny's only son, and Jenny was my best friend," my mom says. "So, yes, I told him he'd always have a place here, no matter what happened with the two of you. And I'm not sorry about it."

I know I should understand her point, but I can't help but feel betrayed. "What did he say?"

"Nothing, really," Mom says. "'Thank you,' I guess. I didn't think he believed me or wanted anything to do with any of us anymore."

I knew the feeling.

"But then, three years later, he knocked on the door." She hands me a plate to dry. "He was in town, and he didn't want to leave without saying hello."

"Well, that was big of him."

"Oh, stop it. It was nice," Mom says. "But it was pretty obvious he wasn't 'passing through.' He didn't have anywhere else to go. So, of course, we insisted he stay with us for the holidays."

"Of course," I say with an eye roll.

"You should know, he was very concerned about upsetting you."

"How kind."

"I thought it was," Mom shrugs, turning off the water and flicking her fingers into the sink.

"Was he the only one concerned about upsetting me?" As the words are coming out, I realize I feel angry—but I don't

36

stop. "What about my own parents? Didn't you consider how this would make me feel?"

"Marin," Mom says. "Stop. This isn't like you. All this meanness."

Oh yes, Mother, when it comes to Max, it's me. One hundred percent me.

She grabs the towel from me and dries her hands. "You know that unkindness just makes you get old before your time."

"That's true," Dad calls from the living room. "Rots your bones and makes you constipated! Look at your Aunt June! She looks like she's at least eighty because she's such a terrible person. And she's younger than me!"

"Still eavesdropping like a champ, I see," Mom calls back. "Makes me wonder if you pretend you can't hear me when I'm standing right next to you."

"Huh?" Dad says—and not quietly.

Mom rolls her eyes, then turns back to me. "He didn't want to stay, but we insisted. I felt like I owed it to Jenny. And honestly, he didn't seem like himself. I don't know what happened to him over those three years, but I don't think it was good."

My hearts stumbles over this. During those missing years, especially at the beginning, I'd wondered where Max was, what he was doing, who he was doing it with. I'd resigned myself to never knowing, but now one comment from my mother and that curiosity is back.

"I get that, Mom, but you should've told me." I pick up another dishtowel and dry a glass, even though I've dried it twice already.

She turns to face me. "You're right. I should've told you. But you weren't home, and it felt like it wasn't worth making you upset. Besides, we thought it was a one-holiday thing."

"But he came back," I say.

Mom nods. "The next year. And then the year after that. And then. . .we just came to expect him."

And they came to *not* expect me. The realization of that settles on my shoulders.

"He was better the second time, but I still got the impression he was aimless. And he didn't have that spark." She looks at me. "You know Max's spark. . ."

I groan. "Yes, Mom, I know about his 'spark.'" I wish I didn't, but I did. He could charm a whole room with a single smile.

"He has an apartment in Chicago, but he's hardly ever there. His job takes him all over the world, and I felt like he needed a place that felt like home. So, I made sure to tell him again—*he could always come here.* I would certainly hope Jenny would've done the same for you if the roles were reversed."

I would be a first-class jerk to argue with that.

I get it. I do. Mom loved Jenny like a sister. And I loved her like a second mother. I understand why she would feel the need to watch over her only son.

But I feel conflicted. This feels like my own mother chose my ex-boyfriend over me. And after the way Max and I ended, that hurts. And I feel betrayed that no one told me.

With the last dish dried and put away, there's a familiar calm that settles. I can hear Dad's TV from the other room, the *whirr* of the dishwasher, and see the flicker of the Christmas lights speckling the walls through the windows.

"I'm going to bed," I say. "It's been a really long day."

It had been, but I knew I was going to sink into my frilly pink double bed and scroll TikTok for the next two hours. The truth was, I needed solace and solitude more than I needed sleep.

"Okay, honey," Mom says. "Let's make the best of this."

I give a half-hearted thumbs up. "I'll try."

She gives me a hug. "It's all I ask. Maybe this is the year our family is finally put back together."

Yeah. Or maybe it's the year I relive my greatest heartbreak every time I see Max's face.

Chapter Six

Max

After dinner, Lydia scolded me for trying to help with the dishes, so I came upstairs.

It was then I realized I had a problem.

Since Marin's brother Teddy would be home in just a few days, Lydia had put me up in Marin's old room. And this wouldn't be the first Christmas break I've slept in her bed.

I've already been here a week, so I'm pretty much settled in —and now I'm trying to pack up and get out—hopefully before Marin catches me in here.

I look over and see my editing set-up. Computer, double monitor, camera rig.

Yeah, that's going to be another problem.

It's not easy to tear down. I'm in the middle of it when she walks in.

"What the. . .?" She lets the handle of her suitcase go and because it's overstuffed and off balance, it flips backwards, hitting her in the thigh. "Ow!"

She tries to kick the suitcase and misses and instead kicks

the door, smashing her foot and crumpling over in a heap on the floor.

"Are you kidding me?!" she says to no one in particular.

I stand and watch. Her utter contempt for inanimate objects that don't do what she wants hasn't changed since high school.

I dip my toe in the shallow end of this encounter. "You okay?"

She gets up off the floor, holds a hand up as a warning, and I obey. I have no interest in getting my head or any of my limbs chewed off.

"I. Am. *Fine.*" She says through gritted teeth, giving the suitcase a shove with her other foot for good measure. "*What* are you doing in here?"

I play dumb. "Your mom didn't tell you?"

"Oh! Hey, Marin?" Lydia calls up the stairs.

Marin looks chagrined. "Let me guess," she says this to me while her mom continues talking, "I have to sleep in the sewing room."

Lydia finishes out with, ". . . in the sewing room!"

Marin's whole body says *great.*

"It's okay, Lydia, I can move, I'm packing up my stuff now!" I call down, eyes focused on Marin.

She frowns.

I can hear Lydia's footsteps heading our way. When she appears in the doorway, neither Marin nor I look at her. "Nonsense. You're already settled in, and that stuff," she flicks a hand toward my computer, "won't fit in my sewing room. I'm sure Marin doesn't mind sleeping on the futon. It's really comfortable! Well, for young people anyway. I always feel like a pretzel when I lay on it, but my body doesn't bend like it used to. Just ask your father."

"Mom!"

I chuckle at Lydia's comment. She and James love to embarrass their kids, and any hints that they have a sex life certainly does the trick.

"I'll get you some sheets and Teddy's old comforter. You'll be just fine in there, won't you, Marin?" She doesn't wait for a reply, but instead hurries down the hall, presumably to turn her sewing room into a makeshift guest room.

She leaves me standing face-to-face with Marin.

And she doesn't look happy.

"And I'll ask again. What are you doing in here?" Marin repeats, as if I've done something wrong.

I shrug. "This is where your mom put me."

"In my *room*? Don't you think it's sort of strange?"

Another shrug. "I've learned not to argue with Lydia. It's almost as bad as arguing with you."

She glares at me. I know I'm on thin ice, but I can't help myself.

"Why are you packing?" she asks.

"Are you scared I'm going to leave?"

She shoots me a look. "Hardly."

"Chivalry's not dead. I was going to go sleep on the futon." I say. "It's what you want anyway, right?"

"Is the futon in the middle of I-90? Because that'd be a great place for you to sleep."

She's quick, and anyone else could take this as an insult— but I can hear what she's really saying.

Where was that chivalry eight years ago?

"I don't need any favors from you, Max."

The fire in her certainly hasn't subsided, but my desire to douse it increases every time she looks at me. I was a jerk, and I never made it right—even when I realized I could've handled our break-up better. Even when I realized I was an idiot.

Distance and time bring an unwanted clarity.

I shrug. "Suit yourself then. Your bed is comfy." I plop down on the end of her bed.

She crosses her arms over her chest and nods toward my computer. "What is all that?"

"Editing equipment," I say.

"What do you edit?" She keeps the interest out of her voice, but I still feel like I've made some headway if she's curious.

"Video," I say. "I do corporate work, mostly, but I've got a couple of side projects I'm working on, too."

"From all your *traveling?*" There's a deeper meaning in this question, and I can't pretend I don't know that. It wasn't my dream to travel alone.

We were supposed to do it together.

I sit up. "Marin. . ."

"I'm going to bed." She turns abruptly, grabs her misshapen suitcase, and starts down the hallway.

A few seconds later I hear a thump and an "Ow!! *No good, stupid, rotten, piece of. . .!*"

I stifle a laugh, and just in time, because seconds later, she's back.

Without a word, she walks straight over to the armchair in the corner and picks up her old teddy bear, George, the one with the red stitching on his foot. She tucks him under her arm and disappears down the hall.

I stand there, waiting to make sure she's not coming back before unpacking the clothes I'd just packed up. It feels wrong to stay in her room, but I know Marin. She's too proud to let me be kind, so I might as well stay put. Maybe tomorrow I can break down my computer and move myself into the sewing room. It's just a couple of weeks. My projects can wait.

I didn't expect to see her—not after years of absence from her parents' house—but now that she's here, I'm floundering. I'm conflicted. All of the feelings I'd convinced myself I no longer had are back, and all I can think about is how much I've missed her.

I close the door, then find my pajama pants in the half-unpacked duffel on the bed. I take off my T-shirt, throw it in the bag, and plod toward the bathroom, suddenly aware of how tired I am. I open the door and am jarred by the sound of a scream.

"Oh my gosh!"

My eyes go wide as they make contact with a half-dressed Marin, shielding herself with a pink T-shirt.

I freeze for at least three (*maybe five*) seconds and we're just staring at each other in various states of undress.

"Max!"

I slam the door shut. "Sorry!"

"Don't you knock?!"

I try to respond, but her bare shoulders are now etched in my mind. Finally, I blurt out, "You could lock the door."

She whips it open. She's fully clothed now.

Darn.

"We need some ground rules," she says.

She's adorable. The makeup is gone. Her long, blond hair is piled on top of her head in a loose bun, and she's wearing a pink *My Little Pony* T-shirt and leggings. So, the girl I loved does still exist—you just have to get underneath the makeup and the stuffy, professional clothes to find her.

"Why are you looking at me like that?" She folds her arms over her chest.

"Like what? I'm just standing here."

"You don't have a shirt on," she says.

I grin. "You noticed."

She rolls her eyes. "You have to knock before you come into this bathroom. In case you didn't realize it on all of your many visits to *my parents' house*, it connects to the sewing room."

44

I toss a glance toward the room where Marin would sleep through the open door on the other side of the small Jack and Jill bathroom. The "sewing room" is actually a fourth bedroom, but since there were only ever two kids in the McGrath house, Lydia claimed it.

"You know," I say, "in all the years I've known Lydia, I've never seen her sew one single thing."

Marin sighs. "Can you do that? Just knock?"

"Yep. And you have to lock the door when you're using the bathroom." I casually lean against the doorjamb.

"Fine," she bristles.

"Fine."

"Good."

I pause.

"And you have to wear a shirt," she says.

"Why? Are you having impure thoughts about me?" I smirk at her.

"And you can't do that." She might as well have stomped her foot as she said it.

"Do what?"

"Flirt with me."

"Oh. This isn't flirting," I say, knowing full well that it absolutely is.

She watches me, and I don't dare look away. There's definitely something happening between us.

I shouldn't entertain the idea.

Right?

I can't ignore the fact that for the first time in a very long time, I'm questioning my decision to cut myself off from anything that even faintly resembles love.

She takes a step toward me, and my breath catches at her nearness. "Please. Just, don't mess with my heart, Max." She grabs the handle to the door, and I suddenly realize that I've completely misread the situation.

There was nothing playful coming from Marin. Only pain.

As she is shutting the door on me, she ends with, "You already shattered it once."

For the first time since I walked out of Marin's life, I get a glimpse of the fallout I left in my wake.

Chapter Seven

Marin

I don't sleep. Like, at all.

It's a combination of hearing my dad snore all the way down the hall plus the lumpy futon my mom swore would be as comfortable as my old bed.

And Max.

Let's be honest, it was mostly Max.

Knowing that he was *right there*, just on the other side of my little pink bathroom, sleeping in *my bed*. . .shirtless. . .well, that made falling asleep impossible.

He had muscles. Like, actual muscles. The kind you get when you work out at the gym. Or star in a Marvel movie.

I can't say the same about myself. I'm pale (thanks, long work hours), and never have time for the gym (thanks, long work hours). It's possible I'd be mistaken for a vampire if I were out late at night on my own.

Lying in the dark on a slant, surrounded by bolts of fabric and plastic five-drawer cabinets full of buttons and thread, I try to take an objective look at myself. It's hard when all I can see are the flaws.

And it's not lost on me that my mom put me in a room where things go to be stitched back up.

It's not just my appearance that seems to have taken a dive. It's my life. Seeing Max reminds me of the person I was supposed to be. Of all the things I was *supposed* to do. Travel. Meet people. Tell stories that excited me. Make films that mattered. Be in love.

Since I graduated from the University of Illinois, I've done exactly zero of those things.

Sure, I live in Colorado—a beautiful, scenic state. But even though I'm surrounded by nature's beauty, and I'm in a job I love and was pretty much born to do, I still feel like this is a trial run. That someone is eventually going to find out that I've been faking it this whole time.

And really, this whole Christmas special *is* a trial run. It's down to me and one other reporter—two women poised to take over the station's favorite show, *Good Day Denver*. I deserve it, but the truth is, Sophie Soto deserves it too. Sophie is every bit as driven and hard-working as I am. It's going to take a miracle to come out of this as the winner.

As soon as the thought enters my mind, I want to lock it up in a box. I don't want to be in competition with Sophie or anyone else, but, as Steph has so often reminded me, that's the way this business goes.

I whip the blanket off, drag my legs over and set them on the floor. I'm tired of my own internal monologue. It's obvious that I'm not going to sleep—so I work.

Whether I want to or not. Whether Max is here or not.

I check the lock on the bathroom. Then I reach over and jiggle it one more time, just to be sure. I have to shower, and I really—*really*—don't want a naked repeat of last night. Having my shirt off when Max opened the door was bad enough. And seeing the look on his face was even worse.

And he didn't hurry to look away.

I wouldn't read into that, though. He's a guy. Guys like half-clothed girls, even pasty ones. And whether I'd intended to be or not, that's what I was in that moment. Pasty half naked girl.

Line up and take a number, boys.

I turn the faucet toward HOT and pull the knob. The pipes whine their familiar tune as the water makes its way up to the shower head.

I stand under the fantastic, steamy pressure. It's something I always miss about this house—the shower hits you like one of those fire hoses they use to wash rhinos at the zoo.

In the stillness, my mind spins with the memory of our break-up. The look on his face, the desperation I felt, and the words he'd said.

I've tried to forget those words a million times.

I'm not in love with you, Marin.

They flash in my mind like a neon sign. And this shower can wash away the sleepiness I feel, but not the memories I'm swimming in.

I try to hurry through a modified version of my morning ritual, aware that the bags under my eyes rival the size of the suitcase that assaulted me earlier. It's not a great look for on-camera work, but zero hours of sleep will do that to a face.

Once I'm ready, I head straight to the kitchen, where I pour myself a big mug of coffee. I open the refrigerator, praying that Mom had my—*Yes!*—peppermint creamer. I pull the bottle out and set it next to the steaming mug when I hear someone enter the kitchen behind me.

"You still drink coffee with your creamer?"

Max.

What is it about a man in a pair of joggers and a gray T-shirt that spikes my heartrate? It makes zero sense. I mean, don't get me wrong, if he was wearing a suit and tie, I'd probably be drooling on the floor, but this look—I don't know why, it's working for me.

I don't let on, or try my best not to. Instead I turn back to my coffee. I can feel him watching me as I pour a perfectly acceptable amount of creamer into the mug, filling it so full it almost overflows.

"I was thinking. . ."

I face him. "Congratulations."

He raises a brow and leans against the counter. "So, this is how we're starting the day?"

I take a drink of my coffee. It's the perfect mix of peppermint and chocolate.

"Yep."

A standoff in the kitchen at 7:36 AM. You could almost see the metaphorical tumbleweed—made of tinsel, because, you know, my mom—blow across the floor between us.

"You're going to spill that," he says.

"I'll be fine."

He turns to grab the orange juice out of the fridge. He seems to know exactly where it is, and is super comfortable maneuvering around my parents' kitchen. I don't like it.

"I took a chance, looks like I was right," he says, nodding to my mug.

"What does that mean, 'you took a chance'?"

"Your mom only had half and half," he says. "You like peppermint creamer." He leans over toward my cup. "Judging by the color of your coffee, you *really* like peppermint creamer."

"*You* got this?"

He shrugs. "I was up early." He says this so nonchalantly, as if this isn't incredibly thoughtful. Why would he do that?

"Why would you do that?"

He frowns. "Trying to be nice? I'm not a bad guy, you know."

I pause for a three-count, then turn and pour my coffee down the drain. My heart hurts at this sacrifice, but it must be done. The wall of anger must stay intact. I glance over and see Max's quirked brow. I can't tell if he's hurt or amused.

All at once, I feel like a child throwing a temper tantrum at Disney World.

I mentally right myself. "Don't be nice to me, Max. In fact, I'd prefer if you weren't. It would make this a lot easier."

He stands straighter and waits for me to face him again. "I was thinking we could call a truce."

"A truce," I say, dumbly, as if it was the most ludicrous word in the dictionary.

"Yeah, you know where two people stand down and decide to get along for the sake of the other people in the house?"

It sounded like a mature way to approach this unfortunate situation, and I'm not oblivious to the fact that of the two of us, Max is being the grown-up here.

But stubbornness has always been one of my fatal flaws.

I lift my chin. "Why?"

"Because all your mom ever talks about is how she wishes she could have her whole family home for Christmas. You and Teddy will both be here, and I don't want to ruin that."

"Then maybe you should leave." The words are out before I can stop them.

We can add "tactless" to the list of my fatal flaws. I have a feeling this trip is going to expose them all.

The expression on Max's face is so earnest I know it was cruel. He watches me, probably aware that I'm wrestling with this. Like my mother said, all this meanness isn't me.

He takes a step closer to me, and I feel the unwanted rise of goosebumps on my arms at his nearness. "We were good friends once."

That was before I fell in love with you.

That was before you broke my heart.

He squeezes my arm in the most platonic way any man has ever touched a woman, and I still feel a flip in my stomach.

"Think about it, okay?" As he removes his hand from my skin, he drags a finger from my elbow to my wrist, and I nearly shiver at the touch.

If he notices, he doesn't let on. He simply flashes a smile, puts his AirPods in, and walks out the back door. I assume he's going for a run because, of course he would, and I'm left here in his wake, wondering how much a plane ticket back to Denver would cost two weeks before Christmas.

This is not good for me. None of it.

I'm having feelings. And not the mean, angry ones that I rely on to keep me from getting hurt again.

The warm, fuzzy ones that might just convince me that everything I used to believe about Max could be true again.

Thankfully, I'm saved by a knock on the door.

Seconds later, Steph is ushering me back into the kitchen while texting and talking on the phone through her headphones.

"Sure, she'd love that." She pauses, gives her head a little shake and points to her headphones. "We're here for all the Pleasant Valley charm." She looks up at me and rolls her eyes, and I wonder (not for the first time) why she agreed to come on this trip in the first place. She's hedging her bets that Tim will pick me, because a promotion for me means a promotion for her.

"Absolutely," Steph says, using her professional voice. "Great. We'll get it on Marin's calendar."

When she hangs up the phone, she gives me a once-over.

I'm not dressed in normal work attire, and it's clear she doesn't approve. But jeans and a form fitting red flannel are appropriate attire for Pleasant Valley, so I took a chance.

"This isn't what's going to happen while we're here, is it? You're just going to let yourself go? Because if you want to win back that hot ex-boyfriend of yours, this—" she waves a hand from my head to my feet and back again—"isn't going to cut it."

I pour myself another obnoxiously full mug of replacement coffee and contemplate the half and half. With the peppermint mocha sitting right there, I can't bring myself to do it. The sacrifice cup was really just for Max's benefit anyway. I pour the creamer into my mug deciding I'm not conceding to Max if he isn't here to watch me drink it.

Ooh. It's really good.

"What is that?" Steph asks, nodding at my creamer.

I frown. "Do you really not know?"

"I sent Danny out for Starbucks," she says.

I laugh. "There's no Starbucks in Pleasant Valley, Steph. I don't even know if there's anywhere to get anything other than black coffee."

She grimaces. "Why are we here again?"

I've been asking myself that question since we arrived.

"Who was on the phone?"

"That was the coordinator of a brand-new Christmas event —a Christmas cocktail competition."

I take another sip. The contraband creamer warms me from the inside out. "Why were they calling you?"

"They want you to be a judge."

I recall the bit of the conversation that I'd overheard. "Wait. You told them I'd do it?"

Steph is back on her phone. "Of course. It'll be great for the show."

"Steph, I don't drink! How am I going to judge which one is best?"

She shrugs. "If it tastes good or gets you drunk, it wins."

I groan. How can any cocktail taste good to a non-drinker? "Are they all going to have alcohol in them?"

She looks at me like I just asked her how long minute rice takes to cook.

"Are you serious right now?"

I wince. "I mean, kind of?"

"You're also judging the snow sculpture contest, and we'll tour some strolling thing with the mayor and. . .I think you're doing something with chili? I'll ask Ashley, she's got it all in the calendar."

"Steph, isn't this supposed to be about *my* Christmas traditions?"

She barely looks up from her phone, waving a hand at me. "It is. I mean, this is all junk that's happening in your po-dunk hometown."

"It isn't, though. Not if you're scheduling everything. No more judging contests, and I don't want to 'stroll with the mayor.' I'm going with my family, like I do every year."

Now she meets my eyes. "Do I need to remind you how long it's been since you spent a Christmas here?"

"I know how long it's been, Steph."

"Eight years." A voice says from behind me.

My mother has entered the kitchen with an armload of grocery bags and Danny trailing behind. She probably caught him outside and forced him to carry his own armload of groceries—and from the looks of it, she loaded him up. "Eight years of my daughter not being home for Christmas." Her tone is chipper, a pure contradiction to what she is saying.

"Here we go," I mutter under my breath.

"I'm teasing, Marin. I do think it's wonderful that you've

worked your way to the top without sleeping with sleezy men. It's important in the workplace to not compromise your morals for a hot boss with a bad marriage." My mother hasn't worked outside this home in at least twenty-nine years, so I have no idea how she's formed this opinion.

General Hospital, maybe?

"I do think it was a little cruel of your boss not to let you go home every third year or so, but what do I know? I'm just the mother." She flashes a phony smile and glances at Danny, who is standing off to the side, still holding a load of groceries. "Oh, set that here. I'll pay you in cinnamon rolls and coffee."

Danny does as he's told and my mother heats up her "best batch of cinnamon rolls ever." She shoves them in front of Steph and me, and they are no match for my willpower. I serve myself two of them, and if Steph doesn't hurry, I'm going in for a third.

"We need to get moving," Steph says. "We've got content to film."

Twenty minutes and three-and-a-half cinnamon rolls later, I'm stuffed to the gills and preparing for my close-up. The plan for our time here in Pleasant Valley is pretty simple. Using a mix of on-air segments and livestreams on the station's social media, we'll share tidbits from Christmas in my hometown. The goal is to try and get as many viewers as possible to tune in because that is one major metric Tim will use when making his decision between me and Sophie.

Steph and I came up with a whole list of different events to cover, along with trending social media we can use to get our videos seen.

Sophie is from Tucson, so she's not going to have the small-town Christmas charm or the freshly fallen snow that I will (hopefully) have. Still, I know my co-worker will come up with something great.

And I want to cheer her on. She's great at her job.

But I also want this show. I'm great at my job, too.

As we track what's working, we'll adjust our plan accordingly, making sure to give the people what they want most.

This morning, Steph wants to go live with a feature on one of my mom's most prized collections. When she pitches the idea to my mother, the woman practically stops breathing for five full seconds, then, without saying a word, she leaves the room.

Steph is standing by the counter, pouring herself a cup of coffee, and she slowly turns to look at me. "What just happened?"

"Twenty bucks says she's going to change and put on lipstick."

Minutes later, Mom returns. Her lips, as expected, are now bright red, almost an identical shade to the gaudy Christmas sweater she's wearing.

I frown. "What is that?" I nod toward the sweater.

Mom puts her arms out and shakes her chest like a Vegas showgirl, jiggling all the bells that are sewn on to the front of the sweater. "It jingles!"

"You can't wear that on the air."

"Sure, she can," Steph says with a grin. "It's festive." My producer waggles her eyebrows at me, and I know this is a losing battle. "Maybe you could take some Christmas fashion tips from your mother, Marin."

"You do look a little disheveled this morning," my mom agrees. "The plaid is nice, but honey, you're too young for such big bags under your eyes. Do you have any lipstick?"

"I thought the idea was to show viewers a peek inside a holiday at home. I'm not wearing a pantsuit and red lipstick to eat cinnamon rolls and tour my own house."

I give myself a once-over. I blame my appearance on my

lack of sleep, but I'm not about to confess that. My mother—
and probably Steph too—would read into it.

Instead, I get mic'd up, grab some neutral lipstick, and take
one last drink of coffee.

Here goes nothing.

Chapter Eight

Max

Running always clears my head.

Well, *almost* always.

I've been a runner since middle school, and in hindsight it's saved me thousands of dollars in therapy. Actually, it was a therapist who pointed out how great it is for my mental health. That same therapist also pointed out that pushing Marin away might be something I regret one day.

I'm up with the sun, as usual, needing this brand of therapy a little more than usual today, especially after my failed attempt at a truce with Marin. A smart man would keep his distance, but when it comes to her, that's the last thing I want.

Outside, I stretch my tight muscles, surprised how warm it is for December. The seasons seem to be confused.

I start off down the gravel driveway, knowing that this wouldn't be an easy run. The McGrath house is large and sprawling, with a yard that makes it feel like a private oasis. But if you turn right out of the driveway and go up the hill, you'll stumble upon my childhood home.

I turn left.

Most times I've been back in Pleasant Valley, I've been able to tamp down the pain to a minimum, but with Marin here, I'll need a whole new level of suppression.

I didn't sleep well, but I don't think that's why I'm slow and sluggish to start. If my therapist is to be trusted, I can assume that my subconscious is trying to tell me something. It could be a mile or ten before I figure out what it is.

Thankfully, my revelation hits around mile four.

I need to talk to Marin. Like, really talk to her. Did I really think I could get away with not addressing the past? Marin would call me out on that so fast, and I knew it.

Letting her go was the kind thing to do. The right thing to do. At least, that's what I'd always told myself.

But I could've handled it better.

And I never apologized.

I'm at the bottom of a hill nearing my fifth mile when I have another revelation, this one not so welcome. I don't just want Marin to forgive me. I want her back in my life.

But why would she ever agree to that?

My quads burn at the challenge of the hill. I reach the top and push myself to keep going, synchronizing my breath with my footfalls, working hard to keep it steady.

And what am I thinking? Do I want us to be friends, the way we were all those years before I kissed her in the hallway?

Or do I want free access to hold her in my arms, to grab her hand when I want to feel her skin underneath my fingers, to kiss her goodnight at the end of a long day?

It takes three seconds for me to know the answer to these questions. I want it all. I want the friendship and the romance. I want Marin.

My pace quickens to an all-out sprint as I hit mile six.

My reasons for leaving haven't changed. It was never about

a lack of feelings for her—quite the opposite. The fact was, I loved Marin *too* much.

And I'm afraid that hasn't changed.

Marin

Steph is communicating with the station back in Denver, where they're preparing for the morning show. She hands me an earpiece so I can hear the morning anchor, Roger Newton. He'll be in my ear, doing a lead-in, and I'll be ready when he tosses it to me.

I glance over at Danny. He's helping my mom with her microphone, and she seems so excited she might spontaneously combust.

"Okay, Mom, the key is to just be yourself, okay?" I say.

"Oh, sweetie, I can talk about Christmas all day long."

"Well, they're only giving us four minutes, so let's keep it brief." I suddenly have visions of my mother being impossible to shut up.

"Four minutes? Well, that's not going to be enough time," she says plainly.

"Just focus on the highlights, okay? Hand-carved Santas, and how it's a tradition in our family. We'll get to the other stuff throughout the week."

My mom peers over at the collection of wooden Santas, made for her by my grandfather before he passed away. My favorites are *Santa on Tractor* and *Santa Gets Stuck* (that one is just the fireplace with black boots sticking out), but *Sunbathing Santa* is definitely in the top five.

I can practically hear my grandpa chuckling as he carved

that big, bare belly, then added a pink sunburn to the pale, peach skin.

"Yes! I've been wanting to hear about these cute little dolls ever since Marin told me about them." Steph turns to my mother with a smile.

"I wouldn't exactly call them 'dolls,'" my mother says absently, picking up *Santa Kissing Mrs. Claus*.

Steph's face freezes for a moment, but she's quick to move on. "We'll start by asking you a few questions about why you love Christmas so much, and then focus on the story behind these adorable little—" she fumbles for a word—"figurines." Steph makes a sweeping gesture toward the shelf where Mom has meticulously set up all of the hand-carved statues.

"Okay," Mom says, smiling. "I like this idea!"

I smile at her, and we start our pre-filming rituals like a well-oiled machine. For all her bluntness—which is refreshing—Steph is an excellent producer, keen and adaptable. She can read a room like no one I know. Sometimes I wonder if she'd ever want to step outside the confines of the local news and jump into a bigger project with me.

This, of course, makes me think of Max.

Then again, what doesn't?

He's really the only other person I ever talked to about *the big dream*. When you're young and full of invulnerable optimism, dreams are as easy as *"Oh, I'll just try that."* Everything seems attainable—doubly so if you've got someone alongside you.

Max being here is definitely why these types of things are consuming my thoughts all over again. He's here, in this house, buying me coffee creamer and looking at me with those eyes.

But no. That dream died when Max left.

I do my best to focus on affixing my mic to my not-Steph-approved plaid shirt.

Steph pulls a tube of concealer from a sleek "emergency" fanny pack she wears around her waist and dabs it on my eye bags. "Did you sleep at all?"

I feel Mom's eyes on me.

"Not much," I say, then quietly add, "turns out futons aren't so great for grown adults."

Steph's eyebrows ask a question, but I give my head a little shake and the subject is dropped.

Like I said, she can read a room.

Danny gets into place behind the camera, and Steph holds up a placard to help him white balance the camera. As I position my mother between me and the shelf of wooden Santas, she squeezes my arm.

"This is so exciting," she says.

It's fun to see her this overjoyed—and to think that I'm partially the reason makes it even sweeter.

"I'll guide you through it, and if I have to cut you off don't be offended, it's just because I have someone in my ear telling me when to wrap it up."

"So, someone will be talking in your ear while you're listening to me?"

"Yep."

"And that doesn't bother you?"

I shake my head. "You get used to it."

But the truth is, it did bother me. The stories I told at work were always short and to the point, and I never got to thoroughly listen to my guests because I always had one ear listening for the voice telling me I was out of time.

"Ready?" Steph takes a step back next to Danny and we all go quiet. I hear Roger through my earpiece, closing out the previous segment, and then, I get the cue.

Danny flips on the light above the camera, nods at me, and I'm off.

"Good morning from Pleasant Valley, Illinois, where I'm standing here in my parents' living room—"

"Oh, it's your living room too, Marin," Mom cuts in.

"Well, yes, for this holiday season, Mom, but I do live in Denver." I say this lightly and smile at her.

"But all my kids know that this is home whenever they want it to be." Mom says this straight into the camera, smiling, hands clasped, and I realize that this isn't going to be the easiest interview I've ever conducted.

My mother is going to go rogue.

And what does she mean "all" her children? She only has two—me and Teddy. My stomach rolls knowing that she's included Max as one of us.

Which he absolutely is not.

"During my time here, back home in," I nod toward my mom, "*our* living room, we're going to be touching on some of our favorite family Christmas traditions. Every family has their own—stockings on Christmas Eve, maybe it's matching pajamas while opening presents—but one tradition for our family that I love hearing about are these very special, hand-carved Santa figurines. Why don't you tell us about these, Mom?"

She couldn't be happier to answer. She loves talking about the Santas. They're all a little different, all a little imperfect—each one unique. And there's beauty in that. Mom is always trying to find the life lesson in everything, and I've realized the older I've gotten that these stories she tells really do impact a person, whether they realize it at the time or not.

I'm proud of Mom's brevity in sharing about the Santas. I smile in approval and ask a simple question.

"So, with so many to choose from, I'm wondering, which one is your favorite, and why?"

She glances over at the display, about to pick one, when behind me I hear the front door open.

Oh dear Lord please don't let it be. . .

"Oh, shoot, I'm so sorry I didn't know you were filming. . ."

Steph's eyes dart toward the entryway, and then widen, and I know exactly who has walked in the door.

"Oh, Max, come here, tell us which of the Santas is your favorite," Mom says, waving him in.

I try not to show the panic on my face.

"Oh Mom, that's not necessary, we're talking about *your* favorite." I'm a fish who's been pulled from the water, flopping around on the deck of a boat.

"Don't be silly, Marin, these are here for our whole family to enjoy."

But Max is not our family.

Telepathy is not one of my mother's many gifts. She continues to wave Max into the living room.

Danny pokes his whole head around the camera and looks at me, confusion on his face. I paste on my smile and take a step to my right to make room for Max, and Danny widens the shot. Max's expression matches my cameraman's, but Mom is blissfully unaware how awkward she's just made this.

The worst part of all of this is that Max is shirtless. And sweaty. And glistening.

Why isn't he wearing a shirt? It's December. In Illinois. I would point this out, but there's no way I'm going to give him the satisfaction of knowing that I noticed.

Mom turns toward Max, who is frozen in the doorway. "Well, come here!" She smiles at the camera. "This is Max. You probably remember him from the porch." Mom frowns. "Have they already seen the footage on the porch?"

I only stare.

This doesn't stop her. "Max is the son of my very best

friend in the world and he and Marin used to date, once upon a time. We all thought they were going to get married, in fact."

Kill. Me. Now.

My viewers are going to see me actually die live on TV.

"Hey. . .Mom, let's go ahead and get this right back on track, can we do that? Great, let's do that! Santas, and the carving? With the wood?"

Word salad. Where are those improv classes now?

I continue like I'm skiing down a hill having never learned how to ski.

"Mom, pick a favorite Santa and we can post it on our socials later. Maybe we could get a shot of all of them and the viewers could vote."

"I like the one of Santa riding a bicycle," Max says from the doorway. He takes a few steps into the room, and I want to go fetal. My body has a traitorous reaction to his nearness, and I'm fairly certain *lust* is written on my face.

"But the one of Santa with Rudolph is pretty special too."

"Oh?" Mom picks it up. "Why?"

"Because the night you got that one was the same night I realized I liked Marin as more than a friend."

I turn. "It was?"

"It was."

I look at him.

He doesn't look back. He takes the statue from my mother and turns it over in his hand. Then, with a nostalgic smile, he says, "Remember we had that challenge to see who could name all of the reindeer names." He looks at the camera. "I won, by the way."

"No, you did not," I point at him. "I've known that song since I was a kid."

"She has," my mother agrees, to the camera, hand on heart. "It's a requirement in our family."

"I think she was flustered because before we started the game, I told her she looked pretty, so she missed a few."

"I don't remember that."

He looks into my eyes, squinting a little. "I do."

At this point I have forgotten the camera is on, and that we're live. It's *West Side Story's* Dance in the Gym, the Sharks and the Jets have faded away and it's only Maria and Tony.

"You didn't say anything."

"Are you kidding? I was way too scared. Taking things from 'just friends' to 'maybe more' isn't easy." He smiles into the camera. "Beautiful women are intimidating, am I right?"

My skin tingles at the compliment.

Mom still seems lost in thought over what was supposed to be the simplest question ever. She picks up *Santa in Workshop* and gives a definitive nod. "This one. This is my favorite. It's classic and traditional, just like Christmas should be."

There's a pause, and I distantly hear a voice in my earpiece, but I can't quite make it out, nor do I want to. It's telling me something about how it's my turn to talk, because we're live, but Max is still standing beside me, and I'm now caught up in the memory of that night.

It rushes back and, like a flood, I couldn't stop it if I tried.

Chapter Nine

Marin

Our families always spent Christmas together.

Teddy, Max, and I always found ways to get into trouble. We'd peel back the tape on our presents and peek inside, or we'd throw little pieces of paper in the fireplace. We'd hide during the grandparents' arrival because Max's grandma smelled like gardenias and she insisted on kissing us on our cheeks, leaving behind the imprint of her bright pink lipstick. We'd fall asleep in the living room under the twinkling lights of the Christmas tree while our parents played gin rummy at the dining room table, the sounds of their soft laughter lulling us to sleep.

And now I remember—that year Teddy fell asleep early and Max and I stayed up late talking.

Max and I had always been "just friends." But that night, with our sleeping bags next to each other and my brother in a food coma from eggnog and thumbprint cookies, something between us shifted.

It was like I knew, even in my fifteen-year-old naivety, that Max wasn't looking at me like I was just a friend.

Maybe that was why, months later, when the time came, I gave him my whole heart, without holding onto a single piece of it for myself.

I'd never make that mistake again.

I finally—*finally*—see the red camera light in my peripheral vision. I'm still staring at Max, who has a quizzical look on his face.

Just off camera, Steph is waving to get my attention, her eyes all psychopathic murderer.

"It seems Marin is lost somewhere with the ghost of Christmas past," Max says, turning to the camera with ease. "But she'll be back later to tell you about another one of the McGrath family traditions." He winks at the camera, slings an arm around me, and my mother lifts her hand in an exuberant wave.

After a beat, Danny flips off the camera and says, "And we're clear."

I shrink out from under Max's sweaty arm. "What was that?"

"That was me saving your butt," he says.

"I didn't need saving!"

His mouth turns up. "You didn't? It seemed like you did."

"You definitely did," Danny says.

"Danny! Really?" I turn to face Max full on. "I didn't need you in the interview. What were you thinking?"

"I was thinking it would be rude not to come in when your mom asked me to," he says. "And now I'm thinking—" he rubs his *very muscular* stomach—"I'm hungry. Do you want me to share my thoughts with you all day long or is this just a right now kind of thing?" He starts toward the kitchen.

I look at everyone else in the room, and they all shrug comically at the same time.

They're no help, so I follow him into the kitchen.

"Max, I'm working here. This is my job."

"Oh, I know, Mare." He starts opening the cupboards again, like he owns the place. He pulls out a small frying pan and a larger frying pan, then gets the eggs and bacon from the refrigerator. "We all know that you came home for Christmas to work."

There's a twinge of a dig in his tone. I cross my arms over my chest. "What's that supposed to mean?"

"Nothing." He feigns innocence.

Not buying it.

He adds, "Why? Do you feel guilty?" He pulls the chocolate milk from the refrigerator and pours it into the blender, along with some powder from a canister that's bigger than his head.

"No! I don't. . .!"

He hits the power button on the blender and shrugs at it, as if to say *I can't hear you!*

Frustrated, I yell, "Just stay out of my interviews, okay?!" Before I can stop myself, I add, "You shouldn't be here anyway!"

But Max turns off the blender mid-sentence so the "—*shouldn't be here anyway!*" part reverberates loud enough for everyone in the house to hear.

I pause. Stubborn and tactless. Regret twists inside of me, and I hate that it does. I need to get myself under control.

"Marin Josephine McGrath."

My gaze hits the floor at the sound of my mother's reprimand.

"Apologize to our guest."

I'm ten years old again, and Max and I just got into a fight because I told him and Teddy no boys were allowed in my treehouse.

"Mom. . ."

"This is my house, and as I've already said, he is welcome here. You are *both* welcome here," she says. "And I won't tolerate fighting. Not at Christmas."

As he pours some chocolate concoction into a tall glass, he shrugs. "I thought what I said was kind of sweet."

"Uh, and so do our viewers, apparently," Steph says, eyes glued to her phone.

I snap my head to her. "What?"

"The comments on the livestream are crazy." She scrolls. And scrolls. She is still scrolling and says, "Everyone wants to know the scoop on Marin's ex-boyfriend."

If I had a pillow I'd scream in it.

Of course, they do.

Beside me, Max cracks an egg into the pan. "What can I say, the camera loves me almost as much as you do."

"Say, Max. . ." Steph says this as if she's just gotten an idea. "You should be in more of our interviews."

Oh no. I need to Shut. This. Down. I'm shooting darts at Steph with my eyes, but she's not looking at me.

She continues, the idea gaining speed. "Maybe you could do a few Instagram Lives with Marin? Or a few remote spots? Maybe a tag team interview or two. . .I think people would really respond to that." She's looking at her phone—and not at me—as she says this.

If she *had* been looking at me, maybe she would've seen the horror on my face. Maybe my eye-darts would've landed.

"Aw, they're trying to come up with a ship name for you two," she says. "Marx? Maxin? Marix?" She grimaces. "You guys don't have a great ship name, do you?"

I want to bolt out of the room like a ball from a cannon.

"Oh. My. Gosh. This is *so* cute." Steph holds up her phone. There's a picture of a heart around our two faces with "M + M" written over the top.

Well, that's a punch in the gut.

Even Max stops moving for a split second.

I can only groan and leave the room.

There must be a Christmas-themed rock I can climb under around here somewhere.

Chapter Ten

Max

I can see James down the hill, hauling lumber from the back of his truck and into his woodshop. He's a second father to me, filling in the unwanted gap when my dad died.

For a long time, I stayed away—not because of any lofty aspirations of my own, but because being with Lydia and James only highlighted what I no longer had. After a few of years of aimlessness and a whole lot of choices I regret, I spontaneously came home.

And there they were. Running down the road to greet me with open arms.

With coffee in hand, I make my way down the hill to the woodshop, letting myself in, where I find James putzing around near one of his machines. He's not fully retired yet, but he always saves all of his vacation time for December. Drives Lydia nuts having him underfoot all day long, which is probably why she didn't put up a fuss when he said he wanted to build a woodshop. What a great way to get him out of her hair.

He glances up and sees me standing in the doorway. "Max, my boy! Come check out my new miter saw!"

I chuckle as I step inside. "Another new one?"

"Don't tell Lyddie," he says. "I'm pretty sure she got me slippers for Christmas, so I look at it as 'righting a wrong.'"

"Solid choice. Let's see how that plays out."

He's looking at the saw with such pride that I'm surprised Marin wasn't named Makita.

He looks up, and I see it—the moment he reads my mail. Instead of badgering me, he says, "Help me unload this lumber?"

I set my coffee down and do as I'm told. James is slowing down, but he's still the hardest working man I've ever met. It's inspiring, really, though I often wonder if he gets bored going to the same job he's had for thirty-five years. Did personal bankers get bored?

"So, Marin's back," he says without looking at me. He drops a stack of 2x4's onto the saw horses and heads back outside.

"Yep." I follow him, making a mental note of how many 2x4's he grabbed so I can grab at least that many—it's a pride thing.

"How's that going?" He picks up another stack of lumber.

"Chilly."

James laughs. "If holding grudges was an Olympic sport, she'd have the record for gold medals."

"Well, she has a right to be angry with me," I say, picking up my own stack.

"It's been a long time, though. She needs to move on."

"Move on from me?"

He looks at me, eyebrow quirked. "You don't want her to move on?"

"Well. . .yes. I mean, no. No, I do." A pause. "I think." Another pause. "I mean I did. That's why I broke up with her in the first place. I knew she deserved better." That was part of it, anyway.

"You sure?"

The way he says it makes me feel like he has information on the subject that I don't. And since the subject is *me*, this is troubling.

"Yeah, I mean, I knew I wasn't in any kind of state to have a relationship. It wasn't fair to her."

"And you were afraid." James is out the door again, but I don't move right away.

When I finally join him outside, he's sliding the ends of the last stack of lumber onto the lift gate of the truck. "You take this one."

I do as I'm told, and when we're both back inside, he walks around the workbench and starts looking lengthwise down each 2x4, eyeing their straightness. He's wearing reading glasses which still look wrong on his face. James has always been strong and sturdy. It's odd seeing things like his eyesight start to weaken.

"I wasn't afraid," I say.

"Yes, you were." He's so matter-of-fact that I believe him. Then he adds, "Ugh, this wood's totally whomperjawed." He sighs. "And you should tell her the truth about it." He's right, and he's still not looking at me.

I try to explain. "I broke up with Marin because I didn't want to bring her down. I didn't want her having to worry about me or look after me. I wasn't the same guy after," I still have a hard time saying it, "my parents died." It sounded like a good, selfless reason. Never mind if it wasn't the whole truth.

He finally looks up. "But that's not what you told her."

I look away. I'm still ashamed of the things I said to her, and even more ashamed knowing that James and Lydia know about it.

He sets a board on the "good" stack. "What about now?"

"Now. . .I don't know. I want to be friends with her again."

He smirks. "Uh-huh."

"What aren't you saying, James?" I pick up my coffee mug and hold it in both hands, as if that could shield me.

He makes a line on one 2x4 with a square and sticks the pencil in his mouth. "You'll figure it out."

"Can you just tell me?"

He laughs. "Where would be the fun in that?"

I chuckle with him. "It'd be easier on me!"

"Easy is never the goal." He brings the marked wood over to his new miter saw.

I take a few steps over to where he's standing. "James, come on. You're the wisest person I know."

"Well, I've got you fooled."

I pause. "So, how do I get her to talk to me again?"

"How'd you get her to talk to you in the first place?"

"I think you guys made us talk."

"No guarantee Lydia won't do that again. All I'm saying is, if you and Marin find yourselves locked in the basement one day, you know who's responsible." James chuckles. "But I don't think that's true. I think there was a period of time where Marin wasn't friends with you and Teddy."

"There was. She banned us from her treehouse."

"And what did you do?"

"Made Teddy help me paint the inside of it pink and filled it with her favorite things."

"Well, there ya go."

I frown. "James, I don't think Marin wants a pink treehouse anymore."

"You sure about that?"

I can't see his point.

"She didn't want a pink treehouse," James says. "But when

75

you painted it, you showed her that you were thinking about her."

I think about her all the time. I don't admit this out loud, and yet, I imagine James already knows.

"Oh, I didn't realize you guys were both here." It's Marin.

I turn in the direction of the door and find her standing there. She's holding two cups of coffee and thankfully, she isn't being trailed by a cameraman.

"Mare-Bear!" James is so jolly he's practically Santa Claus. "What brings you down to the man cave? Want to see my new miter saw?"

Her smile is very obviously forced, and probably meant to drive me away.

I stay put.

"I wanted to see if you'd be up for letting me interview you," she says.

"For your show?" James isn't exactly looking at her, but I am.

I always thought it was impressive that Marin was on the news, the way she'd taken her love of people and television and stories and turned it in to a career. In a way, she reinvented herself. Got herself a new dream.

And she was good at it.

I know because I've seen her. More than once. Her stories post online as well as air on TV, and every once in a while, I'd go on a *Marin-binge*, giving myself permission to check in. To search her eyes for happiness and contentment—two things I want for her more than anything else.

I'd also pause it on her left hand and look for signs of a relationship.

Yeah. I never quite got over her.

"Yeah, Dad," she says, pulling me from my thoughts. "For my show."

"Sure!" he says, chipper. "What will we talk about?"

Her eyes dart over to me, and still, I don't move.

"Your woodworking? The gifts you make, that sort of thing?"

"Sounds fascinating." He sticks the fat pencil in his mouth again and zips a tape measure onto a piece of wood. "Let's do it."

"Great." She doesn't move. "Maybe later this afternoon? Or tomorrow? Is there a time you'll be out here—" her eyes dart to me, then quickly back to her dad—"alone?"

I acknowledge the dig with an amused smile, which, as expected, seems to irritate Marin.

"Sure, hon, whenever you show up, I'll be here." James barely looks up. "Easier than getting in your mother's way."

Marin stands there for a few awkward seconds, then finally says, "Great. I'll be back down later."

And with that, she's gone.

"Well," James says, hand on the miter saw. "Sorry for the bad pun, but. . ." he squeezes the trigger and the saw roars to life, and he pulls it down, precisely cutting the 2x4 on the line he drew. "You've got your work cut out for you."

Chapter Eleven

Marin

Max is everywhere.

I try to avoid him, but every time I turn around, there he is.

Bathroom. Kitchen. Woodshop.

And every time I get a text message, it's Steph, sending me more proof that my viewers are as smitten with my ex-boyfriend as I am trying not to be.

It's late afternoon, and I can't take sitting around the house anymore. I've been hiding out in the sewing room, but it's getting stifling, so I decide to get out and tour downtown Pleasant Valley on foot, filming the sights for future videos. I've got the freedom to go live on our social media whenever I want, so if anything interesting is happening, I can loop in my viewers. Mostly I'm just looking for B-roll for the stories we've got planned over the next few weeks.

I raid the hall closet for my old pink puffer coat and a stocking cap, and head out to my rental car, but as I'm pulling out of the driveway, I happen to glance up into my mirror and see my mother standing in the way, frantically waving her arms to stop me.

I gasp, my stomach in my throat, as I slam on the brakes. When I open my eyes, Mom is standing beside the car motioning for me to roll down my window.

"Mom, are you crazy? You realize I almost hit you, right?" I say, still trying to slow my pulse.

"Oh, stop, I had it under control," she says, like it was no big deal. "You didn't tell anyone you were leaving."

Oh. Was I supposed to? It's been so long since I've had anyone to alert about my whereabouts, it's just not something I do anymore.

"I need you to pick out the Christmas tree this year," she says.

I frown. "Yeah, I thought that was odd that it wasn't up. Don't you normally have it completely done the Saturday after Thanksgiving?"

"We were waiting for Teddy," she says. "I have the little ones up in the other rooms, but I like to do the big one as a family."

How many years had they decorated that tree without me? Did someone else put my ornaments on the branches?

Did Max?

I shake the thought away. "So, what's changed?"

"Teddy just called. He got caught up with some work things, and he's not going to be home until next week. We can't wait that long to get a tree."

"Okay, well, then why don't we all go? You and Dad and me? You love picking it out." And she's so particular about it, I don't want that responsibility to fall on me.

"I have my cookie exchange later, and your father is not to be trusted with a saw."

My frown deepens. "He has a woodshop, Mom. He's using some new saw right now."

She stops. "A new what?"

Uh-oh. Dad probably bought it for himself and didn't tell her.

She sighs. "That man. I'll deal with him later. Can you just? You know, handle the tree?"

"Okay, so you want me to go out to the tree farm, pick out a Christmas tree, chop it down and haul it home?" I pause. "In my rented Nissan Sentra?"

"Don't be ridiculous," she says.

Just then, the garage door opens and I see my father's old, red pick-up truck backing out.

"You're going with Max!" She waves at the truck and starts yelling. "Max! Don't forget, it has to be at least eight feet tall! And full! I don't want all the bare spots like the one James picked out last year."

From the safety of my car, I see Max nod, and I decide not to immediately look away. Instead, I watch as he easily holds a conversation with my meddlesome mother, and her whole face brightens as she speaks to him through the window of the truck.

All at once, any mushy feelings I have about Max harden into a block of irritation.

I'm not saying I'm jealous, but he definitely seems to have an easy rapport with my parents.

I wonder just how often Max has been here. Does he come for Thanksgiving and Easter too? What is he really doing here, in Pleasant Valley, at my parents' house over the holidays? Hasn't he found anyone else worth spending quality time with?

Mom is waving me over, and I see straight through her little ploy. I'm not certain she wants Max and I to get back together, but she certainly wants us to get along. I wonder if she put him up to that truce in the first place. Surely Max doesn't expect me to play nice after the things he said.

Even if it had been eight years.

If you asked me why I hadn't been in a serious relationship since college, I would point straight at Max in lieu of answering.

Not interested in your truce, pretty boy.

"Marin, hurry up! The engine is running!"

I kill the engine on my own car and force myself to walk toward the truck. When I reach it, Max leans over and opens the passenger side door for me.

I stare inside, realizing I'm about to get into a confined space with the enemy, and that enemy is wearing a flirtatious grin as easy as his flannel shirt.

Both have me all out of sorts.

His arms are propped up on the steering wheel at the elbows and he's watching me contemplate my fate.

"I promise I'm harmless." He's smiling at me.

I pull myself up into the truck and close the door. I draw in a deep breath and glance at Max.

"Drakkar," we both say in unison.

I can't help it, and I hate myself for letting it out, but I laugh. Another tidal wave of thoughts come rushing back.

Sometimes a memory is so ingrained with something as simple as a smell.

I grew up here—with Max. It wasn't the first time my dad had lent us his truck, either. We went to our junior year homecoming in Big Red.

"I bet there's a bottle in the—" I open the glovebox, and sure enough, there's a sleek, oblong black bottle of my dad's cologne. "Some things never change."

After a brief pause, Max says, "Yeah, but some things do."

I look over and find his flirty smile has faded. I want to ask him what he means by this, but I'm afraid of his answer.

I choose silence.

He takes in a big breath. "Ready?"

"Yep," I say, but I am anything but ready to be alone in a vehicle doing couple-y things with Max.

He makes a left turn out of the driveway.

"The other way is quicker," I say, trying to figure out how he plans to get to the Christmas tree farm. He never was very good with directions. "You can turn around in Monty's driveway up ahead and go back the other way."

I see his jaw clench, and the slightest little twitch of discomfort washes over his face, but he gives a shrug. "Nah, I like the scenic route."

I realize in a flash why he didn't turn right.

The image of the house where he grew up enters my mind. Steve and Jenny had purchased a small fixer-upper just up the road from our house, only months after Mom and Dad moved in. While we were too little to remember it, I've seen the pictures, and the transformation of their home was astonishing.

They did all of the work themselves. Nowadays, they probably could've made a fortune documenting a renovation like that, but back then, they did it purely for love.

Love of family.

Love of home.

Has Max finally made peace with his loss? For months after the accident, I tried to be there for him, but he never wanted to talk about it. Eventually, he pushed me out of his life completely, and I had to force myself to stop wondering if he was okay.

But now, I can't help it, I'm wondering again.

There are several minutes of quiet. Not quiet, exactly, with the amount of squeaking and rattling of the bones of Big Red.

But it's one of those moments when you can feel you and the other person are searching for something—anything—to say.

"You know she totally set this up." Max breaks the silence.

I stare out the window. "She's been trying to do that since we were four."

He chuckles. "Right?"

I shake my head. "I'm sure she's still carrying the torch of M + M. I think she took our break-up almost as hard as I did."

I "oh-shoot" turn my head quickly and look at Max, then look away. The words are out before I can stop them, and I instantly want to take them back. I don't want to talk about our break-up. Not now. Not ever.

And I especially don't want him knowing how hard it was for me.

I'd moved on. I was doing really well. My job was the new love of my life, and while it wasn't something I'd originally sought out, I'd grown to love it, and it mattered a lot to me that I did my best.

It really did. And I don't feel bad that I want to be good at it. That I want to be the best.

I should probably unpack that with a therapist, but I know I won't. I don't need someone else to tell me I'm overcompensating for the lack of meaningful relationships in my life. I already know.

Max has gone quiet, and I know I need to change the subject—fast. Of course, my mind is completely blank, and what comes out is—"So, are you dating anyone?"

It *is* the question most on my mind, but definitely not one I ever intended to ask out loud.

He turns his head slightly, keeping his eyes on the road. "You've been dying to ask me that, haven't you?"

I don't have to look at him to know the smirk is back. I can hear it in his voice.

"I'm just making conversation," I say.

"Uh-huh," he says. "Well, to answer your burning question —no. I'm not dating anyone. What about you?"

"Wouldn't you like to know. . .?" I smile to myself smugly, trying to remember the last time I went out on a date.

"Okay, so that's a no," he says.

My reaction is bigger than I want it to be. "No, it's not a 'no!'"

"I would *definitely* know if you had a boyfriend."

My frown deepens. "How? We haven't spoken in years."

"Your mom would've told me. She keeps me updated on your love life."

I briefly wonder what she's said about me. "She does?"

"Yeah, back when you were dating some guy named *Buck* —" a side eye as he says his name—"she wanted to make sure I understood you were moving on."

I desperately try to gain back control of this conversation. "Who says I would've told my mom?"

He scoffs. "You tell Lydia everything. You always have."

Not everything. Not anymore.

"But. . ." He gives me a side-eye. "Maybe you've got some secrets?"

"Maybe I do."

"Like. . .what ever happened to *Buck*?" He chuckles.

"He was. . .*fine.*"

"No one named Buck is fine."

He has a point. Buck and I lasted about two months, and I finally told him it was over when I noticed that his ringtone was "The Right Stuff" by New Kids on the Block.

I pull my phone from my pocket and film the drive. It's peaceful out here in the country, though the cornfields are bare and brown. The sky is slightly overcast, and there's a chill in the air, but this—this is what I miss about living in the Midwest.

This all makes it feel like home.

"I don't have a boyfriend," I say. "Not that you really care."

"I care," he says, eyes on the road. "I've always cared."

The words hang in the air between us.

He quickly adds, "And whatever happened to Jeremiah? Or better yet, Jed? Tell me you didn't just go out with him because of your weird crush on Martin Sheen in *The West Wing*."

"I didn't have a crush on Martin Sheen," I say. "Not like the crush you had on Hannah Montana."

"She was hot!" he says.

"Was it the wig, or the Southern accent that did it for you?"

He looks incredulous. "Um, *both*. Duh."

I scoff. "And for your information, I had the utmost respect and admiration for President Jed Bartlet. I wish he was a real man."

"And that's why you went out with Jed, right?" Daylight is fading, but not enough to conceal his grin. "It's gotta be. Your mom showed me a picture."

"Is there anything she *didn't* tell you?"

He shrugs.

"In return, she's told me exactly nothing about your love life," I say.

"I know." He takes his eyes off the road for a brief moment and looks at me. "That's driving you nuts, isn't it?"

I flick a hand in the air. "I couldn't care less." I'm doing a terrible job of convincing myself.

"Mmm-hmm," he says. "Keep telling yourself that."

"Don't flatter yourself, Max," I say lightly.

"I don't need to," he says. "You flatter me every time you look at me pretending like you don't care."

Before I can respond, he makes the turn onto the gravel road that leads to the tree farm.

Memories like a flood, again. I'm ten or eleven or twelve—it doesn't matter how old, because it was always the same. Max and me and our families, pulling into the tree farm to hunt for the two trees we'd take home and decorate for the holiday season.

It was a whole production, complete with hot chocolate and carriage rides and stargazing. This, by comparison, feels awkward and bare.

"It feels wrong without everyone, almost like we're out running an errand. Why didn't my parents want to do this with us?" I ask absently.

"They did." Max points up ahead to the makeshift parking lot, where my mom and dad are getting out of Mom's car.

"She told me she had a cookie exchange," I say.

"Maybe she just wanted us to ride together," Max says.

I put my phone away with the slight shake of my head. "Some things never change."

He pulls into the parking space next to her car and kills the engine, then he looks at me. "But some things do."

It's the second time he's said it, but it feels like it has a different meaning this time.

I'm even more curious, but of course, he's out the door before I can ask him what he's referring to. Himself? Our broken relationship? Me?

These are questions that need answers.

But as he joins my parents in the parking lot, looking like their long lost son, I'm distracted by how out of place I'm starting to feel.

Mom is standing on my side of the truck, motioning for me to get out. It's the three of them, Mom, Dad, and Max, standing side by side, looking like they fit together perfectly. When I open the door, she claps her hands together. "Let's go get a tree!"

It was like I got up from my seat at the movies to grab a drink refill.

And when I came back, someone else was sitting in my seat.

Chapter Twelve

Marin

"Isn't this wonderful? All of us together again, hunting for the perfect tree!"

Mom is downright giddy.

I am downright annoyed.

"The first thing we have to do is get some hot chocolate!"

"What happened to your cookie exchange?" I ask.

She looks briefly confused. Has she really forgotten this was the reason she claimed I had to be the one to go get the Christmas tree?

She stumbles over her reply. "Oh! Right, I had the day wrong. Do you believe that?"

No, Mother, I absolutely do not.

She pops herself on the forehead with the heel of her hand. "I really need to pay closer attention to these things, especially during the holidays."

"Uh-huh."

She leans in closer. "So...? How was the drive?"

"Frosty," I say.

"Marin." She points at me with her eyeballs. "Max told me

he asked for a truce. He made the first move—extended an olive branch."

"And I should take that branch and throw it in the river. All he did was say we should be nice to each other for *your* sake—it wasn't some grand gesture or something."

"Does it need to be?" she jingles. I tilt my head slightly in "*only my mom*" realization because she's wearing a reindeer headband. A jingly, Christmas reindeer headband. I'll even bet it. . .

My mom reaches up and presses an unseen button. "It lights up! Isn't it adorable?"

I wish my pink puffer coat would swallow me whole. "Of course, it doesn't need to be some grand gesture."

"Okay, then." She walks off as if she's just made a point, but if she did, I can't figure out what it was.

I look around. Pine Creek Tree Farm is bustling with activity. It's prime tree-buying time, and the families of Pleasant Valley have come out in droves.

It occurs to me that I should be filming this, if for no other reason than to put it on our social media.

Nearly two weeks of social media and live segments on the morning show will all lead up to our big "Home for the Holidays" show broadcasting the night before Christmas.

The Christmas Eve show is the one that really matters. That's the one that will determine whether it's Sophie or me taking over *Good Day Denver*. All of these smaller videos would hopefully pique interest from the viewers.

Interest in something *other* than Max.

I pull out my phone and navigate to the *Good Day Denver* social media page. I open the camera, hold the phone up selfie-style and click the button to record.

"Good evening from chilly Pleasant Valley, Illinois." I shiver a little. The temperature has dropped considerably, and it's actually starting to feel like winter. "This is Marin McGrath, and I'm excited to bring you a snapshot into another one of my favorite family Christmas traditions." I glance up and find Max watching me from a few yards away. His arms are crossed casually, and he seems perfectly content to stare.

I turn around so I don't have to see his face, but somehow his expression has been burned onto the back of my eyelids, so every time I blink, there he is observing me.

"Hunting for the perfect Christmas tree is a long-standing McGrath family tradition. We come out here to Pine Creek Tree Farm, which is on the outskirts of Pleasant Valley, practically in the middle of nowhere. Families come from miles around, all vying for the perfect fit. . .but my mom will tell you we always find the best tree of the bunch."

I adjust my phone ever so slightly, and in the background, I catch a glimpse of Max behind me. Still watching.

I'm used to working in front of people. It doesn't bother me that I have to be "on" or say the occasional cheesy line. But this? Doing it all with Max watching me? This is unnerving. I'm unnerved.

I'm also live, and more and more people are tuning in.

Focus, Marin.

"We always start our adventure to the tree farm with a trip to the hot chocolate shed." I start walking backwards in the direction of the little red shed where the Williams family serves hot chocolate, hot cider and their famous apple fritters.

"This tree farm has been in the Williams family for decades, and it's woven into the fabric of Pleasant Valley like a 1970's afghan. Many of us look forward to this outing every Christmas. I'm not sure if it's the tree hunting or the treats that keeps us coming back, but—"

At that precise moment, my leg connects to the wheel of a parked tractor, which somehow, I did not see until it was too late. I stop talking abruptly and my feet come out from under me. I let out a loud shriek and drop my phone onto the gravel driveway, but as I fall, I feel a pair of strong arms catch me around my waist.

When I finally get my bearings, I glance up, and see that Max is holding me at an angle, my feet dangling from his arms. It takes me a minute to figure out what has just happened, and another second or three to see that my camera is still filming, and we are still live.

"A 1970's afghan?" he says. "That's the reference you used?"

"Oh my gosh, would you put me down?" I hiss.

Max helps me to my feet, picks up my phone and looks straight into the camera and says, "I guess this makes me Marin's knight in shining flannel." He turns the camera on me, full-on reporter's voice. "Marin, what would you say caused your spill? Are you just clumsy or did the image of me in your rearview knock you on your—"

I snatch the phone from his hand and brush myself off, but the camera is now facing Max, and he must know it because he flashes a grin so beautiful it leaves me feeling slightly bewildered.

"I think she's flustered," he says.

I hurry and spin the camera around so I'm back in the frame, and I do my best to laugh it off, but I'm staring at my red cheeks and disheveled hair, and it's pretty obvious that he's right. I'm flustered.

"We'll be back later," I swipe a hand across my brow to get the hair out of the way, but it doesn't help, "with more on our hunt to find the perfect tree!"

I click the camera off and turn to Max. "What was that?"

He stares at me innocently. "Comedy gold, that's what that was!"

"Why didn't you signal me or something that I was going to run into that tractor?"

Max chuckles incredulously. "You're mad at me because you walked into a parked vehicle?"

Fair point, but I'm not letting his logic get in the way of my argument.

"This tractor hasn't moved in 50 years. It's literally decoration."

"This isn't going to work," I say.

"What, this thing between me and you?" He takes a step toward me. "It is a little overwhelming."

My jaw goes slack, and I tuck my phone in the pocket of my coat. "I told you not to flirt with me, Max."

I start walking—around the giant red tractor, which, in hindsight, is pretty hard to miss. Max follows me.

"I'm not flirting," he says, innocently. "Just trying to lighten the mood."

"Please," I say. "You were flirting with me in front of everyone on Instagram Live."

His eyebrows raise in what I take as fake surprise. "No, I was helping you recover from tripping over a big parked tractor."

I clench my teeth together so tight I fear I might break a molar.

"You should learn to laugh at yourself. People would eat that up."

I start off in the direction of the hot chocolate shed. Anywhere at this point to get away from Max. "You don't even know what you're talking about."

"I know this version of you is fake," he says. "I mean, at least you're wearing your own coat now—not that black drapey thing you had on when you got here."

I spin around. "I'm a newscaster, Max. There is a certain—"

I fumble around, waving my hand as if the right word is going to fling off my fingers and finish my sentence—"expectation."

"You sound like the captain of the debate club looking to win your next trophy." He's followed me, and now—again—he's only a few feet away.

"And when was the last time you were on the news?" I start walking again.

He quickens his pace to fall into step beside me. "All I'm saying is that people usually connect with honesty, Marin."

The gall. I can't even stand it right now.

"Is that right?" I stop walking and face him. "*You* want to talk about honesty? You of all people have no right to judge. *None.*"

It's mean, but I feel hurt and so I justify it in the moment.

He goes still. "You're right. Sorry."

I feel the heat rise up the back of my neck and I should stop while I'm ahead, but this is a snowball that's already rolling down the hill, picking up speed. "You can help me by not helping me. I don't need help. Especially not from *you*." I force myself not to look away. "And I don't need you to flirt with me. Or my viewers."

Frustration, hurt, and confusion, pent up for eight years, start to spill over.

"We aren't friends, okay? We aren't anything. So, if you have to, I don't know, be at my house to hijack my holiday and hold my family Christmas hostage, maybe just stay away from me?"

I feel a shaky combination of vulnerable, angry, and out of breath.

His eyes soften, he takes a breath, and then he looks down at the ground between us.

"I don't think I can."

He takes a few steps toward me, then stops and levels his

gaze. He's staring at me so intently I swear I could count the flecks of gray in his blue eyes.

My entire body tenses, ready to run away or straight into his arms.

He doesn't think he can? What does that mean?

And how can I be so angry with him and so drawn to him at the same time?

I rise up one more time, and finish off what I should've never started saying in the first place.

"Nobody in the whole world has ever wounded me like you did, Max. You think everything is fine, that things can just go back to the way they were." I have no idea why I'm still talking, but I end with something that makes me feel relieved to say and horrible that I said it out loud.

"Just leave me out of your plan and out of your life. Just. Leave. Me. Alone."

My feet are like cinder blocks. And Max's face is crestfallen.

I turn around on shaky legs and trudge off in the direction of the hot chocolate shed, praying that Max gives me space to gather my thoughts...while at the same time wanting him to follow.

Chapter Thirteen

Max

Well. *That went just great.*

This is what I'm thinking to myself as Marin storms off to get her hot chocolate.

She's right, of course. She's always right. I've been so caught up in trying to win her over I never actually stopped to realize just how much I hurt her.

I thought pushing her away was the right thing to do.

I can hear James' voice in my head.

"You sure about that?"

It's not like I haven't thought about Marin over the last eight years. I have. Often. But I've always been able to keep those thoughts in perspective. I took comfort in the fact that I'd done the right thing in letting her go. I didn't like it, but that was the way it had to be.

The first three years after graduation were filled with drunken nights and dark-eyed women—because when fate gashes a life-sized hole in your soul you try to mend it with whatever gets you the numbest the quickest.

Casual and uncommitted were all I could manage when it came to the opposite sex.

And it was easy, because no one had ever tempted me to want more.

I see Marin's pink coat moving in the line at the shed.

Until now.

Lydia motions me over, and I wave back, walking over to join them near the shed. I'm careful to keep my distance from Marin. The least I can do is respect her request, hard as that's going to be.

"I'm so happy we're all here like this," Lydia talks to everyone all at once, with a wide smile. "All that's missing is Teddy." She looks at Marin. "It's like you two switched places this year."

Marin's face falls slightly and no one else notices—but I do.

Once we've all got our hot chocolate, we venture out into the great expanse of the Christmas tree farm. Even after all these years, James and Lydia have very different ideas on what the best tree should look like, so I brace myself for a long evening of entertaining bickering.

Not that there was any question, but Marin's pace makes it clear we are not walking together.

She starts off a few steps in front of all of us, but at some point, she leaves the group completely, and I'm left to trail after her parents on my own.

I wander through the rows of trees, listening to James and Lydia debate every single branch of every single one.

"What exactly are we looking for this year, dear?" James's question is not without sarcasm. "Every time I think I've figured it out, you change the style."

"Well, *I* don't change the style. The style just *changes*." Lydia laughs. "It's not like I'm the one controlling the trends—

heaven knows if I was, skinny jeans never would've been so popular."

"Okay." James eyes flip to me, as if he's bobbing in the ocean and I'm on the life raft.

I lift my hands as if to say, *"Don't look at me."* He's on his own with his wife. And I'm clearly not the person to consult when trying to better understand a woman.

"I'll know it when I see it." Lydia runs a hand over a beautiful White Spruce. "The tree will let me know it's the one."

There's something slightly mystical about her tone, and I remember how hard it was to stop believing in Santa Claus with Lydia around. She just had a way of keeping the Christmas magic alive.

I knew this tree was important to Marin's mom—it had to be the perfect canvas to showcase her ornament collection. It would be proudly on display in the living room, right in front of the bay windows.

Of course, she'd already decorated the smaller trees in many other rooms in the house, but this one? This was the crown jewel—the focal point of her Christmas display.

James falls back as she moves to the next tree in the row. "I don't know why I try," he says as aside to me.

"I don't know why you do either," I say back, voice low. "Our only purpose here is to chop it down and haul it home."

James nods in agreement. "Pack mules."

Being here reminds me of my parents, who never seemed all that caught up in finding the perfect tree. They were much more likely to choose one that looked like the kind of tree nobody else wanted. My mom was a big believer in giving things a chance, a second chance, even a third and a fourth. She said grace was like that, and we should always give grace in abundance. Even to ourselves.

But what if a person didn't deserve grace? She never covered that.

I veer over a row, and then another, to the smaller trees, lost in thoughts of years gone by, when I stop short.

I see a tree my mom would've loved.

It's sparse in places, but the needles are soft. I lean in and smell, and one brief inhale tells me it would fill an entire house with the piney fragrance of the holidays.

I step back and stare, wondering if this is the magic Lydia is talking about. It's almost like, for the first time in a very long time, I can feel my parents.

It's a tree. This is ridiculous.

But for some reason, I can't walk away.

I'm overcome with memories of years and years of holidays where my mom would ask my dad to stuff a little Charlie Brown tree in the back of our minivan and lug it home. And somehow, she always made it look beautiful.

I feel my chin tremble slightly as pain and loss bubble to the surface. I can usually shake these feelings away, but this time—I can't.

I look at the tree again, and I can see my mom's face. I don't know how she did that, how she took things that other people would walk right past and turn them into things that deserved to be seen.

She did it with people, too. Always seeing the good in everyone.

I'm struggling to hold back the tears, but a few betray my will and slip down my cheeks. I wonder if she would see past my mistakes and see the good in me. I'd certainly abandoned everything they taught me in my grief.

I'm trying to make up for it now. Was it enough?

"Hey." Marin's voice pulls me back to the present. She's standing on the opposite side of the tree, watching me.

How long has she been there?

I turn away and wipe my eyes. "Oh, hey. Sorry, it's cold out here, making my eyes water."

She looks at me like she can tell I'm lying, and for the first time I really hate how well she knows me.

I force a smile, and clear my throat, hoping it will clear my head as well. "Think your mom would go for this one?"

She looks at the tree. It's maybe six feet tall. It's bare. It's plain. She looks back at me. "No, but your mom would've loved it."

That same strong emotion pushes tears to the surface again. I'm trying to hold it back, but doing a really poor job of it.

Marin hasn't been home long enough to know that I made a pact with her mom and dad. We don't talk about my parents when I'm home for the holidays. I should probably mention it to her because this isn't a topic I'm willing to discuss.

Clearly.

"I bet it's hard," she says. "Being here for the holidays without them."

Is she trying to rip the scab off of the wound?

"Maybe we could get this one too?" she says. "Sort of as a tribute to your mom? Her style was always so whimsical."

I look at her, and I can feel my eyes are wet. She watches me. And I see that she's not trying to wound me—she's being sincere. It's unexpected, after she lashed out in the parking lot.

Unexpected, but not unwanted. This is what I've been wishing for—a point of connection with Marin.

But I don't want the connection to be my parents. I just. . .can't.

The earnest look in her eyes is part of what drove me away all those years ago. I didn't like feeling so vulnerable, or seen like that—I still don't.

The problem was that anytime I'm around Marin, I might

as well have been as naked as the day I was born. She always could see right through me.

It takes no time at all to realize that hasn't changed.

I clam up, push those emotions back in their usual box and tuck them in their normal spot on the back shelf in my heart, and plainly say, "We should probably get back to your parents."

Her face falls.

Internally, I'm kicking myself. It's the first time she's been nice to me since she's been home, and I'm ruining it.

She sighs. "Right." She slowly turns and walks away.

I look back at the tree. It still wants me to take it, but I can't. It's been years and years but it still feels too soon.

Chapter Fourteen

Marin

"My favorite part is right—" Steph taps her phone, probably to hit pause on my live video from the night before. "Here!" She bursts out laughing. She flips the phone around and shows it to me.

And yep. There I am, mid-fall, mouth agape, and two big, strong arms swooping into the frame to save the day.

"Just delete it," I groan.

"No way!" Steph said. "There are a *ton* of views on this— it's practically going viral! And the comments are all positive. Well, mostly."

"The positive comments are probably all about Max," I say dryly, taking a drink of my "latte." (Read: coffee + milk.) Edna's Old School Diner, whose logo is a gray-haired lady with a pan in one hand and a ruler in the other, doesn't do "fancy" coffee drinks. This place has been here since I was a kid, and I think the gum that Teddy stuck to the underside of the counter when he was eight is probably still there.

At least the décor has been updated—somewhat. The walls are covered with framed photos and newspaper clippings pertaining to the town. The articles have been kept current, but the frames are definitely the same ones that have been there since the first moon landing.

I do a mental double-take. "Wait, what do you mean 'mostly'?"

Steph looks up. "If you keep making that face, you're going to get wrinkles in your forehead."

I relax my frown. "Spill it."

She grimaces.

"*Steph.*"

She shrugs. "Okay, fine, some people seem to think you're too mean. Specifically, to Max."

I scoff. "What? *Seriously?* Max strings me along for six years, dumps me our senior year of college—right before Christmas, I might add—and *I'm* the one who's mean?"

"They don't know all that," Steph says. "I didn't even know all of that. All they see is this super sweet, charming, and let's face it—gorgeous guy and the girl who is constantly rude and angry every time he's around."

I scan the wall and see an image I instantly recognize. Me, in a promo shot for *Good Day Denver*. Surely the people of Pleasant Valley don't consider me one of their success stories. My mother probably put them up to it.

I let out a silent groan. If they only knew the truth.

I hate that the viewers like him. I hate that they think I'm being mean.

I hate that Steph has a point.

Yesterday, after I lit into him, I felt like a total jerk. I was rude when he was only trying to be nice. He had—as my mom had pointed out—tried to call a truce, but I was the one insisting on keeping the conflict between us alive.

But I was scared to let go of the anger. Because a part of me saw what the viewers saw. My heart isn't safe where Max is concerned.

Still, I acted badly. And I felt stupid and ashamed and guilty.

Then I saw him standing there, away from everyone, staring at that tree. . . and the guilt shifted into something else. My heart broke—but not in the way it had been broken before. I could see the pain behind his eyes, and I knew he was lost in memories of his parents. The tears were evidence enough.

My parents were still carrying on their traditions, the same way they always had.

But all of Max's family traditions had died eight years ago.

Why would Max go along with any of this? Why would he even come back to this town, let alone my parents' house?

Stupidly, seeing him like that turned me into a dumb girl, thinking I could swoop in as savior and make it all better, as if he'd just been waiting around for someone to help him sort through his feelings.

I should've known better—it was like I popped in a DVD of our relationship eight years ago and hit play. I try to get him to open up, and he pushes me away. I might as well play it on a continuous loop.

I was stupid to let myself get pulled into the emotion of it. I won't—I can't—make that mistake again.

"Look, Marin, I've been thinking." Steph finally clicks her phone off and sets it on the table. "I think you should capitalize on this."

I shove a bite of pancakes into my mouth. "On what?"

"This—" she shakes her phone at me. "On you and Max."

I swallow. "There is no 'me and Max.'"

"Well, there was, once upon a time, and the viewers can totally sense it," Steph says. "Sophie went live from a Christmas-themed hot air balloon festival last night. If we want to hook them, to get them to tune in to your segments, to get Tim to give you the show over her—we've got to pull out all the stops."

I shake my head. "No. No way."

"Mare, come on—"

I point my fork at her. "Max isn't a 'stop', Steph. He's a terrible human who broke my heart."

"He doesn't seem like a terrible human to me," she says.

"Fine. He's not a terrible human. Whatever. History stays where it's supposed to stay. In the past."

"I hate to tell you this, but he's not over you." Steph takes a drink of her coffee.

I roll my eyes. "You have no idea what you're talking about."

"I've seen the way he looks at you." Steph folds her hands on the table. "I have footage to prove it."

"I think you're just seeing a little bit of history between two old friends," I lie.

"Yeah, sure," Steph says. "Keep telling yourself that. Listen, I think we can use this to our advantage."

I take another drink. The coffee here is truly terrible.

"If the playful, flirty banter between you and Max is what the fans want to see, let's give it to them. And you'll get tons of views and Tim will take notice and he'll have to promote you over Sophie."

"That is not how I want to get this job." I set my fork down. Suddenly, I'm not hungry anymore. Which is a shame, because unlike the coffee, the pancakes are actually good.

Steph steeples her fingers and touches them to her lips, like she's Mr. Burns in a *Simpson's* cartoon, and her plan is falling into place. "I hate to break it to you, but things out there in the real world don't work like they do here in Pleasant Valley. Here—" she motions circles with both pointer fingers, "—we're practically living inside a snow globe. But out there? We do what we have to do to survive. Even if it means playing up the quote-unquote *history* between you and your beautiful ex-boyfriend."

"Will you stop?"

"I'll stop when his muscles stop."

"Good grief, Steph. He's not beautiful."

"Marin, he looks like Ryan Reynolds. Like, are we sure they aren't related?"

I suddenly wish that Steph was aboard a hot air balloon, floating off into the sunlit distance and way too far away to hear anymore.

"What's the big deal? You still like him—so what?"

"Steph." I pick up my fork. "I do not like him. Being around him is killing me. Everything I wanted to forget—" I stab a forkful of pancakes "—I'm now seeing. Every day. In my *house.*" I shove the pancakes in my mouth and finish talking with a mouthful of food. "And now you want me to make him part of my strategy to get the show?"

"Yes."

"Come on!"

She shakes her head at me. "Oh, yeah, it'll be *super* hard to flirt with your gorgeous ex-boyfriend. I feel so sorry for you, *blah, blah, blah.*"

"You have no idea." I realize that Steph is not a sympathetic ear, and I've probably already said too much. I *should* be pretending that being around Max doesn't bother me in the slightest.

Why am I only just now realizing that would've been a better strategy?

Steph picks her fork back up and pushes her eggs around on her plate. "Do you see how much butter they used in these eggs?"

I roll my eyes. If she's not going to sympathize with me, I'm happy to return the favor.

She puts her fork back down. "Do you want the show or not?"

I sigh. "You know I do. It's the thing I've been working toward since I started."

"Okay, then," she says, as if what she's suggesting is the end-of-discussion solution. "You'll do what you need to do to make it happen."

"It's not that easy, Steph," I say.

"I think it is." She glances down at my notebook. "What's on the agenda for today?"

I don't have to look at my list to know that today is the Christmas Stroll. It's a big event in Pleasant Valley, and one that my mom helped start a million years ago.

There's live music, a parade, a Fire and Ice display, local vendors, food trucks, a city-wide tree lighting, caroling, fireworks, and whatever else they've dreamed up to make this year special.

Mom is still on the committee that helps organize it, so she was up and out of the house this morning before I even woke up. She left me a note telling me where to meet her for the parade this afternoon.

It was written in green ink on red paper that smelled like cinnamon.

All of a sudden, there's a *clang, clang, clang* noise coming from outside the diner. I look up and see shapes moving in the street through the slits in the blinds on the diner windows. Someone pulls the blinds up to reveal people outside. Some are wearing tutus and Santa hats, others are decked out in full-on elf gear. There is the unmistakable sound of jingle bells filtering into the restaurant.

"What is going on?" Steph follows my gaze to the window.

"The Reindeer Run," I say without looking away from the runners. "It's a Christmas themed 5K." I stop short of saying *It was Jenny Weber who started it...*

"No way!" Steph cranes her neck to peer out the window. "Wait. Is that Max?" She looks back at me and waggles her eyebrows. "That man is in very good shape."

"I wouldn't know," I lie. As if I could forget just how very good of shape he is in. I have seen him shirtless. Twice.

Steph clearly isn't buying what I'm selling. "We should get out there in case they run by again." She stands. "Does anyone know if the runners will pass by here again?" She asks this question to the entire diner, and an old man at the counter whose name I might've known once upon a time lifts an arm in a wave.

"Nope, but you can hop on over to Mayberry Street and catch the finish if you hurry," he says.

Steph looks at me, tipping her head forward in disbelief. "You have a Mayberry Street?"

I shrug. "The town is called Pleasant Valley. Are you surprised?"

She scrunches her nose as if to say *ew*. "Let's go."

"I don't want to," I say, like a five-year-old being told she has to share her toys.

"We can go live," she says. "It'll be great!"

I groan. "I feel like this is a competition of who has the coolest things going on in their hometown." What's next, Sophie Soto riding through town on a donkey as part of a live nativity?

Steph drops cash on the table. "Pretty much is, Marin. Now, let's go."

Outside, we're met with a number of spectators lined up along the street. They cheer and clang cow bells as some of the runners pass by.

"Which way?"

"Are we just doing this to chase down Max? Because out of breath runners can't compete with hot air balloons."

Steph raises a brow. "Depends on who the runner is."

I shake my head in disapproval, but start off in the direction of the finish line, which I am very familiar with, considering that this event was a big part of the Stroll when I was in high school.

Max ran it then, too.

And I watched.

Decked out in full Christmas gear.

I can still remember ringing my jingle bells as he and Teddy raced by, then rushing off to another spot so I could cheer them on to the finish line. Max was a great runner, so he was always near the front, and always, without fail, he'd come and find me as soon as he finished.

In those days, the naïve schoolgirl version of me would've told you that Max and I had a very special connection. We always knew where the other one was. We could always sense what the other one was feeling.

Maybe that's why it hurt so much when his parents died. I couldn't feel what he was feeling, because he wouldn't let me.

I had a therapist tell me once that pain you don't deal with always finds a way to come back. It will demand attention.

Maybe that's all that this was. Un-faced feelings that had begun to resurface. Maybe if I deal with them, I can finally be free of them.

I quickly reject that idea as Steph pulls out her phone and clicks a few buttons, opening up a live feed on the show's social media page.

"I don't think this is all that interesting," I say, trying to stay focused on my actual job instead of these irksome feelings that have decided not to leave me alone.

She waves me off and nods to let me know she's started the live video.

I flip a switch.

"Good morning, friends. We are still out here in my hometown, Pleasant Valley, Illinois, with a very fun—and festive—community event we couldn't wait to talk to you about! Our 27th Annual Christmas Stroll is happening tonight, and that means a full day of fun." I stop moving, having almost reached the finish line.

I remember what Max said about sounding like the debate club president, and I try to take on a slightly more conversational tone. "This was always one of my favorite events. The Reindeer Run. Participants and spectators alike dress up in ridiculous outfits, all jingle bells and frilly dresses, and run and cheer and celebrate 'running' into the greatest season of the whole year."

I point to the street sign. "We're standing right downtown on Mayberry Street, where we're waiting for the first finishers of this festive 5K that raises money for a local cause." I realize in that moment I have no idea what the cause is this year, so I start off toward a table where a worker is standing, preparing the medals for the finishers.

"Good morning—" I glance at her nametag—"Keylee. My name is—"

"Marin McGrath!" The woman gives me a once-over. "We went to high school together—do you remember me?"

I stare at her, waiting for a younger version of her face to enter my mind.

"Probably not—you spent all your time with that hottie Max Weber—" Keylee gasps. "Wait, are you here to see him? I've been watching all your social media coverage, and I know he's back in town."

I glance at Steph's phone. "Oh, that's wonderful, we're

actually filming right now, Keylee. Maybe you could tell us a little more about the charity this year's Reindeer Run is supporting?"

Keylee frowns. "You're kidding, right?"

I hold my pasted-on smile. "No, unfortunately, I don't have that information."

She laughs. "Oh, Marin, you're hilarious. Like Max didn't tell you. This year's run is in support of the Steve and Jenny Weber Memorial Fund."

The words hang in the air like a thick cloud.

"What?"

"The non-profit organization Max set up in his parents' names with that boatload of money he got in the court settlement after the accident. How do you not know about this?"

I'm frozen. It's like my brain is glitching—like a skipping record with no one to move the needle.

Steph must sense that this information has jarred me—nobody had ever mentioned this to me before. Not my mother or my father or Teddy—and certainly not Max, not that I'd given him any opportunity to tell me much of anything since I returned to town.

"Maybe you could tell us what the organization does?" I'm shocked I've managed to get my question out.

"Oh, sure." Keylee picks up a brochure from the table in front of her and sticks it in my hand. I look down and come face-to-face with an old photo of Steve and Jenny Weber. Max's parents. And I'm overcome with emotion.

Jenny's kind blue eyes smile back at me, and I'm struck with a tidal wave of grief.

I miss them. Oh my gosh, how I miss them.

And how Max must miss them way, way more.

"I thought for sure when Max bought the house, he'd turn it into a home for orphaned children or something, but that hasn't happened yet." Keylee looks up into the camera and smiles.

"What house?"

"The Weber house?" Keylee flips the flier over and points to a photo of Max's childhood home, the one next door to my parents' house. "That's going to the be the headquarters for the non-profit. They have a whole mission statement. It's pretty incredible."

"Wait. So, Max owns his childhood home?" I glance at Steph and only then do I realize I've had this revelation live and on the air. I wish I could take it back. Especially because Max—and everyone else in the world—could replay this at any time.

"How do you not know this?" Keylee asks. "And how are you and Max not married by now? You two were couple goals." Again, she looks at the camera. "You guys should've seen the two of them. Always together, inseparable. They sort of seemed to have their own language, you know those couples? I think they were voted *Most Likely to Get Married Right After High School* and *Most Likely to Have the Cutest Babies*." She glances at me. "Really sad we haven't gotten to see those babies, Marin."

I hear myself fake-laugh, and then the announcer, who is across the street and standing on a small stage, calls out, "Here comes the leader!"

The crowd (surprisingly large for this early in the morning on a Saturday) cheers, and only then do I see that a few places behind the leader, is Max.

"And look, he's still a good runner too!" Keylee leans forward and points at him, as if my eyes didn't already lock on to his stellar form.

Then, Keylee drapes an arm around my shoulder, still watching Max as he high-fives the other finishers. "I'm a happily married woman, but all I'm saying is, you never should've let that one get away."

I shrug out from under her arm. "Okay, thank you so much, Keylee, for giving us the scoop on this exciting event that helps kick off the holiday season while raising money for what sounds like a very good cause. We'll be back later with the Christmas parade—"

"The viewers are asking if you can interview Max." Steph lifts the phone ever-so-slightly, probably to cover her face so she can avoid eye contact with me.

"Oh—" I look around quickly. "I don't see him. He probably had to go get his medal, but I'm sure we can catch up to him later and find out more about his run."

"And the nonprofit?" Steph feeds me.

"Yes, of course, and that." I shoot her a look.

She ignores me. "Oh, look, he's right there!" Steph scans the crowd with my phone, stopping a few feet away. "Let's see if we can get the scoop."

Steph flashes me a smile, widening her eyes at the same time, as if I'm just supposed to go along with this very obvious plan. Only, that's just it. I'm live on social media, *Good Day Denver* is on the line, and I am clearly not in charge of this ship.

"Max!" Steph calls out. "Marin's got some questions for you, mister!"

His eyes fall to mine, and I imagine he's probably resisting the urge to tell her exactly what she can do with her phone, but after a few seconds, he drops eye contact and smiles into the camera.

"Anything for Marin."

Chapter Fifteen

Max

I can tell by the look on Marin's face that interviewing me after the race is not her idea.

I know all of her smiles, and this one is the *Grin and Bear It*. Eyes a bit wide, too much teeth, tiny twitch in her left eye. I've seen it before. When she was interviewing the pig farmer in the pig sty, for instance.

Nobody else would've seen through it, but that was the benefit of knowing Marin so well.

I wonder if she'd prefer the pig sty to me right now.

"Good morning, Max," she says, using that debate club president voice again. "We came down to share a little about the Reindeer Run, and what do you know, we found out this whole thing is being held to raise money for a non-profit you started."

Oh, shoot.

"The Weber Fund," I say, hoping she can't see my wince.

"Right."

Marin's looking just slightly off to the side, as if making eye contact with me might result in her hair catching fire.

"Yes," I say. If she's going to interview me, she's going to have to work for it.

Finally, her eyes dart to mine. "Would you tell us a little more about this organization?" She's clenching her back teeth as she says this, and I can't help it, I smile.

"Is it physically painful for you to ask me these questions?" I finally ask.

Fake smile. Plastic expression. "Of course not."

"A little bit?" I narrow my eyes at her, hoping my tone reads "playful."

She seems to give in a little. "Fine. Yes. I never would've come over here if I'd known I was going to have to interview you, but you had to go and place in the top five, per usual."

"Oh, my goodness!" One of the race organizers, Keylee, practically squeals this as she walks toward us. "The two lovebirds! Back together again!" She motions for me to lean forward, I assume to put the big medal she's carrying around my neck, but as I do, she stops abruptly. "Actually, Marin, you should do the honors."

"Oh, no, that's okay," Marin says.

"Don't be silly." Keylee practically shoves the medal in her hand. "Your fans'll Eat. It. Up." She winks at Marin with practically her whole face, smiles and waves at the camera, then saunters off, an armload of medals jingling as she goes.

Marin's gaze drops to the medal, and I know she's aware that Steph is still filming.

It's bad, but I enjoy watching her squirm.

"It looks like you got—" another glance at the medal— "fourth place overall?"

"That's right, I felt pretty good," I say.

"And you've been running this race since high school."

"I have." I look at the camera. "Only back then, I had a better cheering section."

A blush rushes to Marin's cheeks.

I look at Steph. "One year, Marin wore a reindeer costume and handed out hot chocolate at the end of the race."

"My mother made me do that," Marin says, dryly.

"And remember the year you had my face screen-printed on a green T-shirt with the words *You're Sleigh-in It, Max!* underneath?"

Marin glares at me. I grin back.

After a pause, she says, "And yeah, so, the fundraising, do you get pledges or. . .how does that work. . .?"

Her voice trails off, and she's holding the medal like she opened a present on Christmas morning and it turned out to be an avocado. I glance at Steph, whose expression seems to say *make something up!* and I can see that Marin is crashing and burning. Fast.

I hate that she's working over the holidays, but I know this job is important to her. And what's important to her is important to me.

Time to paint the treehouse pink.

I flash a smile at the camera. "The Reindeer Run started out as a way to raise money to help deserving local charities and organizations, and I've been a long-time supporter of anything that does that."

Still no response from Marin.

"In fact, Marin's mom and my mom were instrumental in starting the race in the first place."

"Well, it was your mom's idea," Marin says quietly.

"But they did it together, Mare." Then, back to the camera —"Their first charity was a church that did a toy drive for needy kids every year, and that year, they tripled the number of toys they were able to hand out. It was crazy how successful it was. I started running the race back in high school, but I continue as an adult because I believe in any event that pours back into our community."

Marin blinks a few times, like a miner coming out of a cave after a 22-hour shift. "And now the local charity is one you started."

"That's right," I say, and then pause.

I have a choice here.

I can keep this all in and let Marin find out from someone else, or I can tell her myself right here on the air and probably get her a bump on her social media stats.

I hold her gaze for a moment that feels like an eternity, and it's almost—*almost*—like old times. I try to detach my emotions so I can get through this next part.

It should be easier by now, but it isn't. And this is the best way I know how to talk about them.

Quickly and without emotion.

For Marin, I would break my own rules.

Deep breath.

"I started The Weber Foundation after my parents died. I really didn't know what to do right after, I was—" I look at Marin, "—kind of aimless. But then I realized that this was the best way to honor their memory. They did amazing things for other people in this community, and I made the choice to carry on that legacy. Our work is mostly focused here locally, and our goal is to create a community center and after school program for kids and teenagers."

"Really?" Marin looks surprised.

"Really," I say. "Teddy's actually helping me with the music program."

"There's a music program?"

I laugh. "Oh, there will be—plus a lot more. Full video editing suite, art lab, design suite, the works. I'll teach kids about shooting and editing videos, and they'll get to explore all kinds of creative outlets. We're raising funds for equipment now. Other local professionals will volunteer their time to come in and share what they've learned." I look at the camera. "So, if you're out there, and you're a maker or a creator and you want to be a part of it, look us up."

"Does this mean you're moving back here?" Marin asks.

I can sense things have gotten too heavy for an Instagram Live—nobody wants to think about dead parents at Christmastime—so I flash her a smile and bump my elbow into her.

"I will if you will."

Her jaw goes slightly slack, and I memorize her expression. Surprising her has always been one of my favorite things.

She turns back toward Steph and puts on that phony smile. "And on that note, we'll sign off for now, but we'll be back later with highlights from the Christmas Parade." She nods at Steph, and then lets out a long exhale.

"You okay?" I ask. "You look like you're the one who just ran three miles."

She doesn't look up. "What else don't I know about you?"

"I'm an open book, Marin."

She scoffs so softly I almost don't hear it. "We both know that's not true."

I look over and see that Steph is still holding the phone up, like she's filming. Marin follows my gaze, then snatches the phone away.

"It wasn't live," Steph says innocently, holding up both hands in surrender.

Marin clicks around on her phone. "And now it's deleted."

"Look, I can't help it if the public is obsessed with you two," Steph says.

At that precise moment, in an ironic display, three teen girls stop right in front of us. "Oh my gosh, it's M + M!" What happens next is something no man could ever describe—a cacophony of high-pitched squealing, a handful of selfies which I did not properly pose for, and a smattering of "We totally love you guys!" but in triplicate.

When they walk away, Steph raises her eyebrows and shrugs as if to say, "Told you so."

"Steph, I'll see you later," Marin says. "I'll text you the details for the parade. I think my mom is going to make me throw out candy or something."

"Um. . ." I start.

Marin turns to me. I can see she's taken one look at my face and deduced what I'm going to say in about two seconds.

"She's got you doing that too, doesn't she?" Marin asks.

I try humor, again. "It'll be fun, right? We'll see how many kids we can pelt with Tootsie Rolls."

"Perfect." Steph grins. "We'll do the parade on socials and then Danny will be ready for the Stroll later tonight. Think about what I said, Marin, and check your texts. See you later, Weber!" She waves, then starts off down the street.

Marin glances down at her phone, which appears to be lit up with new messages.

She looks at me, then quickly looks away.

We might as well have just gotten dropped off for the eighth-grade dance, the air between us is so tense.

"The non-profit sounds really cool," she finally says.

"You mean that?"

"Yeah. I really do. I can't think of a better way to continue the amazing impact your parents had. And using the house as your headquarters is a great idea."

I frown. "Who said that?"

"Keylee." She points off to the side at what ends up being an empty table because Keylee is no longer at her post.

"No, we're renting a space downtown," I tell her. "I closed

on it a few months ago, and they're doing a build-out now. I can take you by if you want to see it."

"Oh." She seems to be trying to work something out in her mind. "Then why did you buy the house?"

I look away. There are no cameras around, but I feel more exposed than ever, and in typical knee-jerk fashion, I look for an escape route from this conversation. "Do you want to get some breakfast?"

She studies me, as if she's trying to decide whether or not to press me on this. "I already ate."

"Sit with me then?"

More studying, which makes me think maybe I've become interesting to her again. Or maybe that's just wishful thinking.

"Sit and watch you shovel food into your mouth?" She rolls her eyes.

Her phone dings, and she looks at it. Her eyes widen, and then dart to me.

"What's wrong?"

She turns her phone around and holds it up—and I see there's a rather large number at the bottom of the post. "Apparently, our views on that video just tripled compared to the last one we posted." Marin smiles—the first time I've seen a real one since she got here. "Where are we going for breakfast?"

Chapter Sixteen

Marin

"Steph thinks you're good for my brand." I say this without looking at Max, and as expected, he doesn't respond until I make eye contact.

And his response is that trademark smirk.

My gaze falls to his lips, and I find myself trying to memorize the crookedness of that smile.

In front of him is a plate of at least six giant pancakes, four strips of bacon, and three scrambled eggs. He douses the entire plate in syrup and starts cutting it all up, mixing it together like a barbarian.

"You eat like someone is going to steal your food."

He responds by stacking a fork with way too much food and shoving it all in his mouth, grinning like an idiot.

I'm still waiting for a response.

"You're not saying anything," I say.

"I'm eating." His mouth is still half-full, and it's obvious he's being purposefully cagey.

I eye him. "You're dragging this out to make me suffer."

He swallows. "Suffer? Nah, that's a little too harsh. Squirm, maybe..."

"Max, will you just—"

He searches the air, as if there is a floating thesaurus above my head. "Writhe? No, that sounds medieval, like you're on a rack or something."

I shake my head at him.

His face lights as if he's just had a brilliant idea. "*Flounder!*" He loads up his fork again and crams the obscene amount of food into his mouth. "I'm making you flounder."

Yes. You are.

The problem is what I have to ask him, and I have a feeling he already knows. Might as well get it over with.

"I need a favor," I say.

"From me?" The innocence in his voice is maddening.

"Don't make a thing of this, okay? The way I see it, you kind of owe me."

"How do you figure?"

Because you broke my heart! As if he could ever repay me for that.

"Oh...the breakup." He points his fork at me and a chunk of egg falls back onto his plate. "You know, you probably need to let that go."

"Oh, I have let it go," I lie. "Long time ago. I hardly even remember that once upon a time I thought you were the best person in the whole world. Thank you for educating me."

The corner of his mouth lifts, and he scoops another bite onto his fork.

"I made some mistakes in my youth," he says. "But I've grown up a lot."

Not enough to have a conversation about your feelings.

And wasn't that the problem in the first place? He wouldn't let me in. Worse, he pushed me away. Though, at the time, it seemed like our break-up had less to do with his trauma and more to do with me. It wasn't like I didn't wait around to make sure. I could kick myself for waiting.

Regardless, the fact remains: Max is emotionally unavailable.

That's not what a woman wants in a relationship. I remind myself of this twice as I weigh the ramifications of what I'm about to ask him. Given my wobbly emotions, this could backfire. And if it did, it would be my heart on the line.

My phone buzzes with a text from Steph.

The likes and views and comments keep coming in! We need to plan our entire strategy around you and Max! The audience is in love, and Tim has noticed!
Your chemistry is off the charts!
BUT YOU NEED TO BE NICER TO HIM, per everyone.

I turn the phone over on the table.

"What's the favor?" He takes a drink of orange juice, and I pause to calculate the sheer number of calories this man is consuming.

I'm simultaneously jealous and disgusted.

"Steph thinks that viewers are responding to you."

His grin is mischievous, and I look away in an attempt to stop its effect on me. "That was hard for you to tell me, wasn't it?"

I bring my eyes back to his. "It was, actually, yes."

His smile holds.

"But it's not just you they're responding to..." I say this next part really quickly, in hopes that maybe he won't make a thing of it if I do. "It's you and me."

His eyebrows pop up, and he leans back in the booth. "You *and* me?"

"Yep."

"Like, the two of us? Together?" He looks around the restaurant, as if he's about to reveal some government secret. "*M and M?*" he whispers loudly.

"Apparently, we have. . .chemistry." I practically groan as I say this.

He lets out an amused laugh. He's liking this *way* too much.

"And, what, we need to play that up? Is that a requirement for your job?" he asks, still smiling.

"No, it's not required. But it might help me get a new job," I say. "A promotion."

He drops the smile, suddenly interested. "What kind of promotion?"

I haven't told my family this part, and it feels like I'm sharing something special. With Max. "I'd be the host of *Good Day Denver*. Not just a field reporter they cut away to sometimes, but the actual host."

Max appears to be processing this. "That's a pretty big deal, Marin."

I can't help but feel warm. If there's one thing that has remained consistent about Max, is that he knows when to care about the big things. And the little things.

The things that are important to me.

He continues, piecing the whole puzzle together. "You need me to help you land this job and make all your professional dreams come true."

"I don't *need* you." I need to make that very clear—to myself as much as to him. "But it might give me a leg up."

"So, why tell me?" he asks. "Why not just film when I'm around and let our chemistry happen?"

"Well, mostly because I think that would be shady. I'm not in the habit of using people. But also, because I've been off my game."

"Huh. I wonder why."

"Stop it. You know I do better when I have time to prepare."

"You don't give yourself enough credit. You're super quick, Mare. You always have been. And I think what people are responding to is the honesty of you being caught off-guard." He takes another drink of orange juice. "And me swooping in to save you, of course."

I hate that he's right.

He takes another bite and chews thoughtfully. After he swallows, he says, "Tell you what, I'll help you if we don't plan anything."

"Well, we have to plan *some* things. Like there's events, and an itinerary, and—"

He waves me off. "No, no, I'm not talking about those kinds of things. Those things keep. What we say, what we do, how we interact. . .no plans."

I sit with this for a moment.

"Plus, I'm great at keeping you on your toes."

"You're great at getting in my way," I quip. "Besides, that completely defeats the purpose."

He shrugs. "So, it's a no then?"

Why was he making this so difficult?

"I don't need you to teach me a lesson here, Max. I just want to do what I can to get this show. This is what I've been working toward for eight years."

Max drags a chunk of pancakes through the puddle of syrup. "And you're sure it's what you want?"

My shoulders drop as if I'm a tire and someone has just let the air out of me.

He presses. "Have you even asked yourself that question?"

"Of course, I have."

I have not.

"This is what I've been working toward ever since I graduated." I say this with so much conviction I believe it. I threw everything into my career after college. Swore off love and focused completely on my professional life.

My mom made a point of telling me I'd regret this one day, but that day hasn't come. My job is everything to me. And I don't need a guy messing that up.

More importantly, I don't need a guy messing *me* up.

This job is all I have.

"But it wasn't always what you wanted," he says.

"Yeah well, we don't always get what we want, do we?" I don't like that he's making me question everything I know to be true. I stand. "You know what, this was a bad idea."

"Marin, wait." He reaches for my arm, catching me before I can leave.

I glance down at his hand resting gently on my arm, and I'm transported back to college. It's our sophomore year, and we're studying on the quad. Max brought a blanket, and he's lying on his stomach, reading his Economics text book, while my head is nestled in his back, reading a copy of *A Midsummer Night's Dream*.

Occasionally, he'd wind his fingers through mine, or we'd shift places without a word, with a quiet ease of knowing each other *so well*.

I remind myself that ease is now long gone, replaced with this awkward, tense acquaintanceship that I cannot stand. I'd prefer to go back to being nothing to each other—it was easier to navigate.

I meet his gaze.

"Of course, I'll help. I'd do anything for you." He says this so genuinely, I see a glimmer of the boy he used to be. He gives my arm a light squeeze and for a brief moment, time stops.

The diner, the décor, the chatter—it all fades away.

He pulls his hand away, and I instantly miss his touch.

"But you have to do something for me too," he says.

I shake off my traitorous thoughts and plop back down into my seat. "What?"

"Agree to the truce."

I simmer.

He watches me.

I begrudgingly say, "Fine."

"No, you have to mean it. I'm done with you hating me for things that happened a long time ago."

I can't explain why, but this triggers something inside of me. "You act like it's been dealt with. You act like it's just the easiest thing in the world to move past, and move on, well we're not all like you, Max, we can't bottle up our feelings and pretend there's nothing wrong."

It comes out harsher than I intended. But it's true, and I felt every word I just said, even if I didn't intend to say any of it.

He nods. "That's. . . fair."

I continue. "You think it's crazy for me not to want to spend my holidays with you," I say. "I don't think you even realize how much it hurt me when you left. And you and my parents and Steph all want me to be okay and pretend it didn't happen, but I'm sorry, I can't do that." The words catch at the back of my throat, and my eyes cloud over. "You broke my heart, Max."

He holds my gaze from across the table. "I know, Marin."

"I don't think you do." I shake my head. "Not really. If you want to help me with this promotion, great. But it won't be real

—none of it. If you flirt with me and I flirt back, it's all for the camera. For the viewers. For the job. That's it."

"I get it." He nods. "And if that's what it takes to help you get the thing that will make you happy, then that's what I'll do."

"Great," I say.

"Great," he echoes, his tone a little kinder than mine.

We sit in silence for a few long seconds, and I chew on the inside of my cheek, trying to think of something to say.

"It'll be sort of like fake. . ." I search for a word.

"Flirting?" he says in the pause.

"Right," I say. "Fake flirting. Can you handle that?"

"I'm down." I know he's being purposely agreeable to offset my accidental frustration.

"Great," I say again, for lack of a better closer. I stand, this time putting space between me and the table to avoid the risk of physical contact.

"But Marin?" he says as I walk past.

I stop. "Yeah?"

He gives me a slight wince. "It's probably not going to be fake for me."

Our eyes meet, and I feel the electrical current of a familiar, forgotten spark. It traces the perimeter of my entire body, zapping me with jolts that refuse to be ignored.

Max breaks eye contact, and I walk away, feeling like I'm in a trance.

As I reach the door and look back one last time, I think—

This whole plan is a giant mistake.

Text from me to Steph:

You'll be happy to know Max has agreed to fake flirting with me
for the sake of my job.
Good thing he doesn't mind being used to further my career.

I don't think he'd mind being used by you in any capacity.
This is going to be fun!

Right. Fun.

Chapter Seventeen

Marin

I haven't been this nervous to film a story in years.

After the pact I made with Max, my stomach is a hamster wheel, and the hamster running on it is the five-time Hamster Wheel Champion.

The main problem is that Max is unpredictable. I can roll with a lot, I've done a ton of live TV, but I can't juggle him while walking a tightrope. I hoped looping him in to this ridiculous plan might actually help me prepare, but the truth is, I'm more off-balance than ever.

I park four blocks from where the parade starts, which is where I'm supposed to meet my family. Every year, Mom and Dad help with the Pleasant Valley Convention and Visitor's Bureau float, sitting atop of it dressed as Santa and Mrs. Claus.

Even on the years I've missed coming home, they've carried on this tradition, and Mom always sends me photos of the two of them in costume.

Today, however, I walk up and notice they are wearing regular clothes and winter coats.

The temperature has taken a dip, and the only good thing

about that is it's unlikely I'll see Max shirtless again. But as that thought enters my mind, I take note of the twinge of disappointment at the realization.

Get it together, Marin.

"Oh, Marin, there you are! You're late—we were starting to worry." Mom hurries me over by the float and shoves a big, fluffy garbage bag with a hanger sticking out of it into my arms. "This is for you."

I frown. "What is it?"

"The costume." She says this as if we've had a conversation about it and she can't believe I've forgotten. In reality, we've had no such conversation, and I'm wondering if I should worry about Mom's memory.

"What costume?"

Mom laughs. "You're funny, Marin. Come on, you need to get changed."

Steph and Danny walk up. Steph is texting or scrolling, yet again.

"Steph told you, didn't she?" Mom is wide-eyed. "You told her, right, Steph?"

My producer looks up, only briefly. "Oh. No. I forgot." She looks back down. "Marin, you're playing Mrs. Claus."

Now my eyes go wide. "I'm doing what now?"

"You don't have much time, Marin," Mom is shooing me— where? What is even happening right now? "Go over to the diner and ask if you can change in the bathroom."

"You want me to put on your Mrs. Claus costume? Why? Why aren't you Mrs. Claus?"

"Ratings, I think?" Mom shrugs. "Steph, isn't that what you—"

Steph cuts her off with a thumbs-up, still on her phone.

I glare daggers at the top of my producer's head.

"This is going to be great publicity, Marin," she says without looking up. "We'll post it all over socials, and—"

"Steph!"

Finally, she looks at me. "What?" She says this like it's no big deal.

I hold up the costume and shake it at her. "Are you serious?"

She smirks, and nods over my shoulder. "At least you've got a sexy Santa Claus."

No. I squeeze my eyes shut. This can't be happening.

Max is behind me, and when I spin around, I'm fully expecting—yep. He's wearing Dad's costume. The beard is slung low around his neck and he's holding the hat, but there he is, in the full red suit with a fake belly and everything.

I wish that made him less attractive.

How is that not making him less attractive?

"Oh, I see what's going on now," I say.

Mom holds her hands up in surrender. "Don't look at me. This was *not* my idea. But if you don't hurry up, there are going to be a lot of disappointed children."

I'm in a horrible situation not of my own making being told to do things I don't want to do with people I don't want to do them with.

It's like I'm at the DMV.

I don't even have the will to argue at this point—I can see it won't matter. I'm going to sit on top of a float in full Claus-gear.

"Don't forget the *spectacles!*" Mom calls after me as I rush off to find somewhere to change.

Ten minutes later, I return. The Mrs. Claus costume looks like something straight out of the Victorian era, a long red dress with a white apron, and I'm wearing tennis shoes. Mom's feet are a whole size smaller than mine. Max has fully embraced his role and is now loudly greeting people in the crowd as Jolly Old Saint Nick.

I could not feel more ridiculous.

She frowns at me. "You're not selling the part at all, Marin."

"Shocking," I say dryly. "Couldn't be because I don't want to be *playing* this part."

"Bah humbug," Dad says. "You used to love Christmas— what happened to you?"

Max's eyes drift over to mine, and I quickly look away. "I *do* love Christmas! I just don't like surprises!"

Max raises a brow. "Which is why you always found your Christmas presents in your mom's closet before they were wrapped."

"You did what?" My mother gasps as she says this, and I shoot Max an annoyed look.

He smirks in reply.

"All I'm saying is that I don't love wearing costumes in front of the whole town. Whether it's for viewers or not."

"Tim's going to love it." Steph holds her phone up and motions for me to move. "Scoot over next to Max, and we'll take a picture."

"First she has to put on the bonnet and the *spectacles*." Mom has emphasized the word "spectacles" both times she's said it. She rushes over and yanks the bonnet from under my arm. She fixes it on my head, then proceeds to shove the tiny *spectacles* on my face. "It's a good thing the dress is long. You did not wear appropriate footwear."

Miraculously, I don't respond to that.

Once the glasses are on my face, Mom shoves Max and me together, then takes a step back, hands out and arms wide, like she's admiring an art exhibit. "You two look so good together."

Max drapes an arm around me, all the while smiling at the camera.

"What are you doing?" I ask, wondering why he doesn't seem to be nearly as horrified as I am.

"Fake flirting, remember?" he whispers this, and I realize that between the two of us, I'm the one with more on the line here. "It'll be fun. All we have to do is sit up there and wave. Nobody will even know it's you."

"And look—" Mom reappears from who-knows-where carrying a big hand-lettered sign that says *Featuring TV Star Marin McGrath as Mrs. Claus.* "Yours is already pinned to the other side of the float, Max."

I shoot him a look, and he gives me a shrug. "It'll still be fun?"

"Let's just get this over with," I say with a groan.

Mom trails behind us as we make our way over to the float. "Don't forget, one scowly look, Marin, and you'll ruin some poor child's entire Christmas. You need to get into the character of Mrs. Claus and help usher in the festive holiday spirit. It's a big responsibility."

I stop short when I see that our float isn't the leader of the parade.

Normally, as is tradition, Santa and Mrs. Claus come at the end of holiday parades. However, in Pleasant Valley, my Mom made sure to switch things around— she said that the Clauses should be "bringing Christmas *to* the town at the front, not following it up at the rear."

I point. "What is that?"

It's a giant reindeer balloon, and over a dozen people dressed as reindeer are working to keep it secure.

"Oh, that's Rudolph! Isn't he spectacular? It's like our little small-town parade got an upgrade. Who needs Macy's at Thanksgiving when you've got Pleasant Valley at Christmas?"

"That's pretty impressive, Lydia," Max says. "Your idea?"

She beams. "Oh, it was a group effort."

Translation: Yes, in fact, it was my idea. How nice of you to notice.

Max and I climb up to a platform where two silver thrones have been screwed down to the base of the float. Once we're seated, Steph calls for us to look her way, and that's when I see Danny filming us.

I know that tonight, when Roger kicks it over to me from the newsroom, there will be a whole montage of this event. In an effort to not ruin all my chances for that promotion, I smile and wave at them as if this was exactly what I thought I'd be doing when I left the house a half an hour ago.

The float is called *Santa's Workshop*, but apparently Santa and I are supervisors because there is a whole slew of children dressed as elves pretending to make wooden toys.

"Gotta hand it to your dad," Max says. "He outdid himself this year."

Dad is driving the truck pulling the float, and Mom is riding shotgun. It isn't until that exact moment, seeing everything from this vantage point, that I see how much this event means to them both. And just how much work they've put in. Not just for this event, or this float, but for this community.

Mom used to spend a lot of time trying to get me to move back home. Said I could be a local celebrity on the news in one of the nearby mid-sized markets. "There are lots of cities, Marin, and a lot of places that feel the same," she'd said. "It's the people that make a place home."

They both grin and wave out the window, calling out to familiar faces, pointing and smiling, as Dad puts the truck in drive and the float begins to move.

I pray he has a steady foot and makes no sudden stops because the last thing I need is to take another tumble while Steph is filming.

I glance over and see that like my parents, Max is happily

waving to the passers-by. Most of them recognize him, and it seems almost like he never left Pleasant Valley.

I, on the other hand, haven't seen anyone I know.

"How do you still know everyone?" I ask.

Without looking at me, he leans over and continues to wave. "It's not a very big town."

"Right, but you like, really know these people. You're basing your non-profit here. You bought your childhood home." I frown. "You're moving back."

"You're supposed to be waving." He's still not looking at me.

I hesitate for a moment, then force myself to play the part. I focus on the small children in the crowd and the way their faces light up at the sight of my pretend husband, Old St. Nick. I work hard to make sure my face doesn't do the same.

"I just needed a home base," he says.

"But that can be anywhere," I say.

"Smile, Marin. You look like the Grinch."

I force a smile, and he grimaces. "You'd think you'd have perfected your fake smile as much as you use it, but I can see right through it."

"What are you talking about?"

"Your smiles," he says. "So easy to read."

"I have one smile."

"Wrong." He tosses me a quick glance, then goes back to waving. "That smile you've got on now is your *Someone else is making me do this* smile. Then there's the one you use on the air. It's your *Practiced Fake smile*, and you use it to look professional. You don't show your teeth with that one. Then there's your sarcastic smile." He faces me and demonstrates this. "That one is meant to prove a point, and it usually means you're not happy."

"So, according to you, I have no real smiles?"

"You used to," he says.

That stings.

After a few hearty *Ho, Ho, Ho's* to the crowd, he leans over again. "But you save that one. Only the very best people get to see a true, unguarded Marin McGrath smile." He flashes a grin of his own at the crowd, waving to a little girl who immediately bursts into tears. "I promise, I'm not the Santa at the mall! I'm the real one!" Max calls out to the little girl, who stops crying and looks cautiously hopeful. He tosses her a candy bar and shouts, "Don't share that with anyone!"

The little girl laughs, and then waves. Her mom gives a thankful thumbs-up to Max, who gives her a jolly wave.

And he's great with kids. Fantastic.

He looks at me. "A real Marin McGrath smile. That's the smile I'm after. Doesn't get much better than an authentic smile from the one and only."

I sit with that for a few seconds, aware that I've dropped my hand again, and now I'm not wearing any of my smiles. My brow is furrowed, and I'm deep in thought, and I cannot figure out how it is that after all this time, Max still seems to see through the clouded window to my soul.

I hate that he does.

I love that he does.

I hate/love that I don't know which of these two emotions is the one I should be concerned about.

We're about halfway through the parade route when I spot Steph in the crowd. She's filming, so I smile and wave. The wind kicks up, and I have to grab onto my bonnet to keep it from flying away.

"It's so cold out here," I say to no one in particular.

Max leans toward me. "I'm sure your mom has a cape made from real reindeer skins, want me to grab it?"

I can't help it, I laugh. "No, thanks, I'm—"

—Cut off by the sound of a collective gasp from the crowd. As I follow a dozen or so pointing fingers, I notice that in front of us, the handlers are having trouble with the Rudolph balloon.

"That doesn't look good," Max says.

"Is it because of the wind?"

Another gust, another gasp.

Rudolph is having a rough go. Up ahead, the people dressed as reindeer, holding the long white strings, struggle to try and steer the giant balloon. This goes on for a few minutes, and Dad brings the truck from a crawl to a stop.

What happens next is a blur.

First, Reindeer Person #1 holding Rudolph's back right leg loses his grip. It happens at the exact same time as another gust of wind, because Reindeer Person #2, also holding down that leg, loses her grip.

The gasping crowd is almost comical.

With one flailing leg now rising and flapping in the wind, the opposite side of the balloon begins to dip—which causes the front right leg to rise, lifting the person trying to hold it three feet off the ground. Rudolph is now a rogue balloon, and the two handlers do their best (hilariously, I might add) to grab the ropes now twisting and whipping around in the wind. Ultimately, they fail. It's like a giant game of keep-away and Rudolph is winning.

I can practically hear him calling out "Hey Prancer! Hey Vixen! Watch this!"

Between the gusts and the flapping leg, Rudolph now appears to be half-galloping while also standing still, and in an unfortunate turn, the handler who just went airborne lets go of his rope.

Now with two appendages flapping around in the chilly December wind, Rudolph is especially volatile, and we all watch in horror as a tear, on the backside between Rudolph's hind legs, rips through the balloon.

The crowd reacts.

Max stands.

And then the world goes into slow motion.

Rudolph's backside begins to wag, and before I know what's happening, I see that the mishandled balloon is coming for us.

More specifically, I see that we're about to be devoured by two giant reindeer butt cheeks.

"Rudolph's butt is going to eat Santa!" A little kid calls out as we are sucked into the black hole of an upside-down reindeer rear end.

My last thought before my world goes dark is *this is going to go viral.*

Chapter Eighteen

Marin

Eventually, they extract us from Rudolph's backside.

When they do, the first thing I notice is that we are, in fact being filmed. Not only by Steph and Danny, but by pretty much everyone at the parade.

I replay the scene in my head, cringing at what the internet is going to do with this video footage.

Finally, by the grace of God and the spirit of Santa Claus himself, we reach the end of the parade, and it's time to get off this float.

Max steps in front of me, shielding me from the cameras, as I stand to go. "You okay?"

"I mean, no. That was mortifying."

"But also kind of funny, right?" He pulls down his Santa beard to reveal a smile. "I mean, come on. We were just sucked into a giant butt."

It takes a moment for this to register, and when it does, I bite my lip to hold in a smile. A real one.

Max is watching, so I look away, but it's too late. He's seen me trying to stifle it, and when our eyes meet again, I burst out laughing. "A giant *reindeer* butt," I say.

Max laughs. "Can honestly say that's never happened to me before."

My eyes are watering and I'm struck with a genuine case of the giggles just thinking about this horrible fiasco. "This is going to be all over the internet."

"Already is." Steph walks up and shakes her phone at us.

I lean down and grab it from her and relive the ridiculous moment as it plays out on the screen in front of me. "Steph! You posted this!" I say, seeing the name on the account.

Steph shrugs. "Are you kidding? It was hilarious! And catching footage of you guys laughing about it after the fact is even better." She punches Max in the arm. "Good job with the fake flirting."

I look at Max. He looks back, and then we both quickly look away.

Nothing about what just happened was fake, but there's no sense pointing that out.

"I need to get off this float." I hand Steph's phone back to her and make my way to the ground.

"That was really awesome, you guys," Steph says as we both reach her. "So, what now?"

"Now, I change out of this ridiculous costume," I say. I take off the *spectacles* and reach up for the bonnet, but then I catch the grimace on Max's face.

"Yeah, about that. . ." Max starts.

"Now what?!"

"Your mom didn't tell you?" Max asks.

I'm sensing a theme here.

"We have to do a shift at the Santa Shop."

"Ooh, that sounds fun!" Steph snaps her fingers at Danny,

who appears like a maître-d' at the ready, camera in tow. "Let's do an intro video now, then we can get footage of Marin and Max playing Santa and Mrs. Claus at the Santa Shop. Ugh, how adorable. And Marin, do this in character."

"In character?"

"Yeah, as Mrs. Claus. Max, keep playing the part of Santa."

Danny holds out a handheld microphone, and I take it, trying to find the energy to fake excitement that I absolutely do not feel.

"Max, you stand there with her," Steph says.

I look at Max. "You don't have to."

"It's okay," he says. "Can't have Mrs. Claus without Santa, right?"

"Oh, I don't know," I say lightly. "I think Mrs. Claus might actually be just fine on her own. Maybe she's been underestimated her whole life, relegated to the role of some fat guy's wife, but she's *really* the one keeping things going up there at the North Pole."

"Maybe." He looks me right in the eyes, with a bit of a smile. "I could see how Santa might be a little lost without her."

I tell myself not to read into this comment. This is just Max being flirty for the sake of the camera.

But then I glance over and see that Danny has not started filming.

I clear my throat.

"Ready, Marin?" Steph asks.

"Yep." But I'm not. This is a very bad idea. If he's going to be fake flirting with me, someone needs to get that message to my heart because so far, it doesn't seem to realize it.

Danny tips his head around the camera and nods. I assume the position, microphone up and fake smile pasted on.

"Good afternoon from the Christmas Kick-off Parade in

downtown Pleasant Valley, Illinois. I'm Mrs. Claus, and I'm sure you all know this lovely gentleman to my left." I take his arm, all part of the act, of course. "Santa and I just finished riding on this beautiful *Santa's Workshop* float in the parade—"

"—and I'll have to talk to that naughty Rudolph," Max chimes in, in a Santa voice, "and teach him that he can't sit just anywhere!"

I giggle. For real. I relax a little and play into the role.

"Yes, Santa dear, I'm just glad we didn't mix the beans in with his oats for lunch beforehand."

Max *Ho, Ho, Ho's* a laugh at that one, Steph mouths *'ohmygoshthatishilariouskeepitup"* at me with two big thumbs-up.

I continue. "And we are now headed over to Santa's *real workshop* for a fun evening of meeting the children of our little town. The Christmas Stroll is a well-loved tradition here in Pleasant Valley—and it's always on the second Saturday of December."

I turn, now immersed in the playacting of the scene. "Santa, why don't you tell us, what is your favorite part of the Christmas Stroll? With a belly like that, I think it might be the food vendors, the cookie display, or the cupcake tower?" I playfully pat his overstuffed faux belly.

He looks down at me, then back at the camera and his eyes crinkle at the corners in a smile. "My favorite part. . .is *Mrs. Claus.*"

I half-laugh, noticing Steph's wide-eyed nod—this is what the viewers want.

The viewers aren't the only ones. . .and that's the part that worries me.

"I especially love the way her *spectacles* accent her big, blue eyes."

I playfully shove him, but not too hard. "I think Santa needs to lay off the eggnog, wouldn't you agree, folks?"

Max drapes an arm around my shoulder and gives me a once-over. "And that bonnet, I don't know, some might say it's old fashioned, but it's working for me."

"Well, I did wear it just for you," I say, aware that my flirting is rusty at best. "But Santa should probably keep his mind on the job."

Max chuckles another jolly laugh and looks back at the camera. "You can see who really runs things up at the North Pole."

Before I can respond, a little boy runs up and grabs onto Max's sleeve. "Santa?"

I see Danny widen the shot. I know we're not live and can edit out anything that doesn't work, but I hope Max is quick on his feet and finds a way for us to wrap this up so we don't have to do the whole thing again.

He kneels down in front of the boy. "Well, hello there, little boy, what's your name?"

"Henry," he says.

"It's nice to meet you, Henry." Max holds out a hand, and Henry shakes it.

A woman I assume is Henry's mom rushes over and stops short when she sees the boy talking to Santa on camera.

"Nice to meet you too, Santa," Henry says.

"I'm so sorry," the woman rushes forward and puts her hands on Henry's shoulders. "I'm sure you all have somewhere to be." Then to Henry: "Honey, I told you we could try to see Santa later at his workshop."

"But I want to see him now." Henry is matter-of-fact and not whiny when he says this.

"It's okay," Max says, still kneeling in front of the boy.

"What can I do for you, Henry? Is your name on the Nice List this year?"

The boy squints up at Max. "I think so? I watch out for my little sister, Ruby, at school, but she's super bossy so sometimes I hide her pencils in the dog crate and blame the dog."

A genuine laugh from Max. "That's not so bad, Henry. I think we can make an exception to keep you on the Nice List!" Max leans in. "So, what would you like for Christmas?"

"I just want my mom to find a job," Henry says. "So we don't have to move to Tampa with my grandma. And maybe a house where she can have her own room." Henry leans in, too. "She shares with my sister now."

Henry's mom closes her eyes and squeezes her son's shoulders.

Max glances up quickly at Henry's mom, who looks embarrassed that her son would reveal such a personal thing. He then looks straight back to the little boy. "Well, that's an awfully good Christmas wish, Henry. What kind of job do you think your mom would like?"

"One in an office, I think," he says. "With no mean people."

Max smiles through his beard. "In an office with no mean people." Again, he looks at the woman standing behind Henry. "It's your lucky day, Henry. I think I know just the thing."

"You do?" Henry's eyes widen.

"You do?" The woman looks taken aback.

"I do," Max says. "I happen to know of a new non-profit in need of some office help. If you leave your name and number, I'll pass it on to the right people." He stands.

"I'd love to interview for it," the woman says.

"No need," Max tells her. "The job is yours if you want it. . .?"

"Joy. My name is Joy."

"Joy," Max says. "It's nice to meet you."

The woman's eyes fill with tears, and she hesitates for only a moment before wrapping her arms around Max's neck. I see Danny shift to get a better shot.

But Max isn't done yet. After the embrace, he reaches down, messes up Henry's hair and asks, "But Henry, is there anything you want for yourself?"

Henry scrunches his face for a split second, then brightens. "Maybe a new Lego set?"

"Legos. Solid choice. We'll see if the elves have any for me to bring to your house on Christmas Eve. Be on the lookout, okay?"

I have a feeling that boy is going to get the Lego version of the Millennium Falcon or the Hogwarts Castle.

"You two hang around a minute. Mrs. Claus and I are almost done, okay?"

They nod and step back, and Max returns to the space at my side. He meets my eyes, and nods toward the camera.

I realize I'm choked up.

I turn toward Danny and clear my throat. "Santa Claus is always ready to spread the Christmas spirit, and it looks like he's doling it out in spades today." I struggle to keep my composure. "Stay tuned for more from our Christmas Stroll, and Merry Christmas, dear friends. I'm Marin McGrath, a.k.a. Mrs. Claus, signing off."

Danny flips the switch on the camera, and Steph steps forward. "In all my years working in TV, I don't think I've ever seen anything like that. That was *golden*. You really know how to sell it, Santa!"

Max frowns at her, and seemingly at that comment. "I'll be back in a minute, Marin." He walks over to Henry and his mom, and I watch as she pulls out a pen and a small notebook from her purse to write down her information.

"Seriously, Marin," Steph says. "That man understood the assignment."

"He didn't do that for our benefit, Steph," I say. "He did that because he's a genuinely good person."

And he is.

And that makes hating him a whole lot harder.

Chapter Nineteen

Max

Marin looks cute in her costume. Which is no small feat considering what her costume looks like.

We start walking toward *Santa's Workshop*, and I notice she's unusually quiet.

We're stopped by the occasional child, and I keep up my Santa persona, telling them to come visit me at my Workshop, where I'll be for the next hour.

"Elf got your tongue, Mrs. Claus?" I ask when she doesn't engage a little girl who calls out to us with so much excitement we might as well have been celebrities.

"What?" She looks over at me.

"What's going on up there?" I point to her bonnet.

"I'm just," she pauses, "thinking."

We take a few more steps, and I see if I can creak the conversational door open a bit wider.

"Okay, what are you thinking about?"

Another pause. "You, I guess."

I raise a brow in a silent question.

"Are you really going to give that woman a job?"

I sidestep a group of iPhone-addicted teenagers. "Sure, why not?"

"You know nothing about her."

"I know she needs a job," I say. "And I need someone to run the office at The Weber Foundation."

"But is she qualified?" Marin inches closer to me to avoid a bench on her left.

"Job skills can be taught," I say. "I believe in hiring the right personality."

"But you didn't even get to know her personality," she says.

"I know she's raising a great little boy. I mean, how many kids would ask Santa for something for a parent over something for themselves?"

She's quiet again.

"This bugs you?"

She thinks about it a second. "No, it's just unexpected."

"Because you'd convinced yourself I'm a jerk," I say lightly.

She laughs. "I mean, maybe?"

I stop walking and step in front of her. "Come on, Marin. You know I'm not."

"I know I have to tell myself you are," she says.

I hold her gaze. "Why?"

She looks like she wants to say something, but chooses not to. Instead, she crosses the street, and I jog to catch up to her.

"You can trust me." I want to slip my hand in hers. I want to have the same familiar ease we once had.

"No," she says, flatly. "I can't."

A family with three small children stops in front of us, staring up at Santa and Mrs. Claus. Marin's forced smile does nothing to dissuade them, and all three kids start talking at once.

"We're headed over to my workshop now," I say in my best

Santa voice. "Come on over and see us!" I throw in a *Ho-Ho-Ho* for effect.

We make our way around them, and I see that up ahead is an alley between two of the old buildings on Primrose Street. I grab Marin's hand and pull her off the sidewalk and into the alley. It's dark back here, and there are no other people. It's possibly the only unused space in the entire downtown.

"Max?" Marin straightens. "What are you doing?"

"I'm sorry." I look her straight in the eye. "This is actually kind of difficult when you're dressed like Mrs. Claus and wearing those ridiculous glasses."

I reach over and take them off her face, and she swipes the bonnet from her head and looks at me. "Sorry for what?"

I step away. I start looking around the alleyway, as if the answer is written somewhere. "Everything," I say on a sigh. I want to articulate it. I want to explain myself. I want things to go back to the way they were. But I'm not sure where to begin.

I was the one who ruined us in the first place.

But I did the right thing. I was protecting her. I was protecting me.

Right?

Marin is standing next to the brick wall of the old drug store, and I turn toward her, removing my hat and the fake beard as I do. I want her to see my whole face when I say this.

"I'm so sorry for hurting you."

Her eyes are still on me, and I can see—in classic Marin fashion—that she's overthinking this moment. She straightens her outfit and says, "I'm fine, Max. You don't have to say anything."

"I want to explain—" I stop. I'm trying to sort out what I want to say in my mind, but I can't find words.

"Explain what? Explain away what happened? Explain

149

why you left? Give me some magical reason that will make the last eight years of my life make sense?"

I stammer with an answer. I *want* to talk about this, but I feel ashamed and vulnerable, and I don't like it. At all.

"No." She shakes her head. "We can have our truce. We can get through this fake flirtation. But we can't have real moments. Maybe it's better if we don't talk about the past."

She moves closer to me, too close.

"This is what you do, Max. You get this close to letting me in. It gives me hope, and makes me think maybe something has changed."

"It has, Marin, I just. . .I can't. . ." Words fail.

She steps closer and puts a hand on my arm.

"I know. You can't. And maybe that's unfair of me, Max. Maybe it's not understanding of me to allow you space to work through things—but that would just be setting myself up to get hurt again, and I can't let that happen. Not again."

I mentally see the gap between us widening.

She adds, "I've put the past where it belongs. Behind me."

"But I haven't!" It comes out too quickly, too loudly. I see a stray piece of hair hanging over her face and I instinctively reach up to brush it away, my fingers grazing her forehead as I do. I hear her breath catch in her throat.

We look at one another for longer than a moment, and I take a step even closer, my pulse quickening at her nearness.

"Max, I. . ."

My hand falls to her waist. "Marin. There's still something here, right?" I hold her gaze. "I'm not imagining it?"

We're both completely still, the unanswered question hanging above us.

"Marin—" My eyes dip to her lips.

She closes her eyes and draws in a slow breath, and I know I shouldn't, but all I can think about is kissing her.

But when she opens her eyes, I see a fresh resolve. She steps back. "I have to go. Can you tell my family—" Her voice breaks a little. "Can you just tell them that I went home?"

She steps out onto the sidewalk, leaving me standing in the dark.

Marin

I rush away from the dark alley, back to where I parked my car, and it isn't until I'm safely inside that I let out the held-back tears.

I see what he wants. It's me.

I start to see what my heart wants, and it's him.

But I can't. It's a risk I'm not willing to take.

Clearly, we need better ground rules. I need to tell him so. Again.

I draw in a slow breath and try and calm down. My head begins to clear, and I wipe my eyes with the heels of my hands.

Maybe I should draw up a contract. Make Max sign a sworn affidavit that he will not now—or ever—make my heart feel things for him, things I have sworn never to feel again.

As if he has control over what my heart wants to feel.

I replay the way he looked at me, with a desperation that betrayed his silence. I felt a tingle in my fingers, the strongest desire to reach up and trace the outline of his face. I wanted his hands on my waist to pull me close to him. I wanted to believe the words he whispered.

Words that could not be believed.

Max cannot be trusted.

But even as the thought enters my mind, another one

swoops in to replace it. *He said he was sorry.* And I know him well enough to know he meant it.

My phone dings with an Instagram notification from Steph.

Go scroll through the comments on the Reindeer Balloon Butt video. Did you even notice that Max tried to shield you from that thing? I didn't. . .but the viewers definitely did. Apparently, Santa Max is their hero—the stuff dreams are made of. Wait'll they see him with that kid! Marin, he's your ticket. He's going to get you the views you need!

It's selfish. Selfish, and horrible, and self-centered that I'm thinking Steph is right.

I re-watch the embarrassing video and as the balloon begins to topple, Max reaches out, one hand in front of me and the other over the top of his head, tent-poling the balloon, keeping it from coming anywhere near me. I have no idea if Rudolph could've injured me, but Max made sure he didn't.

The memory of his expression in the alley—so earnest, so honest—as he apologized flashes in my mind. It's followed up by a replay of the way he talked to Henry, the way he reached out without a single thought, to help that boy's mom.

Max is a *good* person. I hate that he is, but he is.

But that doesn't make him good for me.

Chapter Twenty

Marin

As I watch happy couples navigate their way through the busier-than-usual small-town foot traffic, my mind whirls back, and I'm in college again. I'm prepping for my first semester finals. Steve and Jenny have been gone just over two months, and Max has grown distant and withdrawn.

I'm patient and understanding about this because I love him, and I loved them, and I can't even begin to imagine what this is like for him. He's just lost both of his parents at the same time.

But if I'm honest, I miss him. I'm struggling with the fact that he won't open up to me.

I want to help him however I can, but he won't let me. I want to be there for him, but I don't know how. I want to grieve with him, but he's made it clear he doesn't want to talk about it. This topic is off limits.

I take one step closer, he takes two steps away.

I reach out, and he pushes back.

I ask and he snaps. Then apologizes, and the cycle starts all over again.

Some nights we go out with friends, and I sit in the booth at the bar watching as he pretends everything is fine, that inside he's not completely shattered. He starts ordering one more drink than usual, then two more.

I am worried that the Max I love is fading away.

That night, I made his favorite milk chocolate chip cookies —he likes them underdone and practically dough in the middle —and I bring them over to his apartment, where I know he'll be studying. I knock on the door.

He pulls it open and stares at me. He's wearing sweats and a T-shirt, his hair messy and disheveled. He looks terrible, and is immediately standoffish. "Marin, what are you doing here? I've got finals to study for."

I breathe. This mood I've seen now so many times is becoming familiar. "I won't stay." I hold up the cookies as an offering. "I made your favorite. To help with the studying."

He takes the plate of cookies and leaves me standing in the doorway. "Thanks." He sets them on the counter.

By now, we've been together for six years. Before the accident, I could finish his sentences and anticipate what he needed. Now? I have no idea what to do or say because what seems to work one day doesn't work the next. I used to know exactly what was going on in his mind, and I miss knowing. I miss being close to him.

I miss *him*.

He lets out a long sigh. "Marin, I. . .need tell you something."

I freeze. *Finally*.

He's finally going to open up, to tell me how all of this—the terrible accident, being left alone in the world—is making him feel. I look at him, expectant. Hopeful.

His eyes dart to mine, and he pushes a hand through his hair. "I don't think this is working."

I drop onto the couch and hear a bag of chips crumple underneath me. I reach behind my back and pull out the Doritos and set them on the coffee table. "You don't think what's working?"

"Me and you."

I blink. I open my mouth to say something, but stop, confused.

"I. . .me and you?" Disbelief and, maybe I missed something? Where is this coming from?

He puts his hands on his hips and his gaze falls to the floor. He draws in a breath and lets it out slowly. "We've outgrown each other. It's clear that we stayed together because our parents wanted us to."

". . .*what*?"

If he hears my question, he doesn't acknowledge it.

"But if the last few months have taught me anything, it's that life is short." He looks up at me. "And I have to do the things that are best for me."

"Max, where is this coming from?" Tears spring to my eyes, ready to spill over. "What are you even saying? I understand if you're hurting, if you've got things to work out. . ."

He snaps. Hard. "You *don't* understand!"

I rise up. "Because you won't talk to me!"

"I don't want to talk to you, okay? I don't want to talk, I don't want to be asked questions, I don't want to have anything to do with you!"

The room spins. Panic and heartbreak and sorrow and fear all roll into a ball inside of me.

I'm in a nightmare—the kind where you know you're sleeping but you can't drag yourself out of the dream's clutches.

I plead, "Max, please. Please, don't. I know you don't mean that."

He looks away. "I do, Marin. I can't do this anymore."

My voice breaks. "We've been together since we were kids. We're supposed to get married. I don't understand."

"You're right, and maybe it was wrong of me to just go along when I wasn't feeling the same way you were."

I can't breathe. "You weren't. . .what? You didn't. . .?" I rush over to him, desperate. "Please, Max. I know that's not true. It can't be. You can't tell me you were with me this whole time because of our *parents*."

"Don't make this harder than it is." He pulls back.

"There's harder than this?" I shout incredulously. "Harder for who? For you? You're breaking my heart, and I'm making it hard on you?" I reach for his hands, like a climber whose rope has snapped. "Max, talk to me. What is really going on?"

He pulls his hands away, hard and looks me square in the face.

"I'm not in love with you, Marin."

My heart stops for a moment. I exhale a whispered "Oh."

"I'm sorry."

I should be a blubbering mess, I should be screaming and begging and pleading—but I'm not.

I pull away and hold in the tears. "Okay."

"I'm really sor—," he says.

"Don't." I hold up a hand, not looking at him, or at anything in particular. I speak slowly and clearly. "You have obviously made up your mind. I'll come back tomorrow when you're not here and get my things."

I think he nods.

I'm dazed. I spin in a circle then finally find my way to the door. He follows me, and when I'm standing in the hallway outside his apartment I turn and face him.

"I thought we would be forever. I really thought we would."

He is silent. His book is closed to me, and I'll never be able to read it again.

I look down, shake my head slightly, and say softly to the floor, "Have a nice life, Max."

I turn and walk away. I didn't understand how someone I thought I knew could be so callous, so cold. I assumed it had to do with his pain, but as the months passed, it became clear that wasn't it. It was me.

Max didn't love me. End of story.

Now, sitting in my car, in the midst of the commotion of the town's Christmas event, tears spring to my eyes as fresh as the day he broke my heart.

Memories, certain ones, have a way of zipping together the past and the present. What was once completely separate is now entangled. What you felt then, you feel now, and you're unable to pull them apart.

I start my car and slowly pull out of the parking lot, thinking about how many months it took me to get over Max—if I ever did at all. I tell myself it's a cautionary tale to keep me from making the same mistake all over again.

But when I replay the moment in the alley, all I can think is *I forgive you.*

In spite of my valiant effort to keep this man out of my life, I can't deny there is a part of me that very much wants him in it.

And when I was standing there, my back against the brick wall of Kline's Drug Store, I kept hearing two words on repeat in my mind—*Kiss me.*

I drive home, angry that the past keeps invading my present and trying to force all of these thoughts away.

I reach the house and pull out my phone.

Hey, Steph. I'm not feeling great. Going to go home and rest. Can you use the footage we took today for tonight's segment?

Are you sick/sick?
Or are you lovesick?

Very funny. Just my stomach.

Could be all the 🦋🦋🦋🦋🦋

Or some bad eggnog.

Fine. I'll handle it. See you tomorrow.

I leave the Mrs. Claus costume on my mom's bed and change into pajamas. I lay down on the lumpy futon and try to barter with God to help me fall asleep quickly.

God, I'm sure, has other things to deal with, and it's a solid hour before I feel even remotely tired. But then, I hear the front door open and the voices that follow.

My parents and Max are home.

Their voices are indistinct, and I go completely still, same way I did as a kid when my parents came and checked on me—even though my flashlight and my book were pressed up against my leg under the covers.

After a few minutes of noise, laughter, and conversations I can't quite make out, I hear footsteps walking up the stairs and down the hallway. The light under the door is blocked out by two shadows that look like feet.

I'm holding my breath.

I know it's Max. And I know he's trying to decide what to do.

I want him to go away.

The footsteps start back down the hall and are followed by the sound of a door slowly closing.

When I hear the click of the latch, I realize that wasn't what I wanted at all.

Chapter Twenty-One

Marin

When I wake up the following morning, I find I've been tagged in at least twenty different videos of the reindeer butt disaster. I would probably laugh all over again at the clever titles and comments on those videos, but I'm not in a laughing mood.

I also find Steph has added me to a group text:

Steph:
Let's do Christmas cookies today, live on Insta!
Mom:
Sounds good to me! I'm always in the mood to bake!
Steph:
Great! Can you let Max know? I don't have his number?

Mom has added Max to this conversation.

Mom:
Max, we're doing Christmas cookies today. You game?
Max:

Sure, if you promise we can do milk chocolate chip
Steph:
That's not a Christmas cookie!
Mom:
Those were Marin's specialty, but I'm sure she won't mind. Will
you, Marin?

I toss the phone on the end of the bed with a loud groan.

I do mind, thank you very much. The last thing I need to do is relive the night Max broke my heart. Again.

I loved those cookies, and now they're attached to a memory I can't even think about for two seconds.

I haven't made those dumb cookies since.

I keep my eyes closed and feel around on the bed for my phone. When I find it, I sit up and text back:

Marin doesn't bake anymore. I'll interview you, Mom, and you
can walk us through your world-famous frosted sugar cookies.

Max:
Great, what do you want me to do?

Maybe sit this one out. It'll be crowded in the kitchen.

And I can't think when you're around.

I get a text from Steph, separate from the group:

That's a mistake. You and Max baking sugar cookies together?
The audience will love that.

I won't love that.

161

Your Santa and Mrs. Claus stuff is off the charts.
Plus, Tim called this morning. He said "Whatever you two are
doing out there, keep it up!"
He said he likes what he sees.

He did?

He basically said you're going to get the job.

Did he say that exactly?

Practically.
Don't change the strategy now

I stare at my phone when another text from Steph comes
in, this time in the group chat:

Max, I have an apron with your name on it. We'll see you all
after lunch!

That morning, mostly to avoid Max, I finally go down to my
dad's woodshop and talk to him about the handmade gifts he's
been making for people for years.

Ornaments, cutting boards that later became charcuterie
boards, family name signs, not to mention furniture that would
double as a bomb shelter if the need arose.

It's a pleasant conversation, and for the first time in a long
time, I feel at ease.

Probably because Max isn't here.

But mostly because talking to my Dad is my oasis.

He must sense something is off, though, because when I close out of the camera on my phone, I glance up and find him watching me.

"How're you doing, kiddo?"

"Fine," I say.

"You sure about that?"

"I don't know," I sigh. "I've got a lot on my mind."

"Job's got you in knots, huh?"

"It does a little," I say. "I'm up for a promotion, and it's based on what I'm doing here at Christmas—so maybe that has me a little stressed out."

I haven't gone into the details about the job, or the competition to host my own show. I don't know why. Like cheerleaders with cardboard cutouts of my face, my parents have sat themselves for years in the proverbial stands of my life, making as much noise as possible.

Why is it hard to share this with them? Maybe because this job has kept me away from them?

"A promotion? That's exciting." He stands to his full height and looks at me. Dad has always been great about celebrating even the smallest successes. To him, even being up for the promotion would be worth celebrating.

I shrug. "I mean, I'd have my own show."

"Marin, why didn't you say anything? That's incredible!"

I smile softly. "Yeah, it's kind of a big deal. To me, at least."

"It sounds like a big deal! Good for you."

"Thanks."

"Worth all the hard work you've put in all these years?" he asks.

I go still and think for a moment. I'm not sure. "I think so?"

He nods, the lines on his forehead deepening as he seems to be contemplating something.

"What?"

"Oh, nothing," he says. "Just that, you seem unsettled."

It's Max, I want to say. *Max unsettles me.*

"Are you happy?" he asks.

"Course I am."

I am not.

"I wonder if this job is all you really want?"

"Why does everyone keep saying that?" I tuck my phone into my pocket and look at him. "Did you all have a conversation about me behind my back?"

"Who else asked?"

"Max," I say, as if he doesn't know.

"Huh."

I sigh. "This job is all I've ever wanted."

He points a finger at me, wagging it slightly as he says, "That's not exactly true."

Being close to your family has both its perks and faults. On the one hand, they often know what you need and help you better than anyone. On the other hand, they remember things you said years ago and don't hesitate to bring them up if you ever change your mind.

"That was a long time ago," I say, musing. "And honestly, I don't even know if that was actually me, or me trying to be cool, or me wanting to have a life that complemented Max's."

"Nah," Dad says. "You've always known yourself pretty well. You've never been one to jump into something simply because someone else said you should. And you're definitely not the kind of girl who would spend her whole life doing something for a boy. Hang on, this'll be loud." He runs a piece of wood over the table saw, cutting a hidden groove underneath.

He flips the switch off, and the high-pitched squeal winds down as I think over what he's said.

"Do you think your job gives you the same joy you had making those videos with Max?"

I think back to the way it started. Max got his first video camera when he was in seventh grade. Since our world was pretty small back then, most of his early videos were of me and Teddy and our parents.

It didn't take long before all of the adults were talking about how talented he was. He'd started making stop motion animation videos using Legos in his basement and piecing together old family videos into new montages to tell completely different stories.

The following year, we spent the entire summer walking around town looking for people to interview, for interesting things that other people walked by every day without noticing.

And we filmed them.

Rather, Max filmed me interviewing them. Interviewing Mr. Hester who'd lost his cat, William Shakespaw. I still maintain that our video is the reason that cat was found safe and unharmed.

We noticed they were throwing away old text books at the elementary school, so we dug into the dumpster and started asking questions—couldn't we donate these elsewhere? Couldn't we at least recycle them? And who decided to throw them away in the first place?

I do not maintain that we are the reason Assistant Principal Delancey later took a job two towns over.

Like college, like the cookies, and like so many parts of my life, this dream of becoming a documentary filmmaker was intertwined with memories of Max.

And once I lost Max, I lost the dream too.

Or maybe I forced myself to get a new dream.

It wasn't like Max was this boy I dated for a while. I grew up with him. Spent summers with him. Our families vacationed together. Being in Pleasant Valley, in my parents' home, in my car, or literally anywhere—they all reminded me of Max.

We were supposed to have this whole life together.

A few months after our break-up, I started thinking practically. Logically. What could I do with my broadcasting skills that didn't involve him—that didn't remind me of him?

I started looking for jobs in television, and I landed a gig on *Good Day Denver* as a glorified intern. I'd worked my way up over the last eight years, and now, here I am, with a real opportunity to lead a real show as a real host. How could anyone think that's not what I really want?

Judging by the look on my dad's face, however, there was something he saw about my choices that I didn't. And, if I'm honest, I'd be wise to pay attention. It wasn't the first time he'd known more about what was best for me than I did.

"All right, spill it," I say. "I know you want to say something."

"What makes you say that?"

"Please, Dad, you have a terrible poker face."

"That's true, I do. Last Christmas your brother and Max took me for a ride. Lost all of December's petty cash."

"I wish I could've seen that," I say without thinking.

There's a lull as we both realize that I could've seen it. I was invited, after all. I'd chosen to stay away.

Would Dad understand that I'd done that to avoid all these feelings I'm facing now—the grief, the emotions, the pain of saying goodbye to the life I always thought I'd have?

"Are you telling the kind of stories you want to tell?" he asks as he fishes another 2x4 from his scrap pile.

"That's a really good question." I think about it for a moment. "I think I am. Sometimes."

He quirks a brow. "Sometimes?"

"I mean, the videos are shorter, I guess, but I'm finding

interesting stories and sharing them." I might be reaching here. The truth was, the show was nothing like the videos Max and I made, nothing like the ones we'd planned to make. The dream was to get married, travel the world, meet people, search for stories, and share everything we found on the way. The tag line was "making the world a little smaller, one story at a time," which is maybe a little cliché, but we were kids. We even had a business name: M + M Creative.

It's been years since I thought about that.

"I guess I wonder about all the things you've given up for this job," Dad says.

"Things like. . .?"

He shrugs. "Well, holidays here, for one. Love, for another. Your mother says you haven't had a date in at least a year. Then there's Teddy who seems to have nothing *but* first dates. Between the two of you, she's convinced she's never going to have any grandchildren."

I groan, but inside, the comment niggles at me. I *had* given up a lot—or rather, I'd chosen to keep certain things out of my own life. Love wasn't a priority because I didn't want the heartbreak. Coming home wasn't a priority because I didn't want the memories.

Dad removes his glasses and looks at me. "Honey, as long as you're happy, that's all I care about. That and you coming home for Christmas every now and then." He smiles at me, but something about it feels off.

Or maybe it's the new revelations swirling around in my mind that feel off.

"I know I've been away, for a long time." I run my hand over the tabletop, brushing off sawdust onto the floor. "But I'm here now, and I have to say, it feels good to be home."

"It's good to have you home." He smiles.

"I mean, other than dealing with Max—it's perfect. Just like

I remember." My phone buzzes, and I pull it out. It's a reminder that I set.

"I have to go," I say. "We're doing a Christmas cookie segment with Mom in the kitchen."

"Thumbprints?"

"Frosted sugar cookies."

"Well," he says, "that'll do. I never met a cookie I didn't like."

Chapter Twenty-Two

Marin

Back up at the house, I find everyone in the kitchen, gathered around a table listening to Max as he tells a story. I stand in the doorway for a few minutes, out of sight, listening—remembering how easy it always was for Max to hold the attention of everyone in a room when he wanted to.

I tell myself that he will *not* hold my attention.

But he's holding it now, and I'm not even in the room.

I'm trying to piece together the details of the story he's telling—something funny that happened when he was shooting in Belize.

I'll never admit it to him, but I did some Googling.

I sleuthed out that Max works for corporations that send him all over the world to shoot videos for various reasons. I don't fully understand how he comes by these jobs, and frankly, I never knew businesses would pay for this kind of work, but it seems like it's taken him all over the world.

I'm trying not to feel jealous or betrayed by the fact that he went ahead and did the thing we always talked about doing together. It's not like I owned the exclusive rights to that dream.

But it's such a punch to the gut. "Let me dump you and then go do all the things we were supposed to do together." It's like planning a wedding and a honeymoon and then discarding the bride and taking the trip anyway.

I know that I could've done the same thing. I could've traveled, sated that wanderlust that had us so rapt as young adults. Instead, I changed my path so it no longer aligned with his.

It's apparent now that maybe that wasn't the best way to punish him.

Still, this is reality, and I'm good at what I do. I deserve that promotion.

I just had to get through filming a fluffy segment with my mother and my ex-boyfriend to prove it.

If only I felt like being flirty and fun today.

I step into the kitchen, and when Max sees me, he stops talking and smiles. "Hey, Mare, there's coffee."

Darn. He's being nice to me. I don't want him to be nice to me because I've just had my little walk down memory lane, and my anger toward him has been rekindled. Also because I'm concerned my softening anger is no match for his lazy grin and the way he looks at me.

"Great," I say. "Mom, we should probably get started."

I walk over to the coffee maker and pour myself a cup, aware that behind me there are probably strange, confused glances crisscrossing from one person to the next.

"Of course," Steph says. "We were just waiting for you."

"Well, I'm glad you were being entertained." I toss a glance at Max and quickly look away.

Steph leans in toward me and hisses, "What is your deal? Be nice!"

I ignore her. I can be fake on the air, but I don't have to be when the cameras aren't rolling.

My mom has already gotten all of the ingredients out of the

cupboards and measured everything out in little glass bowls. I survey the spread while Max leans against the counter, holding his own cup of coffee and staring at me.

I try to ignore him, but I feel like he's purposely trying to unnerve me.

Or maybe I'm just naturally unnerved by him.

The memory of the night before—his body *so close* to mine in the dark of the alley—comes rolling back through my mind like a runaway boulder down a mountainside.

I face my mother and try to brighten my mood. "Did you go out and buy these glass bowls just for this?"

"No, it's a happy accident that I happened to have them. I see them on all the cooking shows!" She hums around the room, pulling three aprons off of hooks by the door. She gives one to me, flips one over her own head, and gives one to Max, which he cheerfully puts on.

"Let the cookie baking begin!" Mom claps her hands together.

Steph lays out the plan. "Okay, so we're going to get the cookies started on the show, but we'll finish them on a separate video that we'll post on social media later."

"Perfect!" Mom nods, then with a serious look, she places a hand on top of mine. "Oh, Marin, I'm not going to share the secret ingredient."

"Mom, if you don't tell people about the almond extract, they won't know what makes these cookies so good. They'll make them and when they don't taste different than every other sugar cookie—they'll think your recipe is mediocre."

She thinks about this for moment, and I don't have the heart to tell her that almond extract in sugar cookies isn't actually that original. Many of the recipes on the internet call for it. But I know she isn't spending time searching for sugar cookie recipes. Not when she already believes she has the perfect one.

"All right," she says, acting like she's decided to disclose nuclear secrets with a foreign governmental ally. "I'll share it. I don't want anyone thinking I make mediocre sugar cookies."

I turn to find Max, still watching me. I narrow my eyes for half a second and then look away again. My mom bustles over to Steph to talk about camera angles and microphones, leaving an opportunity for Max to step over and stand right next to me. When he does this, the hair on the back of my neck stands at attention. I can feel his closeness before he even leans in and whispers in my ear, "Can we talk?"

I want to move away from him, to retreat to a safe place where I don't have to worry about confusing feelings. But every time Max is around, my entire body freezes.

I do my best to summon the anger that was *just there,* but when I do, a completely unwelcome thought flitters through my mind.

He said he was sorry.

I force myself to look away. "We have nothing to talk about. Unless you want to say something about Christmas cookies."

"I'm sure I can think of something."

"Well, save it for when we're filming—that's really the only time we need to be—" I search for a word—"chatty."

His brow quirks. "So, you'll only talk to me when we're filming?"

"I think that's probably best."

"And the truce?"

I've thought ahead for this question.

"We can still be cordial to each other. Cordial is different than friendly. And friendly is different than flirty. You seem to not understand these differences."

"You're right, they all seem like the same thing."

I sigh. "And that is why, as I mentioned—" I lower my voice —"*in the bathroom,* we need some ground rules."

172

His smile is intimate, like we share a secret. "I forgot how much you like rules."

I smile back—my *sarcastic* smile. "I do. So. Rule number one: we only talk when we're filming."

"Only when filming?"

"Only when filming."

"Does right now count?"

I purse my lips. "No. This doesn't count because we're going over the rules."

He nods. "Rules. Got it."

I try to continue. "Rule number two: The flirting—

He cuts me off. "Wait. What if you're crossing the street and there's a car coming? Can I yell out to warn you?"

I make a face.

"Or what if—" he puts his hand over his heart—"God forbid, there are bees."

I'm chagrined. "*Bees?*"

He nods, totally serious. "Yes, a swarm of bees. Can I tell you to jump in the river? Or should I try to fend them off, but without talking?"

I breathe the deep breath of someone who is trying to argue with a toddler.

"Max. It's really pretty simple." I move my hands while I talk. "Filming? Talking. Not filming? *Not talking.*"

"Is that because you can't stop thinking about last night?"

This man is shameless. And maddening. And handsome.

I reach out, grab his arm, and pull him further off to the side, away from everyone else. "No, that's because unlike some people, I don't want to lead you on. I think it's important to be clear upfront, and while I thought I was, the message obviously didn't go through."

"The message that you and I aren't friends," he says.

"That's the one."

"Oh, I got that message. Loud and clear."

"Great." I look back at my mom and Steph, who are pointing to the counter, and then to the lights. "Then we should have no problems."

"But I don't really want to be your friend, Marin."

My eyes snap to his. "You should've thought about that before."

His face falters and he backs up, suddenly a bit colder. "Talking only on air. You and I aren't friends. Got it." He takes a drink from a mug that says *World's Best Grandpa*, which is odd because nobody in our house is a grandpa. "Any other rules?"

I have to physically shake my head to clear it. "Rule number two: The flirtation is completely fake," I say. "Nothing real happening—" I move my hand back and forth between us —"here."

He nods. "Message received."

"Great." I stare at him.

"Great." He stares back.

"Great." I say again, for no apparent reason.

"You guys good?" Steph has finished her conversation with my mom, and now all three of them are watching Max and me.

"Great," we both say at the same time.

"Are you arguing?" Mom asks. "Because I don't want to be on the air with you if you're going to argue." Her face turns exasperated and she looks at Steph. "I wish they'd just admit they like each other and be done with it." She rolls her eyes.

Oh, the melodrama that is my mother.

"We're fine, Mom." I look at Max. I've gone into professional mode, and I can see the moment he notices. "Aren't we, Max?"

"Never better." He flashes a grin I can see right through, but it satisfies my mom.

"Good," she says. "You two need to bury the hatchet."

The hatchet he lodged in my back?

The melodramatic apple doesn't fall far from the tree.

I know, somewhere, deep down, I need to let this go. I know I'm holding on to something that Max has asked forgiveness for. But I also realize that without this wall of anger, I'm too exposed and too vulnerable to spend a single second around this man.

"Okay, I think we're ready." Steph claps her hands together. She's wearing an earphone plugged into a pack on her belt, giving her the ability to remotely communicate with the team back in Denver. "Danny, you set?"

He nods, thumbs up. "Good to go."

"Okay, Marin, let's have you and Max on either side of your mom, since she's going to be teaching you guys how to make these cookies."

"Oh, Marin knows how to bake," Mom says. "I taught her that ages ago."

"I told you, I don't bake anymore," I say.

"But you didn't mean that, surely," my mother says. "You love to bake." She looks at Steph. "It's a great stress reliever."

I did love to bake. Somehow not baking the cookies turned into not baking at all. Another thing I gave up when Max broke my heart. All at once, I'm annoyed with myself for doing that.

I tossed away so many things I loved simply because they reminded me of Max. Why? Why did I do that? I'm supposed to be my own woman—someone who thinks for herself. But the truth is, he had a hand in so many of my choices—and he's not even a part of my life anymore.

"Okay, Lydia," Steph says, pulling me back to the present. "This segment is a little like the one we did about the Santas. It's live."

"Got it," Mom says.

"And you two—" Steph points at Max, then me, then back to Max—"are you ready for this?"

"Yep." We say this in unison again.

I get the feeling Max is about as ready for this as I am, which is to say, not at all.

Steph looks concerned. I do nothing to calm her fears because to be honest, I have no idea how this is going to go.

Chapter Twenty-Three

Marin

I flip a switch. . .but it doesn't work.

I'm having a harder time than usual pushing my feelings aside and slipping into my on-air persona.

I would blame Max or my dad or even just being here in Pleasant Valley, but the truth is, this is my own fault. I'm having revelations about my life, my issues, my baggage, and I don't like it.

Okay, maybe it's a little bit Max. The way he looked at me last night in the alley when he said he was sorry. . .it's left me undone.

I stuff my earpiece in and clip the lavalier mic to my shirt. Then I wait for the voice in my ear to tell me it's time to go.

"How many minutes do we have for this one?" my mother whispers aside to me.

"Four minutes," I whisper back. "So, we have to be brief."

"Another rule," Max says, clearly bothered after our argument.

I shoot him a look as I hear Roger wrapping up and preparing to send the viewers over to me. Before he does, he

177

mentions the parade and the reindeer balloon, and my ear fills with the sound of laughter.

Dig deep, Marin. This is going to be the performance of your life.

In my ear, I hear Roger say, "I bet Mrs. Claus was not expecting that, am I right, Marin?"

I try to flip the switch again.

"Yes, you are correct, Roger, that was *quite* a surprise. But thankfully, nobody was harmed in the deflating of Rudolph the Red-Nosed Reindeer."

"Well, I think you have that handsome man standing in your kitchen to thank for that, don't you? The internet is all a-flutter with talk of how Santa saved Mrs. Claus." Roger's tone is jovial, and it makes me want to throat punch him. I see Steph glaring at me, and I remind myself that this is for the greater good.

"You're right, Roger. Yesterday," I turn and indicate to Max, "this man did save me from being swallowed whole by a giant reindeer's, uh, rear end."

More laughter in my ear, and I feel my cheeks flush.

Max does a slow turn to look at me. Not being able to hear Roger's portion of this conversation must have him confused.

Get it together, Marin.

I look straight into the camera, "But today's a new day, and there is no threat to my life, Scandinavian caribou or otherwise, here in my mother's kitchen."

"Not unless we let Marin cook," my mom says with a laugh. She puts her hands on my shoulders, and gives them a shake. "This girl is a great baker, but a terrible cook. The number of times she's nearly burned the house down. . ."

"Well, that's because Marin likes to follow rules," Max says with a smile. "When you bake, you follow a recipe, but when you cook, you sort of make it up as you go, and Marin isn't a fan of anything that deviates from her plan."

I see what he's doing.

Fine, buddy. It's game on. And you're on my turf now.

"Well," I half-smile back at him. "That's true. Especially when a plan has been in place for a very long time," I lean in to the camera, "and somebody strolls in and blows it all up."

Max leans in to the camera, mirroring me. "Or maybe *life* blows it all up."

"I don't know what you two are on about," Mom says, "But we have cookies to bake!"

We both lean back at the same time, as if we're ready to about-face and walk ten paces, pistols drawn.

I continue. "As I was saying, we're here this morning, live, from my mother's kitchen, where all of the Christmas cookie baking magic happens. Now, I know, many of you out there have your own cookie traditions and recipes, but as my mom always says—"

She jumps right in, "—this is going to be the best batch yet!"

I laugh. "She says it every time."

"But it's always true," my mother says with a cheerful smile.

I pick up a bowl and shake it a bit, shifting the ingredients around inside. "This recipe has been a long-standing tradition in many families, including my own. And today we are going to show you how to make the very best frosted sugar cookies with a not-so-secret ingredient."

"Well, it *would* be a secret ingredient," Mom takes the bowl from me, "but Marin says I have to tell everyone what it is." My mother smiles sweetly at the camera.

"She is bossy like that," Max says with a smile that mirrors my mother's.

I ignore him. "Mom, why don't you tell us a little about where this recipe came from?"

"Oh, sure. It's—" She stops short. I see her face falter a bit, like her smile is trying to hold up a heavier emotion behind it. "It's from. . ."

"Mom?"

She turns to me, stricken. "I'm sorry, Marin, I've just realized something." A look of panic washes over her face. "I feel like I'm under oath, and I can't lie with that camera pointed at me. I don't know why I didn't realize you'd ask me that question."

I frown, look at the camera, then back to her. "It's just Grandma's recipe, right? Passed down through the years. . ." I'm trying to jog her memory.

Mom shakes her head. "No, actually. That's just what we told you kids." She looks at Max and her face falls. "This was Jenny's recipe. It came from her family, and she lent it to me." She looks down, her face ashamed. "My family didn't have traditions like this, so I had nothing to pass down and she told me I could take hers. Said we were all family anyway." She looks at Max again. "I'm sorry, hon," she says. "I know we're not supposed to talk about them. . ."

Wait. What was that supposed to mean?

Max gives her a quick nod, then squeezes her shoulder. "It's fine, they are really good cookies."

Steph waves at us from behind the camera. When I look at her, she motions pointer fingers curling up on the sides of her mouth. *Keep this light,* she's miming, *Happy! Fun!*

"Well, taking a best friend's sugar cookie recipe and calling it your own is hardly reason to apologize," I say, adding good-natured humor to my tone. "Especially if Jenny gave it to you. I think it's okay."

"No, Marin, it's not okay" Mom confesses. "It's because we

180

told Max we wouldn't talk about his parents when he was here for Christmas, and now I've gone and brought it up." She looks at Max. "I'm so, so sorry. I broke my word."

I move on quickly. "How about you tell us what's in this recipe, Mom?"

"Don't give it another thought," Max says. "You're forgiven." He looks at me. "Just like that."

Heat rises to my cheeks. "Well, this was an honest mistake. Not a premediated, intentional heart breaker."

"Still, when a person apologizes," he indicates to himself, "and the other person doesn't forgive them," he indicates to me "that's more a problem with the other person. Don't you think so, Lydia?" His tone is fake happy, like someone who just had extensive dental work and thought it was *Just Great!*

Mom nods enthusiastically. "Of course. If you ask for forgiveness, and the person refuses, that's on them."

Max meets my eyes briefly before turning back to my mother. "I agree."

"Well," I laugh, and turn toward the camera. "I disagree. I think it depends on how sincere the apology is. A blanket *I'm sorry* does little to repair a broken relationship."

I've mischaracterized his apology, and I know it.

"Are we still talking about cookies?" Mom asks. "Because I would start by mixing the wet ingredients in the mixer. . ."

I don't even pause at this. "But maybe a *longer* explanation would do the trick. Some sort of insight on why someone would, oh, I don't know, claim that their feelings had completely changed. Overnight. Without warning."

My mom waves hands over the bowls on the counter, "And those lovely little ingredients are all laid out here for you in these beautiful clear bowls so you can see exactly what's inside. I got them on Rachael Ray's website. You know, I heard she's not a very nice person, but I just love her."

"I'm curious, Marin." Max leans on the counter to face me, but keeps his tone upbeat. "How would you recommend a person properly apologize if the person they're apologizing to shuts them down whenever they try to have an honest conversation?"

"An honest conversation?" I laugh, look at the camera. "This man can't have an honest conversation about his feelings to save his life. He's completely shut off, and refuses to let anyone else in." The humor oozes out of my voice as I say this.

"And. . .and the baking powder? The baking powder would just drop in right here. . ." Mom says, her head pinballing back and forth between Max and me.

"Or, you know, maybe not. Maybe it's just me he keeps on the outside," I say—an old wound has been reopened.

"Or maybe he just needs more time to figure out what he wants to say," Max says, a bit louder, stepping out from behind the counter.

I circle the counter to face him. "Eight years wasn't enough time for him?"

"Maybe not!"

"Maybe he needs another eight!"

"Maybe so!"

We stare at each other for a weighted moment.

Then, I slowly turn and remember who's in the room. And that we're filming.

Max must sense it too, because he glances at the camera, looks down, and then we both move back to our spots next to my mother.

"So, once the wet ingredients are all in the mixer—" Mom is desperately trying to get us back on track. Steph's eyes are bugged out of her head, and I can only imagine Roger is watching us crash and burn from his cushy desk back in Denver.

"Lydia," Max says, clearing his throat. "Why don't you tell everyone what the secret ingredient is?"

"Oh! Yes! It's almond extract," she says, thankful for the lifeline. "You put it in the frosting *and* in the mix, that's the secret, and it adds the most wonderful flavor to these fluffy sugar cookies."

Fluffy sugar cookies passed over from Jenny's family to ours.

"Mom, tell us why it's special to you to make cookies that your best friend Jenny, Max's mother, made for her own family," I say.

Mom glances at Max, her face concerned, and a wave of panic washes over me. The question came from the reporter in me, and I didn't intend for it to be thoughtless.

Max still doesn't talk about them, all these years later, but his wonderful, loving, kind parents deserve to be remembered. Still, my timing is off, and I sense it immediately. Sure, I'm still angry with Max, but I don't want to wound him.

I'm about to backtrack when my mom speaks. "Well," she says, sniffling a bit. "Jenny and I grew up together, and we were best friends. We bought houses next door to each other, and had babies—" she motions to Max and then to me— "within months of each other." I can see Mom's eyes have turned glassy, and I know that this—this is the story that needs to be told.

Is it too much to hope that hearing how much his mom meant to my mom might ease some of Max's pain?

Mom smiles through her tears. "Jenny was special. She could make every day feel like Christmas if she wanted to. She had a certain whimsy, didn't she Max?" Mom reaches over and takes Max's hand.

His gaze is firmly on the counter in front of us, and at Mom's touch, he reacts, pulling his hand away like he just touched a hot iron. He looks at me—not hurt, but panicked.

Like he's scared, trapped, and doesn't know how to find a way out. He pulls the apron off and says, "Excuse me", then rushes out of the kitchen, leaving us standing there.

And I know I've really messed up. In the wake of our argument, this will feel malicious, and I'm not sure how to undo it.

I turn to the camera.

"They say that the kitchen is the heart of the home. So many memories happened in this kitchen, and I know you all out there have memories of your own. And though it might not look like it now. . ." I look at my mom, ". . .this might turn out to be the best batch yet."

I sign off, and when we're clear, there's a hush of silence in the kitchen.

Mom turns to me. "We don't talk about Steve and Jenny."

"I didn't know," I say quietly. "I didn't mean to bring them up like that. The question just sort of slipped out."

"You can't force someone to deal with their grief the way you want them to, Marin," Mom says.

The words land in the soft space of my heart, and I wonder if this isn't the first time I've done that to Max. My heart wrenches at the thought. *Stupid, Marin!*

"I should go check on Max," Mom says.

I take off the apron. "No, Mom. I'll go." I glance up at Steph.

"So much for flirty banter." She sighs. "We're going to need to do some damage control. Marin, go find him and figure out a way to make this right."

Chapter Twenty-Four

Max

This was a mistake.

It was a mistake, coming here, to Marin's childhood home, a mistake to try and get back in her good graces. It's clear she has no intention of forgiving me. In fact, she seems intent on making me pay for the past.

I stop and stand in the middle of Marin's room.

What am I doing?

I grab my sweats, replaying the disaster that just happened in the kitchen. How could she ask that? Even after her mom let everyone know we don't talk about my parents at Christmas?

We don't talk about my parents at all.

I tie my shoes, pulling them tight and feeling a flicker of anger when they don't tie right. I stand and pull a hoodie on over my T-shirt, pushing my arms hard through the balled-up sleeves. It's cooler now, and there's a thin crunchy layer of snow on the road, but the only thing I can think to do is to run.

Run away.

I shove my AirPods in my ears and make my way downstairs on the balls of my feet, hoping the creaks of the stairs don't give me away. I want to slip out unnoticed.

I don't want to rehash any of it. I don't want anyone asking me if I'm okay. I don't want everyone fawning, and looking piti-ful, and apologizing for bringing up my mom in the first place.

I hate all of that.

When people find out about your trauma, they start treating you differently. It's way easier to hide all of that. From everyone.

Marin. I shake my head at thinking her name and seeing her face in my mind.

She'd never intentionally tried to hurt me before, but that was obviously her plan in bringing up my mom again. She cornered me, and on live TV. The Marin I knew never would've done something just to be cruel.

I make it down the stairs and out the door without being seen. As I stand on the porch, I breathe in the crisp, cool air.

Yes, we have an agreement not to relive all of our old memories of my parents—and when Lydia let it slip that this was my mother's recipe, it hurt.

But thinking about it now, it didn't hurt the way it used to.

It was bittersweet. Nostalgic. Seeing my mom through her eyes was. . .lighter, somehow.

It made me miss her.

I start my run down the gravel driveway, and when I reach the end, I feel myself at a crossroads. I can go left, like always.

Or I can go right. Towards my parents' house.

I go right.

My muscles burn with the effort it takes to run up the hill, and when I reach the top, I stop again. I know that just beyond the patch of trees to the right is the house. Full of memories. Reminders of a life I wanted more than anything but would never, ever have.

I force myself to go on.

I pass the evergreens and come alongside a clearing, and there it is.

While Marin's childhood home is a sprawling white farmhouse with a wrap-around porch, my childhood home is smaller, more modest. But Lydia was right. My mom was whimsical, and she had turned this place into a storybook home.

I stand at the end of the driveway and stare at it. I'd paid a handyman to keep it updated and landscapers to tend to the yard, but I hadn't stepped foot inside since my parents died.

They say time heals all wounds. But it doesn't. It's been eight years, and standing in front of this house brings back the same emotions I felt the day I found out.

Eight years of "time" and I'm right back where I started.

There's no pastel-colored Christmas wreath on the door or Christmas tree with bright, colored lights. There's no sound of laughter coming from the kitchen as my mom and dad danced to the sound of Christmas carols coming from the stereo.

I miss them so, so much—but in this moment, I'm filled with something unfamiliar and unexpected.

Warm memories of growing up in that house.

I can see their faces in the window. I can smell the sweetness coming from the kitchen. The time when Teddy and I changed all of the name tags on the presents, and James got Marin's earrings as a Christmas gift. The three of us kids building the snow fort to end all snow forts, and me filming Marin interviewing Teddy with his ridiculous fake Scottish accent.

I laugh to myself.

Time doesn't heal all wounds. Time gives you distance and perspective. The time we had wasn't enough, but it wasn't nothing. I lived twenty-two amazing years as their son. And that was a gift.

I pull the AirPods from my ears and tuck them into my pocket when I hear crunching footsteps approaching.

I turn and see Marin's head bobbing up over the crest of the hill. She's breathing so hard I'm afraid she might pass out.

She reaches the top, and as she looks up and sees me, her foot hits a patch of ice and her feet flip out from under her. She lets out a yelp as she lands flat on her back.

I race over and stand beside her, my shadow shielding her face from the sun. "Are you okay?"

She squints up at me. "I suppose I deserved that."

"You won't hear me argue," I say. "I only wish I'd been filming it." I reach down and offer my hand, surprised when she takes it and lets me help her to her feet.

As much as I wish I could be, I'm not mad at her.

She pulls her hand away and brushes the snowy gravel off of her backside. When she's finished, she looks at me.

"Out for a run?" I ask.

She laughs. "I hate running."

"I know." I try to read her. "So, what are you doing? Stalking me?"

She shakes her head. "I came to apologize."

I raise my eyebrows and nod. "Impressive you got that out without clenching your teeth."

"Don't make this harder than it is," she says.

"You made my apology pretty hard, I'd say I owe you."

"That's fair." She looks away. "Max. I shouldn't have brought up your mom."

"It's fine."

"It's not."

"Yeah, I guess maybe it's not." I kick at some gravel under my feet.

She shakes her head. "I was thinking like a reporter, and not like a friend."

"But we're not friends," I say, summoning a smile.

She covers her face and groans. "I didn't mean all of that stuff I said. I mean, I did, but I didn't. I just—you make me kind of crazy."

I laugh. "Crazy good or. . .?"

She crosses her arms over her chest and looks at me. "I feel awful. After the question was out there, I thought that maybe. . .maybe if you heard how much we all loved your parents it would make you, I don't know, see them in a different way."

I look at the house. "Instead of just 'gone.'"

She looks at her feet. "Yeah. Something like that."

I start walking toward the house, and Marin falls into step beside me. "If Mrs. Claus hadn't run off yesterday, Santa would've eventually gotten around to a more detailed apology."

"No, you apologized. That should be enough." She stuffs her hands in the pockets of her puffy pink coat. "I guess I understand not wanting to talk about things that upset you."

"Yeah, we're both great at avoiding the hard stuff," I say.

She frowns up at me. "You more than me."

I watch her. "But also you."

She goes quiet. "Yeah. I guess also me."

I reach the steps of the house and walk up onto the porch. "This is the first time I've been here since they died."

She's still on the walkway, watching me. I don't mind that she is.

I wait for the hollowing sting of pain to envelop me as I stand in the midst of so many memories, but it doesn't come. Only that same unexpected warmth from before.

She runs her hand along the railing, and then sits on the top step. "I don't think there's anything wrong with protecting your heart, Max. Lord knows I've been doing that for eight years."

"What, you didn't want to let Buck in?"

She laughs, and I love it.

"No, Buck and his veneers didn't do it for me." She goes still. "But I do think there's something special in remembering people who loved us so much. It's a way to, maybe, let ourselves grieve."

I can feel her looking at me.

"Maybe you need to let yourself grieve, Max."

I'm staring at the front door when she says this, and I can't bring myself to look at her. Not now. Not when she's being every bit as understanding as she would've been if I'd given her the chance to be all those years ago.

I was so angry and so broken, and so afraid. So, I pushed her away. And when I pushed, I pushed hard. I knew I had to be brutal to get her to leave.

"Look, Marin—"

"Sorry—" she cuts in. "I'm not trying to tell you what to do."

"No, it's okay." I face her. "I know you don't want to talk about what happened with us anymore than I want to talk about my parents, but I do want to clear the air."

To my shock, she doesn't shut me down.

This is the hard part.

"I was going through a lot. Looking back at how I acted, I just. . ." I search for the right words.

She stays patient, and listens.

"I didn't know how to process anything. I was over-whelmed, and I'm sorry—really sorry—that I hurt you in the process."

She watches me, maybe assessing how sincere my apology is. "So, if you had it to do over, would you change anything?"

I look away. I don't want to lie.

"I don't know. I wasn't good for anyone back then, Mare. I

have a feeling I would've hurt you a lot more if we'd stayed together."

I don't want to tell her all the idiotic things I did after we broke up, or how I still thought about her practically every day, or that it took me three solid years and a Christmas with her parents before I finally found my way back to the person I was.

"I guess that's fair," she says.

I know I haven't told her everything—there is so much more that led me to the decision to let her go—but it's a start. "So."

She half-smiles. "So."

"Can we try this truce thing again?" I ask. "For real this time?"

"Like, actually be friends?" A genuine smile. I'll take it.

"Yeah, like that."

She sticks her hand out in my direction, and I look at it for a moment before taking it.

"Truce," she says. "For real this time."

"For real this time." I nod.

We stand, and I don't let go of her hand. I like the way it feels in mine. It's a connection I'm in no hurry to sever.

"Do you want to go inside?" She nods toward the house.

I shake my head and let go of her hand. "Not ready for that yet."

She tilts her head. "Then let's go ice skating."

"Ice skating?"

"The lake froze over, and I need a little redemption after my behavior in the kitchen."

I'm surprised. "Uh, yeah, that would be nice."

She pulls out her phone. "Plus, it would look great on our socials, we'll do a whole thing about it."

If my smile falters for a second, Marin doesn't notice.

Right. Fake flirtation.

All for other people's entertainment.

Chapter Twenty-Five

Marin

I 'm unsure how to act around Max now that I've agreed to a real truce.

It was critical that I protect my heart. The heartache of the past unfortunately ordained my present. But I'm not sure how to do that without being angry.

I'm grateful for the apology, but questions remain—namely, how did he push me away so easily after everything we'd been through together?

This is the current struggle, and the same conflicting mental dance that's been spinning in my mind for years: how can I be understanding and confused at the same time? How could I want to give him space and *not* want to give him space?

And the kicker—did he really mean it when he said he didn't love me?

It sure felt like it at the time.

I suppose if this truce is going to work, though, I should stay away from topics like his parents and how much he hurt me when he ended things between us. Ice skating? Cookie making? Tree decorating? All safe. It would be so much easier to fake flirt with Max now that we'd mostly cleared the air.

We reach the house and find Steph waiting for us. Danny's been relieved, and for the first time, I wonder what he does all day when we're filming content on our phones.

My guess is a lot of Mario Kart.

"You two better?" Steph asks in a cautious tone.

"Yes," I say, verbal hat in hand. "I apologized for being a jerk."

"I did too." Max runs a hand through his hair, and I picture him in an H & M ad, on an outdoor shoot in the mountains.

It's these kinds of thoughts that are definitely going to get me in trouble.

"I'm going to go change." Max runs up the stairs, leaving Steph and me standing in the entryway.

"Tell me there's a secret peephole behind a painting or something." Steph waggles her eyebrows and grins.

"Ok, *no*, and I'm pretty sure that's illegal," I say.

She squints at me. "You're not thinking about how good he looks in that blue sweatshirt?"

I say nothing.

"And thinking about how he looks *out* of that blue sweatshirt."

"Good. Grief." I make a face. "I'm thinking about my job, remember? The competition? The promotion?"

"Mm hmm," Steph says. "So, we can get back to the flirtatious version of you two instead of whatever the heck that was earlier?"

"Definitely," I say. "We're going ice skating. The lake finally froze over."

"Oh, just in time for you to thaw out," Steph says.

"Ha, ha." I roll my eyes.

"Wait. You're going to be spending the afternoon outside?"

"Yes." I laugh, and add sarcastically, "That's where the lake is."

"It's freezing," she says.

"Yes." I lean my head forward and speak as if I'm showing her a chart that explains how two plus two equals four. *"That's what happens to water when it gets cold."*

"But I don't like the cold."

"Well, here in Illinois, we have a fix for that." I open the hall closet and motion to the many assorted winter coats hanging there.

My mother refuses to throw anything away. Ever.

"It's not like it's warm in Denver this time of year," I say. "Are you really surprised by the weather?"

Steph groans. "I do better indoors."

I trade out my short pink coat for a long, black, insulated one that hits me about mid-calf, pull on my stocking cap, and grin at her. "Ready?"

Steph reaches into the closet and pulls out a blue coat that actually belongs to my dad. It's huge, double lined, has a drawstring hood and big zippered pockets. She slips it on, and her entire body disappears inside of it, her tiny head recessed in the hood cavern. One hand pokes out of a sleeve and I put a stocking cap and gloves in it.

I cup my hands around my mouth and pretend like I'm calling to Timmy who fell down the well. "You look great in there," I shout at her.

She harrumphs, pulling the hood off and blowing a stray piece of hair out of her face. "Why are you so chipper?"

Max comes down the stairs and stops in the hallway. He's wearing jeans and a hoodie, and he's smiling at me. "Are we doing this?"

Steph nods to herself. "Ah. That's why."

I shoot her a look.

"We called a truce," I say, then I look at Max. "A real one."

He nods back.

"Oh, this'll be good." Steph smirks over at me.

Max reaches into the closet and pulls out a black coat, grabs a pair of Teddy's old ice skates from the bin inside and opens the front door. "Meet you guys down there?"

I nod.

After he's gone, I turn to find Steph watching me. "What?"

She shakes her head.

"What?" I repeat. "Max and I finally figured out how to be friends."

"Ah. *Friends.*" Her sarcasm is so thick, I can practically see the air quotes around her words.

"And," I continue, disregarding her tone, "it feels good to say that. Why do you care, anyway? This is good for us, good for the competition, and good for my job. I can put all of my angst behind me and focus on getting the promotion."

She waits, and I feel I need to fill the space.

"And. . .if I have to flirt with my ex-boyfriend to get it, I'm finally. . .you know."

"Going to enjoy it?"

"Pre*pared.*" I put my hand on the doorknob and turn to face her. "I'm in this for the promotion—nothing more."

"You sound like you're trying to convince yourself, but whatever—it'll be better for filming."

"Right." I decide not to linger too long on that thought and lead Steph out the front door.

We make our way outside and find Max down at the lake. He's sitting on a bench, lacing up the skates, and I'm in tenth grade again, running down to meet him.

When I reach the lake, he glances over at me and smiles. In light of our deal, this smile does things to me that are impossible to ignore. I'm sweating, even in this big coat.

Steph hangs back, doing something on her phone, and I sit next to Max and take off my shoes.

"I hope I remember how to do this," I say.

Daylight is fading, and my dad has strung white lights into the trees surrounding the lake. Sitting here now, I'm overcome with how things used to be.

Max, who always seems to be watching me, notices, and frowns. "You okay?"

I turn and smile, hoping he can't see through it. "I'm great."

He stands and reaches a gloved hand out in my direction. I take it, and he helps me to my feet.

"It is actually frozen, right?" I ask.

"It's solid," Max says. He moves to the edge and steps on the ice.

I hesitate, and he doesn't pressure me to take a step, just stands there, waiting while I assess the situation.

"I'm not going to let anything happen to you." He looks straight at me when he says this, and I believe him.

I step out onto the ice, and newborn fawn-like, I buckle ever-so-slightly, but Max steadies me.

"I've got you."

"It's like riding a bike, right?" I'm shaking on unsteady legs as we head out to the center of the lake. We move slowly at first, keeping a tight circle around the lake for a few minutes, and Max still holds on to my hand.

Muscle memory starts to kicks in, and I don't think I need help to stay upright—but I don't let go.

"See? You've got this." Max says. He drops my hand, and I instantly lose my balance, but before my legs completely go out from under me, he catches me by the arm.

I look up at him and laugh. "I definitely don't got it."

"Maybe I should just hold onto you, to keep you from

hurting yourself." He laughs, and I take his hand again, aware that Steph is filming us. I'm also aware that I wish she wasn't.

I can tell myself this is all for show until I'm blue in the face, but I'm not buying it for a second. I like not being mad at Max.

Gosh, that scares me.

We skate around for a while. Max cracks jokes, and I laugh at the appropriate times, and it's harder and harder to remind myself that this is all for the sake of my promotion.

It sure doesn't feel like pretend. It feels natural, easy, and familiar.

There's always a point you come to when faced with a situation or a decision—the point of not caring what the consequences are, or just deciding that you'll deal with them later.

I'm rapidly skating toward that point. On thin ice.

"Okay, Marin, we should film an intro, then we'll piece together shots of the lake, the trees, the moon, you two—and then I'm heading back to the hotel to get under a heated blanket with a warm drink and watch *The Bachelor*."

We head over to the edge of the lake and face the camera. Once we're steady, Max lets go of my hand, and I draw in a deep breath and will the blades of my skates to stick in one spot.

"Maybe talk to each other for this intro, instead of the typical explanation of what we're doing out here?"

I glance at Max, who nods, then smiles at Steph.

"Okay, so, think of it like a conversation," Steph says. She holds the phone up and nods at us. "You two can have a conversation without killing each other, right?"

Max raises a brow in a silent question.

"Yes, Steph, we can," I say.

Steph gives me a thumbs-up, and we're off.

"So, we're out here in my parents' backyard, ice skating on

our lake, which is something we've been doing since we were kids." I glance at Max. "How old were we when this tradition started, do you think?"

"Young," Max says. "Toddlers, probably."

"You'll notice at the center of the lake, my parents have set up a small Christmas tree."

"The Wishing Tree," Max says. "It's a really cool tradition. The entire town makes their way out here in the days leading up to Christmas, and everyone writes their Christmas wish on a little piece of paper, seals it up in a glass ornament and hangs it on the tree."

"Then, as the ice melts, the tree starts to sink, and the idea is that the wishes are released into the world so they can finally come true," I say.

"But really, Marin's dad has to fish them out of the lake every year."

I glance at Max. "That's not true. They're all still in the lake."

He frowns at me. "Are you serious?"

"Yes. The wishes won't come true if someone scoops them out of the water."

"Marin, they wouldn't be able to leave a bunch of glass ornaments in the lake. Pretty sure that's bad for the environment,"

I stare at him. I feel blindsided by this information.

"I always thought those wishes were carried away to heaven like prayers whispered on the wind." I say this with the conviction of a six-year-old knowing without a shadow of a doubt that Santa Claus is real.

Max chuckles.

"Don't laugh at me!" I'm not mad, just feel caught in some practical joke.

"Hey, hey, hey, it's okay," he says, taking my hand—which I

let him hold. "It doesn't take away from the magic of it. Plus, I've had wishes from the tree come true before."

"You've had wishes come true before?" I ask, trying to hide my feelings about this legend my parents had told us ever since we were little.

"Lots of times," he says to me. He pats my hand, lets it go, then turns to the camera. "The legend says that if you and someone else put the same exact wish on the tree, then it has no choice but to come true. Which means, that you and I must've put the same wish on the tree at least once—"

"Oh my gosh. The Christmas we decided where to go to college," I say, remembering.

He nods. "Yep. We swore we weren't going to make our decisions based on the other person, so we wrote down our top choices and revealed them to each other the Christmas of our senior year. That happened right over there." Max points to the boathouse, illuminated by the white lights strung all around the roof. "In the boathouse."

"That was a good Christmas," I say with a smile, lost in the nostalgia of it.

"That was a good kiss."

Heat rushes to my cheeks, and I remember Steph is still filming. "We. . .uh. . .both chose the University of Illinois."

"So we didn't have to let each other go," Max says.

I swim through my clouded thoughts and try to end the interview on a coherent note. "So, I suppose we'll have to put our wishes on the tree this year too, and—" to the camera— "you'll have to stay tuned to see if they come true."

I barely shift my weight when I say this, but for some reason, my right skate decides to check out what's three feet in front of it like a dog seeing a squirrel. I completely lose my balance, cartoon-style.

My hand catches Max's arm. *"Flip Flappin' Flip!"* I bark

the same phrase we used to shout when we were kids because we weren't allowed to swear as I take him down with me.

We land in a pile on the ice.

More specifically, I land on top of Max.

"I swear I didn't write this on the tree." he says.

"I'm so sorry," I say, trying to extricate myself from his body. It's difficult in a big coat while wearing ice skates.

"If you wanted to jump me, you could've just said so, McGrath." He looks at Steph and says, "I had no idea she was this forward, I swear."

"I think you mean 'this clumsy.'" My cheeks are hot with embarrassment. I plant a skate on the ice, but slip forward and land the top of my head in his armpit.

Why do I keep falling down?

Max sits back and lets me push on him in an effort to try and get up without hurting myself. "I think it's a front," he says. "Just an excuse for you to grope me." He grins. "Notice I'm not putting up a fight."

Finally, like a newly birthed giraffe, I stand. "That was not planned."

He pushes up to standing and takes my hand. "Deny it all you want, but we all know you can't keep your hands to yourself."

He's doing exactly what he's supposed to, but I'm flustered.

Instead of protesting, like I usually do, I simply look at the camera, shrug, and smile.

"Cut!" Steph grins, sticking her phone back in her pocket. "The falling thing was *gold*! Good idea, Marin."

I push myself in a short glide over to solid ground, spin around and plop down on the ground. Max looks at me, amused.

"Uh, thanks? It wasn't really planned—"

She's not even listening. "I'm going to edit this and post it.

I'll send stats in the morning." Steph trudges off. Max pushes off of one foot and skates over to me, then sits.

We stay like that for a minute, in the brisk silence.

He lies back and looks up at the sky. "Does it ever get tiring?"

"Does what get tiring?"

"Being 'on' all the time?"

I lie back beside him, leaving space between us for Jesus, as my mom used to say. "Yeah, honestly, it does."

"How did you even end up in television?"

"That's a long story," I say. "My dream sort of went up in flames when the guy I loved dumped me, so I. . ."

"Okay, okay, I get it, I get it." He turns on his side and looks at me, but I keep my eyes steady on The Pleiades.

I point to the dim cluster and smile. "The Seven Sisters."

"Always the one you point out."

"The first one I ever found—and it's one that's less well-known than the Big Dipper or Orion, so when I point it out, people think 'Oh, my gosh, she knows random constellations, she must be amazing and smart.'"

He laughs, and I laugh with him. I thought I was funny just then.

But after a pause, he asks, "Was I really the reason why?"

I look at him, then quickly back to the sky. I shrug in my big coat. "Yeah. It didn't feel right without you."

He reaches over and takes my gloved hand. "I'm sorry, Marin."

"You already said that," I say.

"I know."

"We're good now," I say. "Everything is as it's supposed to be."

He squeezes my hand, and it sends a shiver down my spine.

That, with no skin to skin contact—I can't imagine what a mess I'd be if our hands were bare.

"This is kind of nice," he says. "You not hating me and all."

I slide my free hand into the pocket of my coat, and I feel something hard inside. I pull it out and look at it. "Oh my gosh." I sit up.

"What's that?"

Tears spring to my eyes. "It's a rock shaped like a heart."

Max frowns. "From your other high school boyfriend?"

I look at him.

"From your mom."

Chapter Twenty-Six

Max

"My mom gave you a heart-shaped rock?"

I sit up and look at Marin. She turns the rock over in her hand.

"My first day of high school," she says with a wistful smile. "She said if I got nervous, I could find it in my pocket and I'd know that she and my mom were thinking of me, and they were going to be there when I got home."

"I didn't get a rock," I say.

Marin laughs, then holds it out in my direction. "Maybe you should have it."

I shake my head. "No, Mare. If she gave that to you, you should keep it."

She closes her hand over it as the moonlight shimmers on the lake. The white lights in the trees mix with the blue light overhead to cast a glow on Marin's face, and I can't think of a time she's ever looked more beautiful.

I stand and hold a hand out to help her up. "We should probably get you off the ice before you kill us."

Another laugh. "I really am sorry about that."

As if I minded. I'd take any chance I got to have her in my arms—even if it was an accident.

We put our shoes back on and plod toward the house, skates slung over our shoulders and both of us quiet. I look at her. "What are you thinking about?" I have a feeling I already know.

I'm thinking about her, too.

She looks at me. "Sorry, I know we're not supposed to. . ."

"No, it's okay," I say. "It doesn't hurt as much as I thought it would."

There's a pause, and then Marin pulls the rock from her pocket. "I miss her. Both of them, really. They were a second set of parents to me, and how lucky did that make me?"

I smile. "Pretty lucky. We both were. I had two sets of parents too, remember."

Another pause. Then: "I think I understand why my mom told you you'd always have a place here, on the holidays or whenever. I get it now. She knew she and my dad were the closest thing to family you had." She sighs. "I was really mad about that when I first got home."

I default to adding humor. "You? Mad? Wow, I didn't notice. Were you. . .?"

She smiles again, quipping, "I was, yeah. Surprising, I know. I'm really good at hiding my feelings."

I dig my hands in the deep pockets of my coat. "She didn't do it to hurt you."

"I know," Marin says. "But it did. And it made me feel really left out."

"But. . .that was by choice, right?" I keep my tone light when I say this, but I've suspected she wasn't completely honest about her reasons for missing Christmas all these years.

"Partly," she says. "I really did want to make an impression at work. I felt I had something to prove after you left me. The

204

life I thought I would have wasn't going to happen, and I needed to be independent—figure out who I was without the beautiful Max Weber on my arm."

I laugh. "I don't think anyone's ever called me 'beautiful' before."

She frowns over at me. "Trust me, they have."

"What's the other part?"

Her frown deepens.

"You said 'partly. . .' What's the other part?"

"Oh." She looks away. "You."

"Me? But I'm not even here most of the time."

"Max," she says, like I should know it already. "You're everywhere."

That was maybe a little bit of truth she hadn't intended to share.

We reach the door, but when Marin goes to open it, I put a hand over hers. She faces me, and it's like we're right back where we were all those years ago. Marin and I sneaking off to be together every chance we got.

What would she do if I kissed her right now?

It's a stupid thought, and it would be way too forward. Plus, she just agreed to become my sort-of friend again. What am I trying to do, ruin everything?

"What's wrong?" She's watching me—her eyes full of expectancy, and I remember the look on her face when I broke up with her. It was brutal. And as much as I want her in my life, I can't risk doing that to her again. Not when things are finally better between us.

"Nothing," I say. "I'm just. . .glad we're friends again."

If this disappoints her, she doesn't let on. Instead, she smiles and punches me in the arm with a gloved hand. "Me too."

Marin

We come inside and find my parents sitting in the living room, staring at the naked tree we'd picked out day before yesterday.

With the Christmas Stroll and the parade, we hadn't had a chance to decorate, and judging by the serious look on my mom's face—that was about to change.

"Finally," Mom says. "Where've you two been? I was worried you were out there planning a duel to the death."

"We've put our differences behind us, Mom," I say. "And anyway, I would win."

I look over at Max, who makes a face and mouths the words, *No you wouldn't.*

Mom eyes us both suspiciously. "Like, a real truce?"

I nod.

I notice now she's focusing only on me. "No snarky remarks?"

I hold up my right hand in a solemn vow. "You have my word."

"Well, it's about time." Now, she looks at Max. "Would you mind grabbing the Christmas bins from the closet?"

"Sure thing."

"I can help!" I start off in the direction of the basement, when I notice Max is heading toward the hall closet. I frown. "The Christmas closet is downstairs."

"She moved it." He pulls the closet door open. "It's here now."

"Oh." I should know these things. I know it's my own fault, but I should know more about my own parents than Max does.

"It's fine, Mare," he says, like he's reading my mind. "You're here now."

I nod and take one of the big Christmas bins from him. I return to the living room and set it down. Dad has just made a fire, and I wonder if I should change into shorts and a tank top now or wait till it's hot as blazes in this room.

Max shows up in the doorway with two big bins, carrying them like he's a middle school boy at youth group hauling five chairs to impress the girls.

I pull out my phone and open up the camera, setting it up on the mantle in a position where it can film the scene—all of us, decorating the tree together like one big, happy family. Our audience will love it.

I'm trying to balance the phone up against one of my mother's reindeer statues when Max comes up behind me.

"Filming?" He's looking at me via the screen of the phone.

"Yeah, seems like always, right? I figured a time-lapse would be cool. Is it annoying?"

"Nah, but you could catch more if—" he reaches both arms around me and slides the camera over from time-lapse mode to normal video. "Do this. . .? You have enough storage, right?" He changes the resolution, then looks at me in the screen. "Camera ready, as always." He hits record and disappears.

I feel his absence immediately—it's like stepping away from a bonfire in late November.

I join my parents and Max, periodically checking on the camera to make sure it's still filming.

Mom unpacks white twinkle lights, sparkly bows and ornaments, then pulls two smaller bins out of the larger bins.

"Here we go," she says. She hands me one of the small bins, labeled *Marin's Ornaments,* but I'm too distracted to open it when she hands the other bin to Max. I notice that bin is labeled *Max's Ornaments* in the same handwriting as the bin I'm holding.

Max takes the lid off, revealing unfamiliar ornaments.

They're from Max's childhood. He picks one up and looks at it. It's a guy on a bright yellow dirt bike. "My mom got me this when I turned ten," he says. "She said it would have to do because there was no way she was going to get me a real one." He half-laughs, and I glance over to find surprise on both of my parents' faces.

I'm betting Max doesn't often participate in the storytelling aspect of our Christmas tree decorating tradition, but maybe tonight, that will finally change.

Or not. Either way. I don't care. I'm only here for the video footage.

A lie if I ever told one.

He pulls out another one, it's Blue from Blue's Clues, wearing a green Christmas hat sitting on a beach next to Shovel and Pail.

"Oh my gosh, did I ever go through a Blue's Clues phase—it was the only DVD we had in the car for a while." He turns to me. "Do you remember that?"

I laugh. "I do. I think I still have it memorized."

He hangs it, and we both fish more ornaments out of our boxes, turning each one over in our hands before hanging them.

We spend the next hour, sharing stories, hanging ornaments, stringing up lights, and making the living room look like it's ready for Christmas. The tree is the one thing my mom lets anyone else contribute to, and we deck it out from top to bottom. Not one branch is spared.

Once it's all done, we stand back and look at it. Max dims the overhead light so we can properly appreciate the glow.

"Are we done?" Dad asks.

"All done," Mom says.

"Good. I'm going to bed." He doesn't wait for anyone to say goodnight, just walks straight out of the room and up the stairs.

My mother glances over at us. "This was nice."

I nod. Back in Denver, I don't have a Christmas tree. I'm not home enough to enjoy it, so I never really saw the point.

But after tonight, I understand. It's magical.

"Oh, and Marin, if you want to take your box of ornaments back to Colorado with you, that's fine."

"No," I say. "I think they belong here."

She smiles. "Okay, I'm heading to bed too. Big day tomorrow. The Twelve Shops of Christmas Scavenger Hunt and the next day is the chili cookoff."

"Right," I say. "I've got them on the calendar."

"Marin." Mom comes over to me and looks me dead in the eye. "I know I can't tell you which pot of chili is mine because you're a judge and all, but it'll be the one in the red bowls. Maybe we could come up with a signal or something?"

"Mom!"

She holds her hands up. "Sorry! I just can't lose my title."

I laugh. "Go to bed."

She looks at me, then at Max, then back at me. "Can I trust you two down here alone? The tree lights make this room feel very romantic."

"Mother!" I turn her around and push her out of the room.

"All right, I'm going." She holds her hands up in surrender, then turns to face us. "But no sharing blankets, feet on the ground at all times and—"

"Leave room for Jesus," we all three say in unison.

"We know, Mom."

"Okay, I have to catch your father before he falls asleep," she says. "We will *not* be saving room for Jesus." She laughs as she hurries up the stairs, then calls back down, "One of the perks of being married!"

"That is so gross," I say with a shudder, after she's gone.

"It's kind of sweet," Max says. "They still love each other. I hope we—" He looks caught, like he's just let a thought slip that he had no intention of sharing.

Don't read into this, Marin.

"I liked your box of ornaments," I say, mostly because I'm nervous.

"Thanks. It's the first time I've gotten them out."

"Really?" I don't want to spook him, so I keep my tone even.

"Yeah," he says. "*Way* too hard before."

I pause. "And now?"

"Someone told me that grief is an expression of love," he nods in my direction, then stares at the tree. "It felt appropriate."

"Good."

We're standing in the living room, surrounded by nothing but the quiet of the house. I should go to bed—we have a long day of shooting tomorrow. But I find myself searching for reasons to linger.

"Can you shoot some stuff with us tomorrow?" I ask, desperately trying to land on conversation that actually matters.

"If you want me there, sure."

"Okay, good."

The air between us has changed. Without my wall of anger, I'm openly exposed, and while I should duck and run for cover, here I am, still standing in front of him.

He takes a step toward me, and my heartrate kicks up. If he tries to kiss me, I know I'll let him, and what of our truce then?

"Marin—"

I don't move. He tucks a strand of hair behind my ear and rests his hand there, at the base of my neck. I can feel the heat of it on my skin as his thumb brushes across my cheek.

Skin to skin contact.

My breath grows shallow in my chest. I find his eyes, intent on me, and I have to look away.

"I should get to bed," I say, because I'm an idiot.

No, because I am a smart, brave, independent woman. I'm *not* falling back into old habits.

But it's hard not to fall when you're already losing your balance.

He pulls his hand away and tucks it in his pocket. "Right. Big day of filming tomorrow."

And only then do I realize that the camera is still recording.

Max turns to go, and I force myself not to ask him to come back. Once I hear the sound of my old bedroom door closing, I go to the camera, stop the video and then replay the moment when Max almost kissed me.

And then I replay it another 352 times before finally drifting off to sleep with the phone still in my hand.

Chapter Twenty-Seven

Marin

I wake up the next morning to find my phone on the floor next to my bed.

I tap it to life, and the video from the night before pops up immediately, the last thing I watched before I fell asleep.

I watch it again, this time with fresh eyes, and two thoughts occur to me.

1. *I did a really good job of protecting myself there, because it's pretty obvious he was thinking about kissing me.*
2. *WHY did I do such a good job of protecting myself? I could've kissed him!*

I'm conflicted.

I head into the bathroom, listening at the door to my old room, catching a glimpse of the disappointment on my face in the mirror when I don't hear any sounds coming from inside.

Odds are Max isn't going to walk in on me in the bathroom,

shirtless or otherwise, so I might as well make myself presentable.

This tightrope I'm walking might as well be made of fishing line.

Because every dreamy thought I have about Max is followed up by a very real reminder that this is not going to end well.

I need a healthy dose of reality.

I need some no-nonsense, smack-in-the-face, kick-in-the-pants truth to knock some sense into myself, so I go searching for the one person I can count on to give it to me.

I find Steph sitting at the kitchen table, alone.

"Where is everybody?" I ask.

"You mean, where is Max?" Steph leans back in the chair and looks at me.

"No, I mean where are my parents?"

"Your mother said she had to do some shopping, and I haven't seen your dad."

I nod. "And Max?"

Steph's eyebrows raise in a question.

"I'm just curious."

"Because of this?" She flips the phone around and there's the video I took on my own phone the night before.

"Where did you get that?"

"The videos you take on your work phone automatically upload to the server."

Oh, crap.

How did I forget that?

"How many times did you watch it last night?" She watches me with a smug look on her face.

I sit down across from her, knowing that if I start talking about this, even to Steph, it's all going to come out.

"Marin." Steph folds her hands and leans forward. "You're falling for him."

"No! Steph, come on. It's all. . ." I fumble.

"Fake?" She finishes my thought.

"Yes!" I point at her. "Totally fake!"

She taps her phone, lets the video play for a few seconds, and then taps it again. She holds it up to me and it's paused on the same frame I paused on a dozen times last night.

My skin tingles at the sight of it.

"Doesn't look fake to me," Steph says.

"It's not a big deal."

"Uh huh."

"We're back on good terms, and I'm not going to do anything to mess that up."

"You could just go for it. I mean, he's hot, you're hot. Go be hot together."

"First of all, *no*. And second, we've got history. It's not like I can just wave a piece of mistletoe and have it all disappear in a poof of Christmas magic."

Steph shakes her head slightly. "Look, *everyone's* got history. Everyone has baggage. If you're lucky enough to find someone willing to lug it around for you, you should let them. It doesn't have to be *'til death do you part*. Just go have some fun!"

"You know it doesn't work that way for me," I say. "I'm not a casual dater."

"Tell me about it," Steph says. "Remember when Sue in accounting tried to set you up with her son? You nearly had a panic attack and ducked out before the meal even came."

I groan. "He showed up in sweatpants, Steph. And he was wearing a gold chain. And there was this little tuft of chest hair that popped out over the top of his T-shirt."

"With straight-laced Sue for a mom, I admit, that was unexpected." Steph grimaces. "Look, you're overthinking this." She waves a dismissive hand at me. "The point is you can have both things here. Get the guy. Get the promotion. What in the world is stopping you? It's obvious you are still in love with Max."

"I'm not in love with Max!" I say louder than I intend to. "I can't be! Do you have any idea how much he hurt me? How devastated I was eight years ago? You see this charming, sexy, catch-me-when-I-fall-on-the-ice guy, but that's not what I see, Steph." I feel myself being overly defensive, and bubbles of hurt rise up to the surface.

Sometimes grief looks like fear.

"No matter what seems to be happening in this house, or whatever his feelings are for me, I can't. I won't. I refuse to be hurt again."

"Marin—" Steph starts, but I cut her off, holding up my hand.

"No," I say. And this is out before I think: "I may be confused. I may be conflicted, but my mind is made up. If we need to play things up for the audience and the promotion, great. If I need to fake interest for internet points, great. But I don't love Max. Period."

Steph winces.

I frown. "What?"

"Well, that's good to know."

I spin and see Max standing in the doorway of the kitchen. He's wearing jeans and a green hoodie and he looks like he ran himself through an Instagram filter before he walked in the room.

Caught.

"Max, that wasn't. . ." I take a deep breath, hoping it will make me disappear. "I didn't. . ." I fumble for any explanation that what I said could possibly mean something else. I don't find one. My words were pretty plain, after all.

If Max is upset, he doesn't show it. Instead, he smiles.

"Marin. It's okay."

"No, it's not—"

Now he's the one to stop me by holding up his hand.

"I get it. I thought we were on the path to figure some things out, but I can see that way is blocked off. And as far as ramping things for the viewers—I never minded being your plaything." He smiles.

After what I said, he is still gracious.

I feel awful. And conflicted. And angry at myself.

Worse, I'm pretty sure I was lying, so I'll have to unpack that at some point too.

Max turns to Steph. "I have a meeting this morning, so we'll have to film after I'm done."

"A meeting?" I ask.

"For the foundation," he says. "Catching up with the contractor, that sort of thing. Boring stuff, you wouldn't be interested. I mean, your viewers wouldn't."

But I would.

I'm legitimately curious what Max is doing with this foundation. Curious about the building he's bought and where he sees it going.

"Can I come?" I ask.

He shoots me a look as he grabs an apple from a bowl on the counter. "I'm not sure that's a great idea. I don't want my life to be filmed, Marin," he says. "You're used to putting everything out there on social media for everyone to see, but that's not really me."

"Okay, what if I promise no filming?" I ask.

His eyes dart from me to Steph and back again. "That's not going to help you reach your goal."

I feel my face fall. Maybe what I said *had* offended him. Maybe his graciousness was an act.

"I'll text you when I'm done," Max says. "And you can let me know where to meet you."

With that, he leaves.

Chapter Twenty-Eight

Max

The truth comes out.

I suppose I always knew that it would be darn near impossible for Marin to move past what I did to her—I treated her horribly, by choice and out of necessity, or so I thought at the time. But I let myself hope that yesterday had repaired some of the damage.

I was wrong.

Which means that Marin hasn't changed her mind about me.

As I drive downtown to the old warehouse that will eventually house The Weber Foundation, I make a decision.

I owe Marin for the mistakes I made in the past. I'll help her get her job, no matter what.

Then we're even. I can stop beating myself up for the past.

My conscience can finally be clear.

After Christmas, we'll go our separate ways and that will be that. End of story.

I can do that. Right?

It's not what I want. Not even a little. But maybe this is the smartest way to approach things.

I reach the warehouse and park on the street. I see Brian, my contractor, getting out of his truck. I'm here for an update on the progress, but I'm beginning to question my decision to base the foundation here in Pleasant Valley.

Maybe Marin's tactic of staying away is the smarter way to go. Fewer daily reminders.

Fewer distractions.

Brian stands on the sidewalk and waves at me. I shove my questions aside and get out of the car. I shake Brian's hand and open the front door of the warehouse, and the second we walk inside, all of my questions fade.

This is absolutely the right place to be.

The warehouse used to be a textile company. It's situated on the edge of downtown Pleasant Valley, right near the river. Light pours in through tall windows on all four sides, and the potential in this place is endless. If I wanted to, I could take an office and base my business here too. Or claim the whole second floor. But that would mean moving here permanently—something I never planned to do.

A part of me longs for roots. My job takes me all over the world, but I never seem to land anywhere for any length of time. I have an apartment in Chicago that I hardly ever use.

I haven't even hung anything on the walls.

It's hard when the one place on the planet with the most pain is the same place that feels the most like home.

I figure it's that way for a lot of families. It's just a matter of which one wins out—hurt or home—that determines your living arrangements.

"Let me show you what we've done," Brian says excitedly. His passion reignites my own. He shows me some of the updates and improvements he and his team have made over the last three weeks. The floors will be restored, and while they've added a couple of walls, better bathrooms and a dedicated lounge area, he's found a way to do it without compromising the integrity of the space.

The door opens behind me, and when I turn, I find Marin standing there.

I frown. "Mare, what are you doing here?"

"I followed you," she says. "Sorry."

This is so Marin. Curious to a fault. The type of person who wouldn't stop until she had the whole story.

That's why things started to fall apart between us—because I stopped sharing my side.

She looks at Brian, then at me. "Should I go?"

I look at her for a few seconds, as if I'm making a decision. As if I haven't already realized that I want to know what she thinks about this. I assume she's only grown sharper and more insightful over the years, and I could use a little advice at the moment.

But then the door opens again, and Steph walks in.

I look away.

"We won't film anything," Marin says. "I promise." She takes a small step toward me, and lowers her voice slightly. "I'm here as a friend."

I hate that things between us are tense, and weird, and unfocused. I long for normal, but every time I think we're on our way back to that, something happens to derail our progress.

"Okay," I say, softening a little. "You're still the nosiest person I know."

She smiles at me. "It's not nosy, it's curious."

"Curious. Right." Steph is panting, out of breath. She leans against the wall. "I'm not wearing the right shoes to be running around downtown Hicksville."

I make a face at Marin. "You. . .ran here?"

"Just from the parking—" She cuts herself off and quips, "Don't worry about it."

Adorable.

Marin takes a step into the space. "This is the building you bought."

I nod. "Yep. Do you like it?" I'm not a guy who cares much what other people think of me or my decisions, but I do care what Marin thinks.

Even now, watching her turn a circle to take in the space, I know that I'm nothing but a prop in a video to get her to her promotion.

And yet, I still care what she thinks. Makes me a bit of a fool.

She smiles. "I love it."

And that's all it takes for her to reel me in.

"I was thinking we could do a bank of computers against this wall, and hopefully we'll have a space back there where we can teach music. I know it'll need more renovating, but I think it could be really good for the community." I can feel the passion for this project spring up in my voice as I share the ideas.

"So. Good." She walks over to the office area. "And this is where you'll work?"

"Undecided."

She nods. "Max, I can see it. It's amazing."

I love it when she says my name.

"It's a great space," she adds.

"You really like it?"

She looks at me. "Yeah, I *really* do."

I could be wrong, but this doesn't feel like a show. It doesn't *feel* like pretend. It feels like my connection to Marin is still repaired, like she and I are back in our own world, the one where everyone else drifts away.

I like it.

At my side, Brian clears his throat. "Should I tell you what else we need to finish the job?"

Oh, right. I forgot he was here. "Yeah, of course."

Marin holds up a hand as if to say *don't mind me*, and begins walking around the space. There are building plans spread out on a table off to the side, and she stops to look them over. She'll have ideas, thoughts, insight—and I want to hear it all.

I want her fingerprints on this. On everything in my life, really. You'd think hearing her declare how much she *doesn't* love me would squash that feeling, but what can I say? I'm a glutton for punishment.

Brian and I finish our business. I couldn't be happier with the progress he's made and the plans he has for the next month. I see him out, and when I return, I find Steph on her phone, sitting in the one chair in the entire space.

Marin is standing with her back to me, hands on her hips, looking up, like she's deep in thought.

"So. . .?"

She turns, and I'm right. I can tell by the look on her face. "I have ideas."

I can't help it—I smile. "Let's hear it, boss."

For the next half hour, Marin and I discuss the purpose of the Foundation and how to bring it to life in this space. We sit on the floor, building plans spread out in front of us and begin to imagine different options.

"So is the goal to bring education and fun to the community, focusing specifically on things kids can't learn in school?" Marin asks.

"Exactly," I say. "Things that kids like us would've *loved* to learn. I mean, think about it, if you're not an athlete, if you're not some math whiz, if your creativity sparks elsewhere, you're out of luck because a lot of schools don't have the margin to offer things like this. You'd probably feel a little left out."

"You were an athlete," she says.

"Yeah, but I wasn't as passionate about running as I am about filmmaking," I tell her. "So, we teach them what we know —graphic design, video editing—" I nod at Marin—"Story-telling."

She stops. "Oh, I can't—"

"I know," I say. "I don't necessarily mean *you*, just *someone like you*." As if such a person exists.

"It's an amazing project, Max." She goes quiet.

"Thanks." After a pause, I ask, "What are you thinking?"

Without looking at me, she says, "I'm thinking your parents would be really proud." Now, her eyes find mine.

I hold her gaze for a long moment. I won't run away from the hard stuff again. "Thanks, Mare. That means a lot."

"And cut!" Steph is standing a few feet away and only now do I realize she was filming us that whole time. She tucks her phone in her pocket and grins. "That was perfection, you guys. Even better than the flirting, I think. The long, lingering gazes, the reconnecting on a deep, personal level—people will fill in the blanks! Well done!"

"You said no filming," I say quietly, feeling like a fool.

This really *is* all for the benefit of her viewers.

"Max, I didn't know," she says. "I told her not to. . ."

I snap my head at Marin and my look stops her mid-sentence.

"What's the big deal? You sat in a building and talked," Steph says. "Why keep any of that secret?"

"Steph, I gave my word," Marin says.

Steph looks at me. "This could be good for your little foundation, you know?"

That hits a nerve, and I stand. "Little foundation?"

Steph redirects. "Sorry, *big* foundation. I mean, publicity never hurt anyone." She glances at Marin. "I'll meet you outside. We have to go do the Twelve Shops of Christmas thing, and we're meeting Danny in front of the—" she checks her phone, "Gingerbread House?" She puts on an exasperated face. "That should be riveting."

And with that, Marin's producer is gone.

I'm trying not to be angry. I'm doing a poor job.

"Max, I'll make sure she doesn't post any of that," Marin says, standing.

"We both know she already did."

"Then I'll delete it." Marin says, and I can hear a bit of pleading in her voice. "I told her I didn't want anything fil—"

"It's fine. I know you've got a job to do," I tell her. "Content is king, right?" I walk over to the table and lay the plans back down.

"Max, I swear I didn't know—" She pulls her phone out and finds the video.

"It's fine, Mare." I force a smile.

"No, I gave you my word." She clicks around on the phone, then holds it up. "There. Deleted."

"Thanks."

There's a heavy pause, and I hate it. I don't want this awkwardness to come back. Why can't we find and keep any common ground?

"So. . ." I try to lighten the mood. "Are you ready for the Twelve Shops of Christmas?"

Confusion splashes across her face.

"I have it on good authority that the donut shop is definitely six geese-a-laying this year," I tell her as I walk toward the door. "Somebody told me they had a real goose in there yesterday."

Chapter Twenty-Nine

Marin

I don't want to, but I force myself into work mode.

"The Twelve Shops of Christmas is a longstanding holiday tradition here in Pleasant Valley," I look directly into my own phone, holding it up selfie-style as Max and I walk over to The Gingerbread House to pick up our entry cards.

"Some of the shops downtown will be decked out in a theme, and the theme will reflect one of the twelve days from the famous Christmas carol. So, people like us visit the shops, keeping track of which shop corresponds to which number in the song. Sort of like a scavenger hunt."

Max chimes in, "The maids a-milking one is always an. . .ahem. . .interesting theme."

I chuckle, "Yeah, the local creamery actually brought in real cows one year."

He laughs. "I remember that! Judging by the way it smelled in there, I don't think they thought that one through."

I don't sense the strain in his voice anymore. That's a good thing, right? I continue narrating. "Every participant keeps track of which shop has which theme, and at the end, one lucky person wins a gift basket with an assortment of goods from all twelve shops."

Beside me, Max stuffs his hands in the pockets of his navy blue pea coat, drawing my attention away from the filming. I glance at him and find he's still looking up at my phone. But as I do this, the camera goes wonky and starts filming the corner of his head and the world beyond his right shoulder.

He reaches up and takes the phone away from me, shaking his head at our images on the screen. "I guess we're going to have to let a professional handle the filming today because Marin is too busy gawking at me to focus on her job."

"I was not gawking," I say.

A comment rolls across the bottom of the screen:

I'd be gawking too—dang! No wonder Marin trips over herself all the time!

One glance at Max tells me he also read that comment—I can tell by the amused expression on his face.

"She was definitely gawking." He turns toward me. "Is that drool on your chin?" He reaches out like he's going to touch my chin, and I smack his hand away.

"Please, Max, women aren't that shallow," I say, not sure if I'm trying to convince him or myself. "Women are far more likely to date a man because of what's on the inside—not what's on the outside. Unlike men, who are *only* concerned with how a woman looks." We stop at a streetlight and wait for the signal to turn.

"I take offense to your broad generalization," he says. "I'm a lot less shallow than you think." Then, under his breath, he comically mutters, "I can't help it if I also think you're gorgeous."

I look at him and he grins over at me, raises his eyebrows, as if waiting for me to counter. But, of course, I'm blank. Between the two of us, Max is a much better flirt.

"What's the matter, McGrath? You seem rattled."

I'm floundering. *Dang it.*

"Can we stick to the topic at hand?" I say.

"Well, the most current topic is either the shallowness of men or how pretty you look. Which one do you want to stick to?" he asks.

"You bozo," I say, looking at him through the camera. "I mean the Twelve Shops of Christmas."

"Alright, well, then no one will hear all the other things that I find attractive about you." He shrugs.

I want to hear all the things.

He grins at my pause. "She's curious, folks."

"I'm not curious," I lie. "I'm just trying to do my job, and you're making it really difficult."

"Say the word and I'll tell you," he says. "I have a list."

"Should I be concerned that you're developing an obsession with me?" I squint over at him.

Good flirting, Marin! Do more of that!

"Yes," he says. "I plastered your photos all over my wall."

"My photos are all over your wall because you're staying in *my bedroom.*"

His eyes go wide and a smile creeps across his face as we both realize what I've just said.

The comments roll in.

Ohhh!! I knew it! They're totally together!
I'd let him stay in my bedroom too!
Get it girl!

I freeze.

"Well, now you've gone and stepped in it, haven't you?" Max is still grinning.

"I mean that my mom put him up in my old bedroom, not that. . ." I start blathering.

"I'm on a lumpy futon. In the sewing room! We're definitely *not* sleeping together. . ."

WHAT AM I SAYING?

Beside me, Max is laughing. "No, no, keep going, you're doing great."

It's no use. The internet now thinks Max and I are sleeping together, and no amount of backpedaling is going to save me.

"So, about those Twelve Shops of Christmas..." Max says.

I'm grateful for the save. "I have it on good authority that the donut shop had a real goose inside yesterday, and you know what that means."

Max gasps. "Six geese a-laying?" His question drips with sarcastic irony.

"That's right, Max." I look straight at the camera, trying to ignore the onslaught of comments. "We'll be back later to tell you if we're right."

I click the phone off and groan.

"It wasn't that bad." Max stuffs his hands in his pockets again, and I wonder if they would be warmer if his hands were in mine.

"You're just saying that to try and make me feel better," I say.

"True."

I look over and find him smiling at me.

"I mean, there are worst things than people thinking we're—"

I cut him off with an upheld hand. "Let's not rehash it."

"You sure?" I don't have to look at him to know he's still smiling. "Could be fun to rehash." He clicks his phone on. "What do you think people are saying?"

I snatch his phone away. "I don't even want to know."

He bumps his shoulder into mine. "It's fine, Mare. Really. You don't have to explain yourself to anyone. Despite how all this seems, you don't actually owe anyone insight into your personal life."

We walk in silence for a few minutes, our shoulders still practically touching, and I imagine slipping under his arm, feeling the weight of it draped around me. But then we turn the corner, and I see Steph up ahead, and reality sets back in.

When we reach the Gingerbread House, Steph is all smiles. "That was quite the reveal, Marin," she says. "Announcing to the world that you and Max are getting it on."

I shoot her a look to let her know I'm not amused, but she doesn't seem to care. She launches straight into the plan for the Twelve Shops of Christmas Scavenger Hunt, and Max nods appropriately, as if he's a dutiful student and she is the teacher.

He has so much to be angry with me for. Bringing up his mom on live television. The fact that my producer directly violated his request—and mine—not to have his life broadcast on the internet. My declaration that I do not love him.

And yet, he's still here, still going along with this ridiculous plan. For me.

I tune Steph out as she hands over our scorecards.

Between the two of us—I was the one who was proving to be untrustworthy.

And he was proving to be exactly what I told myself he wasn't—the man I'd always loved.

Chapter Thirty

Marin

I t's the morning after the Twelve Shops of Christmas, and I wake up to the saucy hot smell of chili.

I can practically see it bubbling on the stove just from the tomato/onion/garlic/bean aroma wafting in my room.

I swing my legs over the side of the bed and grab my phone.

32 *Unread Messages and eight voicemails.*

And they're all from Steph.

I click on a voicemail and listen.

"Marin, this is insane. Off the charts. You and Max letting it slip that you're sleeping together is the best thing that's ever happened to this campaign to get you the show. Are you, actually sleeping together or...? Never mind. I know it's a family show and *blah blah blah*, but people are loving it. People *love* you two! We need to strike while the interest is hot, and you and Max need to turn up the heat. There's a metaphor in there somewhere with the chili cookoff thing, but I'll let you figure that out. Go read the comments on yesterday's live. People want to see you as a couple. Can you make that happen?

Giving the public anything less than some genuine PDA would be cruel. Call me!"

I swipe over to the video we posted and sure enough, Steph is right. Comment after comment "shipping" M + M. They're practically begging to see the coupled version of us.

They have no idea what's happening off screen.

I could tell Steph that no, this is where I draw the line, but even I can't deny there's potential in this idea. Maybe ramping up the heat on camera will help me inch ahead in the race for *Good Day Denver*.

I fling myself back on my pillows. This is starting to feel *too* out of my control, and I don't like it.

I head into the bathroom and crack the door to my old bedroom, where Max is still soundly sleeping. I want to rush in and shake him and force him to talk through this whole mess with me, but instead, I decide I'll wait for him to wake up.

Right here, in the bathroom.

I grab my iPad and close the lid of the toilet. I sit and rewatch the video, and I have to say, the viewers are onto something. Max and I do look like a real couple. A *cute* couple.

When I talk, he looks at me like there's no one else in the world, and I wonder if this is all part of the show. Him, watching me, like he's hanging on every word I'm saying.

Did he always look at me like that?

I scroll through more comments:

I knew they were together!
This is the best real life second chance romance ever! #Swoon
Sorry, but Max is too good for her. She's so uptight—I bet her side of the bed is always cold. Max, if you want a hot-blooded woman, give me a call!

I click out of the app with an eyeroll. Steph is right—people are invested in this, for one reason or another. If I'd known fake flirting would escalate so quickly to a fake relationship, I might've thought twice about this strategy in the first place.

Although, I really only had myself to blame for that, didn't I?

I peek into my old room again.

Still sleeping.

I close the door softly, wondering if I make some noise in here if that might wake him up. I flush the toilet, open and close the cupboards, then fish my curling iron out from the bottom drawer and plug it in.

I listen for any signs of life on the other side of the door, but there are none.

I pick up my toothbrush and flick on the faucet when I see the door open in the reflection of the mirror. So apparently, he's just very quiet.

"Sorry," he mumbles as he starts to close the door.

"It's okay," I say. "I've just got to brush my teeth, and then I'll get out of here." I hand him his toothbrush, and he glances over at the iPad on the counter.

"Were you. . .working in here?" he asks.

I flip the cover over the iPad. "No."

He frowns. "Were you. . .waiting for me to wake up?"

"Don't be ridiculous." I put toothpaste on my brush. "But I did want to say something."

"So, you *were* waiting for me to wake up."

"Fine, yes."

"You could've done that downstairs."

"Are you kidding? I've been banging around in here for a half an hour trying to wake you," I tell him.

"You could've just come in and given me a little shake," he says. "The whole world already thinks we're sleeping together."

"Listen, about all that—"

232

"Mare, it's fine," he cuts in. "I'm not concerned about what anyone else thinks. Besides, there are worse things I could get a reputation for than fake sleeping with a beautiful woman."

In response, I shove my toothbrush in my mouth and start to brush my teeth.

He sticks his toothbrush in his mouth, glancing up at my reflection in the mirror periodically. Twice, I meet his eyes and look away. Once, I spit the toothpaste into the sink.

"What's going on with you?" he asks. "You're being weird."

Why is this so hard? It's not like I haven't already asked him for favors—we're already fake flirting, this is just an extension of that. Right?

I swish water around in my mouth and spit that out too. Then, I stand upright, intent on getting it all out, but one look at him, and I chicken out. "This is so stupid."

"What is?"

I sigh. "So, now that I've accidentally—and *falsely*—announced to the world that we're, you know," I move my hands back and forth as if they're going to produce the word I'm looking for.

"Making sweet, sweet love?"

I laugh and gasp at the same time. "Oh my *gosh*, Max!"

He spits. "I'm not wrong."

"They think we're *together*, that's what I was going to say, the viewers think we're . ."

"Together?"

"Yeah."

"Sexually."

I feel my face redden. "Stop it."

"Right? I mean, that's what you implied, so..."

"Yes. Fine. That's it."

He leans against the sink, wiping his mouth off with a hand towel. "Ok, just wanted to be clear. Clear is kind."

I roll my eyes, and then take a moment. How in the world am I going to say this?

Rip off the Band-aid, Marin.

"Steph thinks we should play it up."

He pauses. "Play it up?"

I nod.

"So, what does that mean?"

I don't want to say it. I don't want to ask it.

I take a step away, and then turn around and face him. "It means what do you think about pretending to be, you know. . .my boyfriend."

He looks at me. I can't read him. "You want me to be your fake boyfriend?"

I try to laugh it off. "Ironic, right?"

"That's one word for it." He turns to put the towel back on the rack. I push myself up to sit on the counter next to the sink.

I hate asking. I hate all of it. I hate that his nearness is making my skin feel hot.

I hate going to these lengths to try and prove that I'm the right person for this job. I wish my work did that all on its own.

He faces me. "Will this help you?"

I shrug. "Steph thinks so."

"What do you think?" He takes a step toward me.

We're only inches apart when I finally dare to make eye contact. His gaze falls to my lips and back again, and I hear the shudder of my own breath.

He places his hands on the counter, one on each side of me, and leans so close I can smell the mint of his toothpaste. "You think you can handle pretending that this is more than a little flirtation?"

"Of course," I say, shakily.

"Might jog a few memories you've been keeping buried. Make you feel some things you haven't felt in a while."

"It might." I lock on to his eyes, and I force myself not to look away. "The real question is, can you handle it?"

He shakes his head. "I will absolutely not be able to handle it."

His lips are *right there*. And I can practically feel him daring me to take a step into his arms.

I ran away before, in the alleyway, and I shut myself off after we decorated the tree. Part of me regrets that. But now that we're in this position again, "flight" is still the only thing that comes to mind.

Before I can do anything, Max pushes himself away and takes my hand and turns it over in his.

As bad I know this is for me, I can't seem to move.

"This might be dangerous," he says. "All this pretending. One of us is bound to get confused."

"I think we can do it." But the brush of his thumb across my wrist is like a warning shot to my heart. I'm in deep water with no life vest.

"All right." Max pulls his hand away. "If you think you've got a handle on it, I'm game."

The intensity of the moment flutters away, leaving me standing there suddenly aware that the bathroom isn't all that romantic after all.

I find my voice again. "You're sure?"

He faces me again. "I want to show you that I'm genuinely sorry. Anyone can say the words." He grins. "I'm a man of action."

I hate that I've put my hurt in this context. It's like a contractual agreement.

"So, the plan for the next few days is that you and I are a happy couple."

I nod.

"And that I'm completely smitten with you, in love with every single thing about you."

Another nod.

He holds my gaze. "Shouldn't be too hard." He flips on the shower and closes the curtain to let the water heat up. "Was there something else, or did you want to stay in here and watch me shower too?"

Chapter Thirty-One

Max

My feelings are now more conflicted than ever.

I know Marin needs me to get her promotion. The trouble is, I don't care.

I can say I'm going along with this for the sake of her job, that I'm just looking to right an old wrong, but after the moment in the bathroom this morning, the way she raced out when I made the comment about the shower, the way my body reacted to her nearness—I know the truth. Who am I kidding? I've known the truth since the moment I opened the front door and found her standing on the porch.

I just wish things weren't so messy.

Marin and her mom are out shopping for most of the day. I know because she documents everything on social media. I've already scrolled through the comments that led to Steph's brilliant decision for Marin and me to take our flirtation to the next level, and as awkward as it makes me feel, I guess I shouldn't be surprised.

As a tactic to pique interest, it's not unheard of. Look at Jennifer Lopez and Ben Affleck, for Pete's sake.

Marin's audience is invested in this relationship, fake or otherwise, which means they'll tune in, retweet, re-post, and respond.

Which hopefully means she'll get more views than her competitor.

And get the job.

And move back to Denver.

Out of my life all over again.

I shake the thoughts away. *I owe this to her.*

She and her mom return from shopping and Lydia instantly starts fussing over the chili, which she mentioned three times in the short one-minute video Marin posted from inside Taryn's Toy Emporium. I'm sitting at the kitchen table, and Marin rushes upstairs to get changed.

"What's that?" Lydia is looking over my shoulder at the image on my laptop.

I close it. "Nothing."

"Are you moving?"

The image was of an apartment. Nothing gets by this woman. "I'm considering my options."

She opens my laptop and her eyes widen. "Max, you make a lot of money, don't you?" Unfortunately, the rental price is right there in bold red print.

I laugh it off, or try to.

"Wait, this apartment. . ." She looks at me. "It's in Denver."

I take the computer from her and close it. "Yes, but the others are in Vancouver, Santa Fe, and Houston. I'm just looking around."

"Oh, Max," Lydia says. "Marin told me about you helping her get this job she's after. Personally, I think it's terrible and dishonest to deceive people, even if they are strangers, but she assures me that's the entertainment side of her job." She watches me. "She seemed pretty clear that that's all it is—entertainment."

"Yeah," I say. "She's right."

"It'd be easy to get confused." She nods toward my computer.

"I'm not confused. I know where I stand with Marin," I say. "She's made it crystal clear."

"Are you sure?" Lydia always could see straight through me. "Because the last thing I want is for either of you to get hurt again. Things are just starting to feel somewhat normal."

"Yeah, I know." I don't even believe myself when I say, "I won't get hurt. We're friends again, and that's great. I just wanted to see what the city had in terms of apartments—that's all. I'm tired of being homeless."

I'm not exactly homeless, but I'm definitely a nomad. I book out my jobs back to back, and I never exactly *land*.

I want to land.

It crossed my mind that it might be nice to land near Marin.

I'd get to watch her morning show. To maybe meet her for lunch at the Denver food trucks everyone is always talking about. To spend a little bit of time with her.

For as long as we both shall live.

Lydia doesn't look convinced, but thankfully, Marin shows up in the doorway before she can grill me anymore about it.

"Ready to go on a fake date with me?" she asks.

She's wearing jeans and a simple turquoise sweater that brightens the color in her eyes.

Lydia has every right to be concerned.

I grit my teeth and push aside all the unwanted feelings. This is all for show. This is to get back in her good graces.

The problem is that I also want to get back in her arms.

We drive to the community center where the chili cookoff is being held. Lydia and James drive separately, because Lydia

a) doesn't trust someone else to drive her chili and b) is always looking for a way to get Marin and me alone in a car together.

"You told your mom about the fake dating," I say as I park the car.

"I couldn't *not* tell her," Marin says. "Do you know how much it would crush her if she saw us all cute and cozy only to find out it was all a show?"

"Yeah, I can imagine." I put the car in park. "So, how do we do this? Are we at the beginning stages of a new relationship? Are we back to our old routine? What?"

"I don't know." Marin frowns. "I hadn't thought that far."

"Maybe it's new, but familiar?"

She looks like she's thinking it over. "Hmm. Okay, that might work."

"What about public displays of affection?"

"Our first kiss was in the hallway of our school, so. . .maybe?"

"Yeah, but that was back when making out in the high school hallway was like an everyday occurrence," I say. "If we're talking now, I would want you all to myself."

"Unfortunately, you can't have me all to yourself. You'll have to compete with most of Pleasant Valley, half of Denver, and the surrounding affiliate suburbs."

"Fine," I say. "We're into *tasteful* PDA."

She nods. "Maybe we just hold hands. Look at each other longingly. Make eyes at each other?"

"I am capable of all of those things."

Lydia knocks on Marin's window and mouths the words, "We'll meet you inside!"

Through the window, Marin says, "If you just talk, I can hear you, Mom."

"Oh!" Lydia laughs. "We'll meet you inside!"

"Got it." She turns to me. "Are we ready for our first public appearance as a couple?"

"Technically it's not our first public appearance as a couple," I remind her. "That would be the football game after the hallway."

"Right," she says. "We sat at the top of the stands, and you bought me popcorn and held my hand."

I can see the lights of the football field, feel the memory of her hand in mine—I can even remember how she smelled. "I don't remember a single thing about that game," I say.

"Me neither." She smiles at me.

"Things were so easy back then."

It's difficult reconciling what's happened with what is. Feelings and emotions that happened years ago feel as present and immediate as anything.

I shut everyone and everything out so I wouldn't have to mourn what could no longer be. Pushing Marin away was self-preservation.

It was the right decision, though I've spent every day since questioning it.

Tonight was only a chili cook-off, but I knew it was going to remind me that every good thing didn't die with my parents. Friends, family, love, and kindness remained and endured.

I miss it. I crave it. I want it all back. I was so stupid to have thrown it all away.

"You ready?" she asks.

I pull myself back to the present and nod. "Yep."

We walk into the community center, which has been decked out in full Christmas décor. Lights, trees, hanging white snowflakes—it's pretty impressive. On the stage, there are tables, and each of the competitors have set up stations for people to come through and taste their chili. There will be a "crowd favorite" selected by the participants and a "grand prize winner" selected by Marin and two other judges.

From her spot behind her table, Lydia waves.

"I guess they're not concerned that my mother and I have worked out some sort of code to make sure she wins," Marin says. "And they should be, considering how much that woman tried to cheat."

"It's a blind judging," I say. "I'm sure they've got an iron clad system to protect the integrity of the Christmas Chili Cook-off."

Marin's laugh is cut short when Steph races over and squeezes both of our arms. "So glad you guys are finally here. I've been mingling with the locals, and let me tell you, it's been *interesting*." She widens her eyes as she says this, like our hometown is populated with a bunch of weirdos.

I glance behind Steph and see Jeremiah Logsdon strolling around the room wearing pin-striped overalls and a white tank top, loudly explaining the dangers of pesticides.

"Maybe let's keep some of the local color out of the video tonight," Marin says.

"I thought we'd approach tonight a little differently," Steph says. "You two do your thing, and I'll film you throughout the night, then I'll put together a video, but are we all in agreement that you need to make it look like you're taking things to the next level?"

"I mean, everyone already thinks we have, right? Give the public what they want?" Marin says.

"Excellent," Steph says. "I heard from Tim today, Marin. He's highly impressed with your numbers. Says you're basically a shoo-in and you'd have to totally crash and burn during the final show to change his mind."

"Really?" Marin's face lights up.

"It's as good as yours." Steph grins as she walks away. She

turns back and points at us—"Sell me on the romance, you two."

I smile. "Congratulations."

"Well, let's not get ahead of ourselves," she says.

"All you have to do is try a bunch of chili, avoid cheating with your mom, and pretend to be madly in love with me. Boom. Done. Promotion, in the bag."

"Right." Her smile fades. "In the bag."

Chapter Thirty-Two

Marin

I have no idea where Steph went—I've hardly seen her at all tonight—but that hasn't stopped Max from paying the utmost attention to me.

He reminds me of people's names, introduces me to new friends, and even has a full-on conversation with Jeremiah Logsdon because the poor old guy "seemed like he had some things to get off of his chest."

We laugh. We mingle. We talk. We hold hands. He stays by my side, his hand on the small of my back as we work our way through the crowd. He throws away my discarded spoons and tasting cups of chili and does a mediocre job of sharing his thoughts on which one he thinks I should give top ranks to.

He whispers jokes that would make me laugh, if it weren't for the effect his nearness is having on my body. I freeze at the feeling of his breath on my cheek, and when he brushes his lips across my hand, every nerve in my body wakes up, as if they've all been in hibernation until that very moment.

He is just as I remember him.

Kind. Thoughtful. Attentive.

And I'm having a hard time remembering it's not real.

As the evening winds down, Mom finally comes off the stage, sporting a new blue ribbon to add to her collection. She's beaming.

"I knew this was my best batch of chili ever," she says.

I don't have the heart to tell her that of the three judges, I was the one who didn't vote for her chili. One of the organizers of the event made a point to tell me she was thankful I proved I wasn't biased in my voting and she thought Helen Steele had the winning batch too.

"Congratulations, Mom," I say. "Very happy for you."

"Your father and I are going to go get a drink at that new wine bar downtown. Do you kids want to come?"

I glance at Max, who is chatting with my dad a few yards away. "I might just go home. I'm tired."

"Tired of pretending you're pretending?" Mom raises a brow.

"You don't need to worry, Mom," I tell her. "I'm not going to let him break my heart again."

Mom glances at Max, then back at me. "It's not your heart I'm worried about."

I frown, but she doesn't let me ask questions. Instead, she rushes over to my dad, links an arm through his and drags him off like a man without a choice. Which, judging by the look on his face, is exactly what he is.

"You ready to head home?" Max asks.

A quick survey of the room tells me that Steph is no longer here. We don't need to keep up the charade.

But when he reaches for my hand, I give it freely, stepping so close to him as we walk that our arms might as well be glued together.

"How do you think we did?" He asks as we step outside into the chilly Christmas-soaked air.

I feel his fingers wrap around mine. "Good. I think we did good."

He leads me down the stairs toward the parking lot. "Any word from Steph? Is she still skulking around somewhere?"

We reach the car, and I slip my free hand into my pocket and pull out my phone. "I can see if she posted anything."

He releases my hand, and I scroll around until I find a new video. I click on it and hold the phone out so we can both watch at the same time. An instrumental version of *I'll Be Home for Christmas* begins to play behind a shot of Max whispering in my ear. It switches, crisply edited in time to the song, to one of us laughing. Then to one that pans from our faces to our hands, clasped together. Another of his hand on the small of my back. Another of him—watching me as I talk with a woman whose name I don't remember.

It ends with one of us walking out the door and down the stairs, not a sliver of space between us.

As the video starts to replay, I shut it off. "That was literally minutes ago. She could still be lurking around out here." I laugh. "We should go."

He nods, and we get in the car and head back home. With my parents out for the evening, we'll be alone, and knowing that has me on edge.

When we reach the driveway, he pulls in and turns off the engine.

"Thanks for a fun night," I say, trying to keep this light. Trying—failing—to keep my heart out of all of it.

He nods. "Yep."

I slip out of the car and a cool breeze nips at my cheeks. He follows me inside, and we stand in the dark of the entryway for a long moment.

"I'm going to go change," I say. "I've been craving pajamas all night."

"Sounds good."

When I get upstairs, I slip into the sewing room and let out a giant exhale. Now what? Do I stay in here? Lock myself in this dumb, ill-appropriated room hoping he goes to sleep? Or do I go back downstairs and pretend I don't know what's happening between us?

I glance over and see a small box on the futon. It's wrapped in white paper with a blue bow. I open it and find a small stack of graham crackers, a Hershey bar and a baggie of giant marshmallows.

S'mores date? No cameras.

I smile. He must've put this in here before we left. S'mores dates and bonfires were a staple throughout high school and every time we came home for college.

My eyes linger on his handwriting. *No cameras.* But still a date?

What do I do? What does he mean?

I change into yoga pants and a big sweatshirt. I fish my stocking cap out of the closet, along with my coat and gloves, grab a couple of extra blankets and head down toward the lake. Sure enough, there he is, stoking a newly lit fire.

"You got my gift?"

I hold up the S'mores. "You're crazy if you think this is going to be enough."

He laughs. "Not a chance. I have a whole basket over there."

He motions to the log next to him, hands me a long metal stick meant for roasting marshmallows and then holds his roasting stick at me like a knight challenging me to a duel. "Shall we see who can roast the best marshmallow?"

"No, because you always like yours burnt to a crisp," I say.

"Is there any other way?"

"Well, there's the *right* way," I laugh.

He shoves a couple of marshmallows on the ends of our sticks and we sit in silence for a few long moments.

The chill, the warmth, the moment—it's nice.

A flame catches my marshmallow, and in mere seconds, it's nearly black. I blow it out, but it's too late, it's charred and inedible. "Oh, come on."

"Give it." Max switches sticks with me, happy to trade his lightly toasted marshmallow for my blackened one. "I forgot how bad you are at this."

I laugh, but when I look up, I see that his face is serious, and my mother's words come rushing back at me. Is his heart as tangled up as mine?

"I think we did a good job of playing the part tonight." It's the only thing I can think to say, and it's already been said.

"I told you, Marin, it wasn't going to be pretend for me." We're practically leaning against each other, our arms pressed together the way they would've been all those years ago, back when we couldn't get close enough to each other.

He faces me now. "I tried to go along with it, but I can't. Letting you go was the stupidest mistake I ever made."

I look up at him. I want to let myself feel all the things I'm feeling—this is Max, after all.

But this is Max.

This all feels like it did when we were good, and I believed he loved me then. But he made it very clear that he didn't—so how can I trust him now?

I meet his eyes and find them intent on me. I see the desire there, a familiar knowing that always existed between us, whether we said the words out loud or not.

"What happened with us, Max?" I ask.

He sighs and pushes a hand through his hair. "I screwed up."

"You said you didn't love me anymore." My eyes turn glassy, and I blink back the tears.

"I lied." He shakes his head.

"But why?"

He struggles for a moment. I begin to read what his face has been saying every time he talks about the past. About us, about his parents, all of it.

It's hard for him. It's so hard.

He straightens, and I listen. "I'd just lost two of the most important people in the world to me, and the only other person I loved that much was you." He takes his empty marshmallow stick and pokes the fire. "I shut myself off. Told myself I was better off alone. That it would hurt less for me to walk out of your life than to have you ripped from mine. I didn't want to be blindsided again. And I knew you wouldn't leave unless. . ."

"Unless what?"

"Unless I was cruel," he whispers. "I was young and stupid."

I wrap my arms around myself, as if they could protect me. "And now?"

He looks at me. "Now I realize living without you hurts a whole lot more."

There are creased lines of grief on his face.

"Tonight was not pretend," he says. "Not for me."

My heart and my head war with each other. One believes him, one warns me not to.

I want to fold myself into his embrace and stay there until the fire is just embers. But the memory of the pain he caused comes rushing back, eager to reduce me to nothingness all over again.

I'm as honest as I can be in return.

"After you left, it took me months to start living again, Max. I was wrecked. I'm not saying this to hurt you—I'm just telling you how it was for me. It was years before I found a new dream and a life of my own. I can't just pretend none of it happened or that it's not still affecting me every single day just because you're here saying you're sorry."

He's quiet for a moment, and I fear I've said too much. Finally, he utters a soft, "I know."

I turn toward him. "Max, what is it that you want?"

"You." He holds my gaze for a heated moment.

Max wants me. He wasn't pretending.

He takes my face in his hands and kisses me—softly at first, as if he's asking permission.

And I don't pull away. I don't move. I fear I might be dreaming, and I don't want to wake up.

I grab a fistful of his coat and pull him toward me, drawing my body close to his.

His fingers tangle in my hair, as his kiss grows hungry and a rush of memories flood my mind. We're sixteen again in the hallway. Seventeen in the boathouse. We're eighteen and heading off to college. Nineteen, studying on the quad.

His lips, his scent, his touch—it's all familiar, and I savor every second of it, letting myself get lost, not only in his kiss, but in *him*.

He's everything. We're everything. This is all I want.

But wait.

No.

I can't let him be everything. I can't let him be all I live for. Not again. I pull back. "Max, I can't."

His eyes search mine. "Why? Marin, you can't tell me you don't feel this—it's all still there, everything we always had—it's still there."

"I know, but that's what scares me." I look away. "You broke up with me because it was easier than having me taken from you. You didn't want to be blindsided. But don't you see that when you did that—you blindsided me? You made the choice and I had to live with the consequences. I can't do that again."

"You won't," he says.

"It's not a promise you can make." I inch back. "I don't want to risk everything I've built when I have no guarantee that you won't get scared and push me away again."

He looks away.

"Do you know you're the reason I stopped coming home for Christmas? You're the reason I gave up on the idea of making documentaries? You're the reason I got into TV in the first place. You left, and somehow in your absence you still dictated every single decision I've made for the last eight years."

"I'm sorry, I never—"

"No, that wasn't your fault," I say. "I chose to give you that much power, but I can't do it again."

"I understand." He brushes a hand across my cheek. "I really thought I was making the right choice."

"I wish you'd talked to me." I'm fighting back real tears now. "Max, why didn't you just talk to me?"

"I was afraid!" he stands, letting go of my hand. "For the first time in my entire life, I was afraid!"

"Afraid? Afraid of what?"

He slumps his shoulders. "Loving you too much. Losing you. I don't know—I was messed up."

I stand and move toward him. "But you did lose me."

He shakes his head, almost to himself, and then reaches for my hand. "I know. And I regret it more than anything." He looks at my hand before pressing a kiss to my palm. "There's not a day that goes by that I'm not reminded of you. Of what I did, and the choice I made. And I know it's asking a lot, but I want a second chance."

At that, fresh tears spring to my eyes.

"I won't run this time, Marin. And I don't want you to

change anything about the life you've built—it's impressive what you've accomplished. I just want to be a part of it."

I want you too. I just don't know how.

He reads my mind, as usual, and leans in to kiss me on the cheek.

"I know you have to think this through," he says. "Take your time. I'm not going anywhere."

Chapter Thirty-Three

Marin

My lips are still tingling when I wake the next morning.

Pushing Max away last night was the hardest thing I've ever had to do.

And I'm still not sure it was the right thing. It certainly wasn't what I wanted to do.

I'm lying there, staring at the ceiling, when there's a knock on the door and my mom pokes her head in. "Oh, good, you're awake."

I sit up.

"I just wanted to talk to you—" she holds up her phone. "About this."

It's the video Steph posted of me and Max last night. The one that looked more like an engagement announcement than a post for a news outlet.

I let out a groan and hide my face behind a pillow. "It's not a big deal, Mom."

She takes the pillow away and forces me to look at her. "I disagree."

"I've got it under control."

"But Marin, this is dishonest," she says. "You're manipulating the viewers into believing something that isn't true." She eyes me for a few painful seconds.

"It's not *not* true," I say. "I mean, it *is* fake. We're just pretending, but..."

"This is not fair to Max," Mom says. "I think he has genuine feelings for you."

"And you don't think I have genuine feelings for him?" The words are out before my brain gives approval.

Mom's eyebrows raise in surprise.

"Ugh, I don't *know*." I'm practically whining, like a 16-year-old in a teen romance. "I'm confused."

She waves the phone at me. "I wonder why."

"It's not just that, Mom," I say. "It's Max. When he left me —I realized I had no idea who I was without him."

"But look at you now. You're strong and successful and independent."

"And in love with him all over again."

Mom goes still.

"I can't lose myself like that again."

"I understand," she says. "And you've both got some messy feelings to sort through." She puts a hand on my head, stroking my hair for a moment. "It would be a lot easier to do that without the commentary of the entire internet."

I sigh.

"Maybe just consider his feelings, okay?"

"I will. Thanks, Mom."

After she goes, I go back to staring at the ceiling. The answers aren't there.

I try to keep from thinking about it. As if it's not the only thing I've been thinking about since I got back to Pleasant Valley.

I successfully manage to avoid Steph, my parents, and Max for a good portion of the day, but after the sun goes down, I'm back on the clock.

Tonight's event is the Christmas Cocktail Competition, and for reasons that will never make sense, I am a judge.

I know exactly two things about this event:

1. I am supposed to dress up.
2. I am going to drink cocktails.

Nobody has given me any other details.

Which is why I'm now standing in the sewing room in a semi-formal blue dress, wondering if I should've gotten Max a boutonniere.

Steph texts me the address of the event, along with a reminder that she'll be there, ready to film, and my stomach drops.

I don't know if I can do this tonight. I need to keep Max at an arm's length for the good of my heart and I need to keep him close for the good of my job.

I walk over to the full-length mirror on the wall and stare at my reflection. "I am a brave, independent, smart, and successful woman," I whisper to my reflection. "Who apparently just can't let go of the past." I sigh.

The image of my little apartment in Denver creeps into the corner of my mind. I can't call it "cozy" because it's plain and very bare. "But it's sufficient." I say this to my reflection. "And it's mine."

After Max, I worked hard for my life and for my job. It was enough when I got here a week ago, why doesn't it feel like enough now?

I shake off these ridiculous thoughts and open the door, anxious to get the night over with.

As I start down the stairs, I'm seventeen again—a ball of nerves—knowing Max is waiting in the entryway, ready to escort me to the junior prom.

So many scenes of my life where he's the main character.

And now I've forced the both of us into playing the roles of a lifetime.

Chapter Thirty-Four

Marin

Max is waiting at the bottom of the stairs, holding a single white rose.

I know he's chosen it because it's my favorite. I want that to not mean something, but it does. He knows me. Better than anyone, even still.

Our eyes meet, and he smiles, a genuine smile, and I can't help it, I'm smiling too.

"You look incredible," he says as he hands me the flower.

He's wearing a neatly tailored black suit with a white shirt with a blue pocket square, and I don't have to consult my viewers to say without hesitation that he's a ten.

Or maybe a twelve.

My eyes drift across the room, where my parents are standing, watching us. My mother's eyes are laced with concern, which is honestly surprising given how much she always wanted Max and me to end up together.

But then, Max and me falling apart didn't only break my heart, it broke hers too, splitting her family into pieces that still haven't mended.

"I say, you look *smashing*," my dad says in a faux British accent. "Both of you."

Mom smiles. "I can't say I condone the drinking."

"I'm an adult, Mom." And *alcohol's not the biggest threat to my senses here.*

She waves me off. "I know, I know, but still."

"I'll make sure she gets home safe," Max says.

"We're heading to the airport to pick up Teddy," my mom says. "But we'll keep you posted so you don't worry about us." She smiles, and sends us on our way.

I pull a dressy coat from the hall closet, and Max takes it from me. "Here, let me."

In the car, we talk about Christmas gifts and the fact that Teddy still hasn't shown up. We talk about the lights on the houses in the neighborhoods we drive through to get to the brewhouse down by the river where this event is being held.

We talk about all kinds of things, but we don't talk about our fake relationship, our real relationship, or anything in between.

I'm not mad we're avoiding the subject. Because frankly, it's not only seeing him in the suit that's got my head swimming —it's the way he looked at me when I walked down the stairs. It's the way his fingers grazed my shoulders when he helped me with my coat. It's the way he opened the car door for me, carefully placing the bottom of my dress in my hands as he closed it.

I glance at my reflection in the side mirror and find no trace of the strong, independent woman I'd told myself I would be. Only a lovesick girl with a crush that won't quit.

We arrive at the brewhouse, and I don't wait for Max to open my door. If his chivalry is going to have this effect on my weakened heart, I'm going to have to start combating it somehow.

I meet him at the front of the car and he smiles. "You really look beautiful."

"Max, I—"

But I'm silenced by Steph, who squeals out the door in a black dress. "Look at you two! The toast of the town!" She holds up her phone and snaps a few photos. "Are you ready for this?"

I'm not a drinker, but I could use something to take the edge off—something to help me forget this little battle between my feelings and my brain.

My brain should win, right? It's got to win.

"Point me to the cocktails!" I link an arm through Steph's and she pulls me inside, where she introduces me to the organizers—mostly restaurant owners—then to the contestants: a few bartenders, some professionals, one stay-at-home mom—who have each created a signature cocktail. I'll try them all and fill out a scorecard as I do.

"Have fun!" One of the men hands me a stack of scorecards and sends me on my way.

I notice that the stack is thicker than I expected. How many mixed drinks are at this event?

"They don't recommend more than a few sips at each station," Steph says. "We're not trying to get drunk here."

"Definitely not." Although. . .would that help me cope with my racing heart and unwanted mental conflict?

I walk up to the first station and find a tall, fancy glass with bright green liquid inside. I smile at the bartender standing behind the table and "cheer" my drink to him. I turn around and search the room for Max, but come up empty.

"He went to check your coat," Steph says.

"What?" I toss a quick look over my shoulder, then back to the crowd. "I wasn't looking for Max."

"Uh-huh," she says.

"Max is bad for me," I say. "I've told you a million times."

Bad, bad, bad.

"Oh, yeah, it's terrible to have a sweet, charming, wonderful guy look at you like you hung the moon."

"Oh, stop it. He does not."

She pulls out her phone and navigates to the video from the night before. She taps play and holds it up without looking at me.

I see her point—he *does* look at me like I hung the moon.

"Pffth. That's all pretend." I say this with a dismissive flick of my wrist, taking a small drink of the first cocktail.

This isn't pretend for me, Marin.

I choke a little as Max's words echo in my head.

I shake the thought away and notice the sweet taste of apple hitting my tongue. "Ooh, tangy." I didn't expect the cocktail to be sweet or. . .delicious. But it is. It makes me feel warm on the inside. "This is really good."

I take another sip, and then another, and then I see Max coming toward us, and I panic and polish off the rest of the drink.

Steph takes the glass away from me. "Smooth."

"Sorry, it was good." I look away. "And I panicked."

Max strolls up. I'm not sure how, but his eyes are brighter. His muscles are tighter. His teeth are whiter.

He nods at the empty glass. "How was that?"

I take out the scorecard and give the green drink top marks. "Super great." Then I start off in the direction of the next station.

Behind me, I hear Steph say, "Will you keep an eye on her?"

I spin around and face them. "I don't need to be watched, Steph. I'm not a child. I'm a strong, independent woman." I look at Max. "And I'm doing just fine on my own, *thankyouverymuch.*"

Max and Steph exchange a glance, and then he asks, as if I'm not standing right there, "Did she have more than one cocktail?"

Steph shakes her head.

I roll my eyes and walk away.

The next cocktail is coffee flavored. I smell it, and my face, I'm sure, gives away how I feel about it.

Max grimaces. "No peppermint creamer, huh?"

I take a drink, hold the liquid in my mouth for a few seconds, then spit it right back into the cup.

Max takes it and sets it on the tray of a passing waiter while I fill out the scorecard. (Low marks.)

The third drink is a fizzy cranberry something-or-other. I take a small sip—and then another. And then another. "This one's good. Not as good as the first one, but it's good."

"Scorecard?" Max holds it up between two fingers, but I shake my head.

"Just a couple more sips."

"Pace yourself, slugger."

After a few more drinks, the nervous humming in my belly begins to dissipate, and a peaceful calm slides in, like an ocean wave washing over a sandcastle.

By the seventh cocktail, I'm feeling *much* looser and less anxious.

To my dismay, Max only gets more attractive as the night goes on, and considering where he started the night (at least a twelve), that's a remarkable feat.

I stroll up to the eighth cocktail station and find a bright red drink with a wedge of lime and salt on the rim of the glass. "What's this?"

The pretty brunette behind the table smiles. "A Christmas

margarita." She looks straight past me at Max. "Would you like to try it too?"

He holds up a hand. "I'm driving."

The woman flashes a different smile—a *well, aren't you gorgeous* smile. "Shame."

I wrap a possessive hand around Max's arm and pull him away from the table, giving that drink the lowest marks possible without even tasting it.

"What's wrong, McGrath?" he asks. "You jealous?"

"Ha! You wish!"

I reach the table with the ninth cocktail, and my head starts to feel light and a little bit woozy. Steph appears, phone poised to take video, and she motions for Max and me to play the part.

I shrug into the space under his arm, draping it around my shoulder, then smile at Steph.

"We need to do a full intro, Marin. You up for that?"

"Course!"

"She's had a lot to drink," Max says. "She doesn't understand the meaning of the words 'pace yourself.'"

"I'm fine," I say, talking to the Max in the middle of the three Max's. "I hardly feel it."

Max looks skeptical, but Steph shrugs, and counts me down, giving me a nod to let me know we're live.

I try to flip the switch, but I miss completely.

It's like when you're walking out of the bathroom and your arm moves up to hit the light switch on your way out but you miss and your body keeps walking and your arm desperately wants to turn the light off so your hand keeps swiping and missing until finally, you grab the door jamb to stop you from leaving the room.

Am I rambling? Oh well, time to go live.

"Good evening!" Well, that was louder than I'd intended. I

point a finger at the camera, mentally working overtime to focus. "We're live at the PV Brewhouse, where I am judging my very first —" I sweep the room with a dramatic arm— "Christail contest! So far tonight, I've sampled—" I hold up five fingers "eight different cocktails, some *super* good and some *super* gross. For instance, the first one I had was a sweet green apple that looked like something from Ghostbusters, but the second one was disgusting."

I lean in to the camera, as if we're old friends, and I'm telling a punchline to a story. "Then one of them I didn't even taste because the bartender lady looked at Max like—" I lift my hand to my mouth and whisper loudly— "*she wanted to tear his clothes off.*"

I give Max a once-over. "Not that I can blame her." I laugh and hit him on the arm. "He is quite the attractive man, don't you think?"

He laughs, a bit uncomfortably it seems. "Marin, uh. . .thanks for the compliment, but—"

"Oh, he's just being modest. I think he knows how *beautiful* he is." I look at him again. "But then he's also nice. Like, a genuinely *nice* person. I mean, he set up this whole foundation here in Pleasant Valley instead of keeping all that money for himself, and who really does that? Max Weber, that's who." I sigh. "But when he looks at you like you're the only person in the room—woo-eee—that does a number on a girl."

"So, Marin's not a drinker," Max says to the camera.

"Says you! I'm quite capable, and now *you're* the one who's fumbling for the words." I poke a finger in his chest. "*The foot's on the other shoe now, isn't it, mister!?*"

Max squeezes my shoulder. "Why don't we come back after the winner of the contest has been selected?"

I pick up a yellow drink from the tray of a passing waiter. "That's fine. I'll be back later!"

Max stares straight into the camera. "After we get her some coffee."

I take a sip of the yellow drink—it's pineapple with a kick. I follow the waiter and the tray, and walk out of frame as I say, "I like the sweet drinks."

Behind me, over the din of the room, I hear Max say to Steph, "Clearly this was a terrible idea."

Chapter Thirty-Five

Max

Marin is drunk.

Not just a little buzzed, all out drunk. And it's not pretty.

I've been here before. In her shoes. I did my share of "calming my nerves" in the years following my parents' accident.

I can safely say that the best choices are not made in these situations.

I've been following her around all night, steering her away from bumping into things and taking extra drinks out of her hand and putting them back. Now, it's time to go, and I'd like to move quickly before she embarrasses herself. I've noticed that everyone in the room has filmed us—her— at some point.

What kind of footage are we going to see on the internet tomorrow?

"Max! Oh my gosh, we should dance!" She grabs my hand and tries to pull me out onto the dance floor, where very few people are actually dancing.

Thankfully, almost everyone in the room is in a similar state as Marin, and no one seems to notice.

A slow Christmas carol comes on, and Marin presses her body against me. I can feel her shape against me, and it's killing me to keep my distance.

She wraps her arms up around my neck and looks at me, her eyes wide, expectant. Beautiful.

Yeah, I want her. Everything inside me wants her. How can I not?

This kind of attention is exactly what I want from her. But not like this.

She leans in and kisses my neck. "You smell *so good.* Just like you always do. You smell like Max."

"Marin, we should probably get you home." I step back, but she's still clinging to me.

"Good idea," she says. "Let's go home. *There are no people there.*" She steps back, wobbles a little, and I slip an arm around her to try and steady her.

She laughs. "Just like the lake!" She turns toward me. "You're always saving me, Max."

"Oookay, let's go get your coat."

We walk past the margarita station, and Marin stops and looks at the woman behind the table. "He's going home *with me,* lady."

The woman's eyes widen, and I give Marin a tug to my other side. "Sorry."

"Don't apologize to her," Marin scolds me. Then, hisses "*Homewrecker*" at her.

"Marin, we're not even together," I say.

She stops and looks at me. "We should be."

I know we should. But tomorrow, will she say something different? "We can talk about it tomorrow."

"That," she steadies herself again, "my good man, is a plan."

We get our coats and I lead her out to the car, expecting her to fall asleep on the drive home.

But then my phone rings, instantly connecting to the car's Bluetooth. I can see from the name on the display that it's Lydia. And I know if I don't answer, she'll keep calling.

"Hey, Lydia..."

"Oh, Max, hi, are you with Marin? I tried calling, but she didn't answer."

Marin leans over and shouts at the radio, even though that's not how it works. "Hey Mom!"

"Yes, I am," I say. "We're just heading home. The event was...interesting."

"She drank too much, didn't she?"

I look at Marin, whose entire face is pressed up against the window. "It's cold. I like cold. Cold face."

"You could say that," I say.

I look again and Marin is now fogging up the window with her breath and drawing a heart in the condensation.

"Well, I trust you'll get her home safe," Lydia says, but doesn't wait for me to respond. "We're going to spend the night in the city. Teddy's flight is delayed till morning, and it just doesn't make sense to drive back and forth two more times. The gas will cost us more than the hotel."

"Not the hotel I got," James says. "We've got a night on the town—we deserve to live it up."

Lydia laughs. "Will you two be okay?"

"We're great, Mom!" Marin says. "Max and I aren't a couple so no hanky!"

She pauses, furrowed brow. Then, her face lights up in a eureka moment, adding, "and no panky!"

"I'm sorry, Max," Lydia says. "If I'd known..."

"It's okay," I tell her. "I'll take care of her."

"I know you will, hon. We'll talk to you tomorrow."

"Sounds good, have a great night," I say.

"And leave room for Jesus!" Marin shouts as I end the call.

Once we're back at her house, I help her out of the car, aware that she is leaning almost her full weight on me. It would probably be easier to pick her up, but she insists on walking.

Until she trips up the stairs.

She lands in a heap on the top step, and lays down flat on the porch. It's pretty obvious she has no intention of going any further. "Just leave me here."

"Can't do that," I say. "You'll freeze. Come on." I reach down and pick her up, throwing her over my shoulder like a ragdoll.

"Max! I'm upside down!" she shouts.

"It's a good thing you don't have neighbors," I tell her as I open the door and set her down in the entryway.

"You were my neighbor." She wraps her arms up around my neck. "And then you were my friend. And then. . ." She looks up at me, her eyes wide, and even though I know she has no idea what she's saying right now, a part of me wants to hear the rest.

And yes, I know that's pathetic.

"Then you were the boy I loved." She pulls her hand away. "The boy I still love."

The words aren't true, and I know it. She's drunk. She needs sleep. I help her out of her coat, shrug off mine, then pick her up and toss her back over my shoulder. She lets out a squeal like we're playing a game, and when she's upside down, she sticks both of her hands in my back pockets.

"This is firm," she giggles.

I open the door to Marin's room and set her down on the bed. She falls over instantly and says, "My bed!" She draws in a deep breath. "It smells like you. It's supposed to smell like vanilla." Her eyes flutter open. "But you smell good so it's okay."

"All right, you can't sleep in that." This is going to be a problem. "We probably need to get you into some pajamas. Can you handle that? If I go get them for you?"

She appears to be slowly making snow angels on the bed. "Mmm-hmm."

I don't believe her.

I head off to find her pajamas. I know she hangs them up in the bathroom, so they're easy to locate—a pink My Little Pony T-shirt and leggings. Believe me, I've noticed the way she looks in them.

I return with the pajamas and find her sprawled out on the bed. "Mare, I've got your pajamas. Can you put them on? I'll step outside."

She laughs. "Okay."

"Seriously, Marin."

She sits up and looks at me. "I thought you said you liked me."

"I do like you."

She pulls me down next to her so we're both sitting on the end of the bed. She looks at me, wavering eyes trying to focus. "I know it's the alcohol talking. I know it."

"It is, Marin, you don't have to—"

"But it's just taking away my filter. My walls. My. . ." she looks as if she's trying to think of the perfect word. ". . .walls."

I have been where she is, and I know that truth spills out more easily when your brain is saddled with appletinis.

It *is* the alcohol talking, but it might actually be how she's really feeling.

"I don't know how to feel about you." She touches my cheek. "I thought I was over you."

I brush her hair away from her face. "Yeah. I know. I thought I was over you too."

We face each other, and I want this moment to be real. I want that more than anything, but I know it isn't.

She won't even remember this in the morning.

"I don't know what I'm supposed to do with you, Max." She lets out a groan and flops back on the bed. "You come in here with your muscles and your sweatpants and your eyes. Who has eyes like that? They're not blue. They're not gray. They pierce me right here—" She puts a hand over her heart. "And you say the things. All the things. How am I supposed to resist you when you say things like you do?" She looks away. "But you broke my heart."

"I know, Mare," I whisper. "I'm sorry."

"I know you are." She sits back up, with a little bit of effort. "I wonder if we can ever get us back."

We sit there as the seconds tick by, just looking at each other, and I don't have a single doubt in my mind that I would do anything for this woman.

She stands, moves directly in front of me, occupying the space between my knees. She presses in closer, taking my hands and putting them around her waist.

"Marin—"

She silences me with a kiss. It's looser and more open, and I can taste the drinks she's had tonight.

I won't lie, it's a kiss I've craved, and it's a kiss I don't want to stop. Her long, blond waves fall over me, and it's amazing and wonderful and completely wrong.

I pull back. "Marin."

She looks at me. "Max—?" There's a question in her voice.

I don't want to hurt her. Again.

"Isn't this what you want?" She is breathing faster than normal.

I study her beautiful eyes, and I can feel my face tighten. "Not like this."

Her expression changes. She looks down, then back at me, and I see a wave of embarrassment wash over her face. "I'm sorry, I thought..." she's practically on top of me, and struggles to stand, stumbling a little as she does. "I thought this was what —" I reach out to steady her but she yanks her arm away. "I got it."

I know this reaction too. Emotions run hot when mixed with alcohol—what you feel is the utmost of that feeling.

"You should sleep." I push myself up, stand, and look at her.

I can see the hurt in her eyes. "I remember how this feels," she whispers, with an edge. "To be rejected by Max Weber."

And there it is. There are some moments, the morning after, that cut through the drunken fog like a knife. I pray this moment isn't the one she remembers.

"No, Marin—that's not—"

"Goodnight, Max."

She turns slowly. She takes a step, stops, sticks her arms out to balance herself, then leaves the room and shuts the door behind her.

Another decision I've made hurts her, but I did it for us— and I *know* it's the right one.

Chapter Thirty-Six

Marin

My eyes creak open as the sunlight pours in the windows in my old bedroom.

Wait. I'm in my old bedroom.

Panic.

I gasp and sit straight up in bed. I whip off the covers and breathe a sigh of relief when I discover I'm fully clothed.

I press my eyes shut and open them wide again, foggy from sleep.

I have no idea how I got here.

I scan the room, and there, in the armchair in the corner, sound asleep—is Max.

His head is tilted back, and I fear he's going to have a wicked sore throat, but he's there, I assume, for me.

The events of the previous night are hazy, and I remember all over again, this is why I don't drink.

I slowly lay back down, close my eyes, and work to remember what happened. A green drink. A flirty brunette. Max helping me home. Carrying me up the stairs. Me kissing Max.

My eyes pop open.

Me, kissing Max, as if he's an oasis in the desert.

And Max, stopping me.

I pull the covers up over my head. This is the most humiliating thing that's ever happened.

My phone buzzes with a text from Steph.

I pick it up and look at it with some effort—my eyes haven't gotten the memo that I'm awake.

S.O.S.!!!!

Now what? I click the power button to shut the screen off and lay back down, head spinning, still holding the phone.

It buzzes in my hand again. I peer at it through one open eye.

Go look at Sophie Soto's post from today.

It can't be anything worse than what's been posted about Max and me.

Three dots, then another message pops up on the screen.

How did she find out you and Max weren't for real?

It takes a second, but only a second, for this to register.

My stomach drops.

I sit up and navigate to the show's social media where I find a video of Sophie, dueting the video Steph posted of Max and me at the chili cook-off.

The captions scroll by, underscored by the kind of music you'd hear on a criminal investigation Netflix series.

"Marin McGrath has been playacting in Pleasant Valley!"

Oh no.

"An anonymous source tipped us off. . ."

Anonymous source? Who in the world—

"Marin and ex-boyfriend Max Weber are *not* a couple. . .THEY JUST PLAY ONE ON TV!"

I click the phone off, hold it in both hands, and press it to my forehead—which is pounding like a storm. Tears spring to my eyes as my thoughts swim.

I focus, tap my phone back to life and text Steph:

So, what now?

Damage control?
You and Max are going to have to look more couple-y than ever.

Or we could just tell the truth.

And have the internet call you a liar?
The internet is good for some things, but it's great at ruining someone's career.

I shake my head. *What was I thinking?*

"Morning, lightweight."

Max. I had forgotten he was there.

I toss my phone aside and fling my feet over the edge of my bed.

"Wait. What's wrong?" he asks.

The concern in his voice, after everything I've done, unravels me.

I open my mouth to unload everything, the post, last night, how sorry I am, the way I really feel—but I stop.

"Nothing," I say, rubbing my head. I stand, head currently on the spin cycle. I make my way into the bathroom, where I close the door and turn a circle—an animal trapped in a cage.

I look in the mirror and notice something.

I fling the door back open and look at Max, who hasn't moved. "How did I get in my pajamas?"

He looks away.

"I left this room last night," I say, certain that I did.

"Yes."

"And then. . .?" I struggle to think. It's like trying to finish a puzzle in the dark with gloves on.

"And then you came back for your pajamas," he says. "When you bent over to pick them up, you collapsed on the bed and passed out."

I frowned. "I don't remember that."

"No, I didn't think you would." He stands. "I can go get you some aspirin."

I find his eyes. "I made such a fool of myself. Not just with this whole stupid charade, but last night."

"It's fine, Marin." He crosses the room and stands right in front of me.

My world is crumbling, and I want to find a way to make it his fault when I know, without any doubt, that this whole mess is mine to own.

"At the bonfire, you said you weren't going anywhere," I say, forcing myself to get it out—all of the hard, ugly, horrible things I'm thinking.

"I meant it."

"But last night—" my voice catches. "I practically threw myself at you."

"Ah. You do remember *some* things."

"Unfortunately, yes." I cross my arms over my chest, thankful to realize I still have my bra on. Max might've gotten me dressed last night, but he'd been a perfect gentleman when he did it. "I remember you pushed me away."

He steps toward me. "Hardest thing I've done."

I dare to lift my chin and look at him.

"Believe me, the opportunity was right there. I'm a guy. . .but I'm not an idiot." He reaches for my hand. "If anything is going to happen between us, there's no way I'm going to let it be when there's a chance you might not remember it in the morning." He reaches for my hand. "I want you to remember the way I kiss you—"

He leans in and brushes a soft kiss across my cheek. "The way I touch you—" He takes my face in his hands and brushes his thumbs across my cheeks. "The way I convince you what I already know—that we belong together."

I close my eyes, and the room slightly tilts. I must be dreaming. I open my eyes, and there he is, still watching me.

"How do I convince you to give us another chance?"

I press my lips together. Why isn't this easier? Why can't I just say yes? It's not like we can't work things out, we were best friends before we were together.

There's something holding me back, and when I go to speak, I realize what it is.

Pride.

I've been holding out because of my ego.

I'm an awful person, and he deserves better. Everything inside of me is crying out, *Yes! I'm ready!* But the words are locked at the back of my throat.

Max brushes the hair away from my face. "I know it's scary, but this is real, Marin. It's always been real."

My head is spinning faster now—and not, I realize, from the dizzying words Max has said.

The room shifts on its axis, my eyes roll shut, and my stomach lurches.

"Max, I. . ."

"Yes?"

"I think I'm going to be sick."

And then I'm in the bathroom, gripping the sides of the toilet, with Max holding my hair back. My body wracks and clenches as I lose the contents of my stomach.

I can feel Max softly rubbing my back—and I can feel the beads of sweat underneath my shirt starting to form.

"You want me to get the camera?" Max asks, lightening the mood slightly. "Might be good for the socials. . ."

"Please, don't make me lau—" Another bout of nausea washes over me. I rest my head on the toilet bowl. It's cold and offers some temporary relief.

"We'll talk later," Max says, handing me a wet hand towel. "You okay?"

I look up at him like a lost dog and nod, wiping off my mouth and face.

"Let's get you some crackers."

I reach up and he helps me to my feet. I prop myself up with one hand on the sink and brush my teeth, swishing water around in an effort to eliminate the terrible aftertaste. I reach for him again. He wraps his arm around my waist, holding me close, and I stumble into my bedroom. He uses his free hand to pull the covers back, and I crawl in the bed.

I sink into the soft mattress, curl up and embrace the coolness of the pillow case.

He pulls the blankets up to my chin, sits on the edge of the bed, and places a hand on my forehead.

Smiling, he says, "I'd still date ya."

I crack my eyes open and offer a smile. I feel amazingly terrible.

"I'm going to go see if we have any ginger ale and saltines," he says.

I nod, and within minutes, I drift off to sleep.

When I wake up, I have no idea what time it is or which of my memories are a dream.

Did Max tell me we belong together?

Did Sophie Soto out us to the whole world?

Did I dream all of it?

I force myself out of bed like the undead crawling out of a grave and pull on one of Max's hoodies. I inhale it, filling myself with this scent.

This is real, Marin. It's always been real.

I want those words to be true. I want to be with him.

I'm terrified of this revelation, and terrified to give him a part of myself that I've held back all these years.

But everything he's done since I've been back, regardless of my stubbornness—it's all been for me. To help me. To prefer me.

The realization shames me.

I step out of my room into the hallway and follow the sound of voices downstairs. I tiptoe toward the kitchen, hugging the sweatshirt around myself, when a flood of memories rushes back.

How many Christmases did I tear out of bed and into the living room to open presents with my family and Max's family? How many years did his parents shower Teddy and me with gifts while our parents did the same for Max? Our entire lives were all tangled up together, and now that I remembered it all —how could I ever let it go?

In the kitchen I find Max and Teddy sitting at the table, looking like long, lost brothers. They're poring over something on Teddy's computer while my mom stands at the stove and my dad at the griddle.

"Well, look who's finally up!" Mom says. "Rough night?"

"Rough night, rough morning," I say.

Teddy stands. "You look great, Marin." He says sarcastically, walking over and hugging me. "Oof. You smell great, too."

I laugh and push him away. "Leave me alone, Teddy."

278

But I pull him back and hug him again. I tousle his wavy, dark hair, much longer on the top than it used to be. "When was the last time you got a haircut?"

He tugs my hair tie out and throws it across the room, my messy waves falling to my shoulders.

"Marin, are you hungry?" Dad flips a pancake. "These have your name all over them."

I shake my head, stomach cramping. "I don't think I can eat."

"Coffee then?" Dad says.

"I can get it."

"It was so nice of Max to take care of you last night, Marin." Mom has this way of saying things that *sound* like normal conversation, but *really,* she's making a point.

She says this like I haven't said thank you, but as the thought enters my mind, I realize that I haven't.

And I don't, because Steph bursts into the kitchen, in a frenzy.

"Finally!" she says. "We've been waiting for you to wake up."

I do a slow turn. "Where did you come from?"

"She was in your father's office," my mom says. "She needed somewhere to strategize."

I glance at Max. I can't even remember if I told him we've been outed, but I assume Steph filled them all in.

"I think I've got a plan," Steph says, loudly.

I hold up a hand. "You're going to have to bring it down a notch."

I see my mother mouth the word *hangover* while simultaneously cutting a hand across her throat.

Steph sits at the table, next to Max. "I think we have to double down. How do you two feel about a fake engagement?"

At that, Max pushes his chair away from the table. "Yeah,

I'm out. I've got some stuff to do." He exits the kitchen and heads straight for the front door. He shuts it on his way out, and we're all left in a trail of awkward silence.

I want to, but I can't bring myself to follow him. I turn my groggy head to Steph, and I know what I have to do.

"I think it's time to come clean. We need to own this, Steph. We screwed up."

I stop.

"No. Not 'we.' Me. I screwed up. I never should've treated Max like that in the first place. I never should've agreed to play on his feelings. I own this."

"And if it costs you the show?"

I am reticent. "Then it costs me the show. Better that than costing me my relationship with Max—whatever it may be."

Shockingly, my mother doesn't respond to this, but she and my dad exchange a glance, a soft smile and a barely detectible nod.

It's as if they're saying *Finally, she's getting it.*

And I am. Finally. Yes, the job *is* important to me and yes, this new life I've forged *is* important to me. But it's time to face the past. It's time to do the hard thing.

It's time to make it right.

Chapter Thirty-Seven

Marin

Well, I *was* determined to make things right, but it's proved harder than I thought.

It's been days since I've had a real conversation with Max.

If I'm honest, I've been avoiding it. When it comes to a moment where I feel it's right to start, I shut down and change the subject, or avoid him altogether.

I'm embarrassed by so much of my behavior since returning to Pleasant Valley—and really, my behavior since Christmas eight years ago—and feeling vulnerable isn't my favorite thing in the world.

Is it anyone's?

The nail in my own coffin was the world finding out about Max and me.

Ironically, the real joke was on me. We were never fake-anything. He even told me that, multiple times.

He was right there, and my pride wouldn't let me see it.

My video segments as of late have been filled with family traditions and Pleasant Valley events—but not with Max.

The comments have been harsh, but I'm doing my best to weather the storm.

Twice, Steph has tried to convince me to sweet talk Max into fake proposing, but I flat refuse. I'm done pretending, and I'm done using Max.

I know Sophie will likely get the job, and that's fine.

I sit with that thought for a moment. It *is* fine. I'm actually okay with it.

She's good, and she earned it, even if it was a little shady for her to out me the way she did. I was a little shady too, so I suppose we had that in common.

It's the day before the big *Home for the Holidays* show, and I wake up with nerves dancing in my belly that have nothing to do with my job.

I shower and get ready and find Steph sitting in the kitchen on the phone. She hangs up. "You're not out of the running yet, Marin. The big show tomorrow could seal the deal."

I hold up a hand to stop her. "I hope it does, Steph. I hope I get the chance to take over the show and prove to you and Tim and everyone else that I'm good at this. But I'm not going to use my family—or my friends—to do it anymore."

She lets out a heavy sigh and opens her phone back up. "Fine. What's on the agenda for today?"

I've got my back to her, pouring myself a big cup of coffee, and I can't help it—I smile. "Today, I'm taking the day off."

"Marin, the show's tomorrow," she says.

"I know, but I've got something more important to do."

I can feel her frowning. "What could possibly be more important than the promotion of your career?"

Now, I turn. "Every single person living in this house."

I start toward the door, but she follows me. "So, what am I supposed to do today?"

"Take Danny out for coffee. Go see a movie. Visit Santa

downtown. Go shopping at the Twelve Shops of Christmas." I spin around and look at her. "There are so many things to do here in Pleasant Valley, I'm sure you'll find something." I say this last part with all the cheerfulness of a newscaster on the air, grin at her, and head upstairs.

I've got a day off to get ready for.

Max

Another day.

I wonder if Marin will avoid me today, too.

Or maybe I'm avoiding her.

Either way, it's weird with us. Again.

I can't stand the thought of things being this way—awkward and tense and silent. Especially not when I'm more certain than ever that no matter what happens in the future, I want Marin to be there for it.

I've spent the last few days with Teddy, and remembered all over again how much I love that guy. We picked up right where we left off, just like always. He's genuinely excited about the Weber Foundation and especially the community center, and it's nice to have someone to share it all with.

We're at the new building, planning, talking, strategizing—but Marin is always there in the back of my mind.

She should be here for this.

I want her to be a part of it all. I know this entire plan would be so much better with her input, but she's hardly home. She stays out late and leaves early. She's obviously wrapping things up, and I can't blame her.

She heads back to Denver the day after Christmas, and with her she'll take my heart.

I've been making decisions of my own in the meantime, and frankly, I could be way off, but I have to find out. I'll kick myself if I don't.

After a full day at the Foundation and a mediocre pick-up game of basketball followed by a shower at the gym, I get back to the house to find Marin's rented Sentra is not in the driveway.

I'm immediately disappointed.

Time with her is shrinking, and I can't figure out how to connect with her. Have I lost her for real this time? Just when I thought we'd finally had a breakthrough.

I must've scared her off.

Inside, the house is warm and cozy and I start getting that feeling I used to get when it was the Sunday after New Year's before going back to school.

Break is over, the fun is over, no more late nights and late mornings and games and gifts and friends and family. It's time to get back to the grind.

Lydia looks up when I walk in.

"Oh, there you are, Max!" she says. "A package came for you. It's on your bed." She smiles. "James and I are going out tonight, and I think Teddy has plans. Are you okay on your own for dinner?"

"Oh, sure thing," I call out, as I walk up the stairs. "Have a great night!"

"You too, hon." There's a smile in her voice, which I attribute to the fact that she and James probably have scandalous after-dinner plans.

I walk into Marin's old room and see a small box wrapped in brown paper sitting on the bed. There's no postage on it, so it must've been hand-delivered.

I open it to find another, smaller box. And inside, a single glass ornament, a small piece of paper and a Sharpie.

A white tag is attached to the ornament, and on it, the words: *Make a wish?*

I walk over to the window and look out at the lake. It's covered with snow and frozen straight through, but the lights in the trees and on the roof of the boathouse are on.

I take the ornament and head downstairs, noticing that the house is now empty.

I pull on my coat and walk outside, down to the lake, where I see another card tacked onto the door of the boathouse. I pull it off and open it.

It says: *I wish Max would come home for Christmas.*

I frown.

But then a light in the trees catches my eye. The lake is about halfway between Marin's house and my old house. And my old house is lit up like a Christmas tree.

I flip the card over.

First, make your wish.

I take the marker from my pocket and scribble my wish down, then trudge back outside where I stand in the yard, staring out at the house.

The house where I grew up. *My home.*

I get in my car and start the engine, heading down the gravel driveway. When I reach the end, I turn right, and something inside me buzzes. I'm not sure if I'm nervous or anxious or filled with dread.

When I pull into the driveway, I see Marin's car. She's sitting on the porch, wearing her pink coat and a stocking cap and looking as much like home as the house itself.

I get out of the car and walk toward the porch as she stands to her feet.

"Welcome home, Max Weber." Her smile is tentative, and I'm whisked back to the night I let her go. She showed up that night to comfort me, and I pushed her away because I was scared of my own feelings. But I'm done pushing.

If Marin asked what I was thinking, I would tell her. If she wanted inside, I'd fling the door wide open.

I wasn't about to repeat the mistakes of my past.

I look around, and she grabs my hand. "No cameras tonight, Max. It's just you and me."

I feel the grin creep across my face, narrowing my eyes "Are you sure?" I look around quickly. "Steph isn't hiding in the bushes somewhere?"

"I'm sure." She laughs. "Is this okay?" She motions with her head at the bright, colorful lights strung to the edge of the roof. My attention falls to a pastel-colored wreath hanging on the door, also surrounded by lights.

"Is that—?"

"It's your mom's wreath," Marin says. "She was always a fan of non-traditional Christmas decorations."

I laugh. "Yeah, she was. Drove your mom *nuts.*"

"I think your mom was onto something. It's festive and fun. And we could use a little of that in our lives." She takes a step toward the door, but I pause. "Is this okay? We don't have to go inside if it's not."

I look at her. Before, when she asked if I wanted to go inside, the answer was a resounding no. I wasn't ready.

But now, with her standing here beside me, I felt like I could do anything.

Even face the past and everything I'd lost. I suppose I was starting to learn that I still had a whole lot to be thankful for.

Chapter Thirty-Eight

Marin

"I'm ready." Max gives a single nod.

I know it's a risk, bringing him here like this, and if he'd said he didn't want to walk through the door, I would've sat right down on the porch with him and looked at stars until the sun came up. Whatever he wanted to do—I was going to follow his lead.

But he assures me it's okay, and I'm secretly thankful, because I want him to feel the warmth of this home again.

I push the door open, and Max follows me inside.

"I know you feel like you don't really have roots," I say.

"That's true." Max slowly looks around, taking it all in. "I'm a bit of a nomad."

I want this to mean something special to him. I have that nervous *I hope he likes it* feeling you get before a loved one opens a gift.

"I wanted to remind you that you do."

In the corner of the living room is the wonky tree we found at the Christmas tree farm, decorated with the ornaments my mom kept in a box for him, along with strings of popcorn and more colored lights. I tried to make it look as much like one of Jenny's trees as I could.

My parents helped, and I think we mostly got it right.

On the mantle is a whole line of framed photos—his parents, him and his parents, both Max's family and mine, and then, a new one of Max and me.

I watch as he takes it all in. He picks up the new photo. "What's this?"

I smile. "Steph took it. I wanted you to have something new to remember me by when I go back to Denver."

He sets it back down, his smile faltering. Why did I mention Denver? I don't want to think about how I have to leave him again.

He looks around the room. The furniture isn't the same, of course, but I've positioned it in the same places as the sofa and chairs that had been here when we were kids. My mom lent me a few of Jenny's things—an old afghan, a few throw pillows, a stuffed dog she called their "guard dog."

I stifle a laugh looking at that ragged, stuffed dog again, because as kids, Max would hide behind a chair and whip it at Teddy when he came into the room, yelling, "*Guard Dog!!*"

So many good memories here.

Did Max remember?

"You're sure it's okay?" I knew it was a risk putting so much of his parents on display like this. "Not too pushy? I'm not trying to force you to have feelings you don't want to have."

He meets my eyes and nods. "No, it's good. I think it's about time they were a part of my holidays again." He continues to look around, into the connected dining room and at the presents under the tree.

"I found the Lego set you bought for Henry and wrapped that up—" I motion toward the gift. "And I also found the gift cards you got for his mom."

"Snooping, as usual."

I smile—a real one. "Naturally."

"It's amazing, Marin, thank you."

We stand still for a few long seconds, and I know I need to be the one to speak. I have things to say, but they're stuck behind the lump in my throat. At the back of my mind.

But this is why I've brought him here, so I summon the courage and blurt it out before I lose my nerve. "Max, I'm sorry."

He frowns. "For what?"

I stuff my hands in the pockets of my coat. "For the fake relationship. For being so angry. For taking so long to let you back in." I hold his gaze. "For all of it."

"Don't be sorry, Mare." He takes a step toward me. "Just tell me you've come to your senses."

I smile. "You mean, like realized you're the best thing in the world, and you're worth a second chance?"

"Yeah, like that."

I shake my head. "Nope. Haven't come to my senses." I grin at him, but feel myself turn serious almost immediately. "I was so stupid and stubborn." I look away. "I waited for you, you know. I kept thinking maybe our breakup was about your grief, but when you didn't come back, I guess I thought it wasn't about the accident or what you'd lost. It was about you and me. And that's when I started to believe that you really didn't love me after all. That this wasn't just you lashing out. It was the way you honestly felt."

I know I have more to say. It's now or never.

He moves toward me. "I hurt you."

I look up at him. "Max, you were grieving, you had every right—"

"But I hurt you."

"But you apologized." My gaze falls back to the floor. "It was my pride that wouldn't let you back in."

He tucks a finger under my chin and lifts my eyes to his. "We both made mistakes. I pushed you away. I couldn't figure out how to let you in. I gave up on us. But I never stopped loving you, Marin. Not for a day."

Tears cloud my view of him. There's no feeling like shame being forgiven.

He's blurry, which is a shame because he's such a nice view. I close my eyes, and tears stream down my cheeks. He swipes them away gently with his thumb.

He reaches in his pocket and pulls out a small piece of paper, then holds it out to me. "Since you told me yours."

I take it and open it up. "I wish Marin would give us a second chance."

My voice catches as I read it out loud.

He takes my face in his hands. "It's always been you, Marin."

I inch up on my tiptoes as Max draws his face down toward mine. Its familiar and new at the same time, and his kiss melts away any trace of residual pride.

I'm ready to let it all go. I'm ready to try again. I'm ready to make his Christmas wish come true.

He pulls back, as his hands wrap around my waist. "I think this is, without a doubt, the nicest thing anyone has ever done for me."

I press my palms to his chest. "I don't know if you'll live here, but at least for the holidays, I wanted it to feel like home."

"Thank you." He pulls me closer. "It does feel like home. But not just because of the house—because of you. I'm realizing that home, for me, is wherever you are."

I look at him, and the past melts away. Something inside me settles, maybe for the first time in eight years.

I remember the best part and suddenly straighten.

"I know it's not Christmas yet, but—" I walk over to the tree and pick up one of the small, wrapped gifts and hand it to him.

"Well, that's not fair," he says. "I don't have your gift wrapped yet."

"Open it," I say.

He sits on the edge of the couch, and I sit next to him, watching as he tears the paper from the small box. He removes the lid and reveals the crisp, white business cards inside.

"How did you. . .?" He pulls a card from the stack and runs his finger over the raised M + M Creative logo, the same one we came up with all those years ago. He frowns. "You're not quitting your job."

"Heck, no," I say. "I've worked hard to get where I am, I'm not hanging it all up for some guy."

He laughs, and I love hearing the sound.

"But I want to dream big dreams with you, Max. The traveling, the meeting new people, the searching for stories—I want to do it all."

"With me." He says this as if he needs to confirm it.

I nod. "I think we deserve a second chance, don't you?"

He kisses me again, then pulls away and looks at me, a crooked smile playing at the corners of his mouth.

"What?" I ask.

"I was just thinking that Christmas wishes do come true."

I couldn't keep from smiling if I tried. I'm deliriously happy, and I know it's because I'm finally—*finally*—where I belong.

Chapter Thirty-Nine

Marin

We spend the next few hours in Max's house, sharing stories, reminiscing about past Christmases, and laughing—a lot.

It's like all the memories Max had locked in the basement of his mind have been brought out into the open, and he's ready to reminisce.

And it's beautiful. I'm honored to be a part of it.

We order pizza and drink way too much Coke. After we're done eating, we sit on the couch—his arm wrapped around me, my head on his chest—staring at the orange flames as the fire dies out.

It's been so quiet for several minutes, and I assume he's fallen asleep, but then he whispers my name.

"Yeah?"

"What if I move to Denver?"

I smile. "Do you *want* to move to Denver?"

"I want to be wherever you are," he says, squeezing me a bit tighter. "I want to be there to cheer you on. To see you succeed. To make faces off camera when you're on location."

"How thoughtful of you," I say with a smile.

"But really—you were right. You've built this whole, amazing life, and I missed so much of it already." He sighs, and I can feel the rise and fall of his chest. "I just want to be a part of it."

"What about the foundation?" I ask.

"Teddy's going to run it," he says. "We worked out all the details, and your dad's going to help."

"Wait, what? Teddy?" I sit up and look at him. "He's going to move back here?"

He nods. "Guess he figured out what I've known for a while—that this place and these people are special."

I shift my position so I can see his face. "Are you sure you want to leave here?"

"Are you going to be here?"

I shake my head.

"Then I'm sure."

I kiss him. It feels good. It feels right. He shifts forward and kisses me back, and it stirs all of the feelings I've been avoiding. I don't want to hold back any part of myself from Max.

The kiss is simultaneously long and way too short.

I pull away, a new question on my mind. "What about your house?"

Max smiles. "I have an idea about that. Will you help me?"

"Of course. What is it?"

He stands and holds his hand out to me. When I take it, he pulls me up and presses a sweet kiss to my forehead. "I can't believe I'm going to say this, but I think it should be the grand finale for your show."

"The grand finale? I wasn't going to go all out. I was just going to film from our family Christmas Eve celebration. You know, go traditional."

He scrunches his face. "Boring."

I smirk. "I've subjected you all to enough of the show. It doesn't really matter if I win the competition or not, I just want to let the chips fall or whatever."

"That doesn't sound like the Marin McGrath I know and love."

I start to respond, and then his words register. "Wait. Did you just say you love me?"

"Never stopped." He takes my hand. "We've got some storyboarding to do."

I follow him, but the words have stuck on repeat in my mind. *Max loves me.*

The dining room table becomes our makeshift work area, and together, we plot out what has to be the most brilliant idea for an eight-minute *Home for the Holidays* segment I've ever seen. All thanks to Max.

Our creative energy is firing off of each other as we craft a perfect story—not for the sake of our audience, but for the sake of some special people right here in Pleasant Valley.

We kick around shot ideas, cutaways, and framing, and I write a loose script. By the time we're done, we're both exhausted and spent, but energized at the same time.

We collapse on the couch and I drift off to sleep leaning on him, his arm around me. Safe. Calm. Familiar.

The next thing I know, it's morning, and the smell of coffee wakes me up. When I finally open my eyes, I find Max standing in the dining room, cup in hand, looking over the shot list we came up with the night before.

In the silence only a perfect morning could offer, I take a moment to admire him—this good, kind, wonderful man who was always, always, supposed to be my person.

I stand and make my way to his side, slipping my arms around his torso as I try to see what he's seeing written on the scratch paper spread out across the table.

"Does it make sense in the light of day?" I ask.

"It's perfect," he says. "It's better than anything I could've come up with on my own. We're a good team."

"We are." I smile up at him. "We should get going—we have a lot to do to make this happen."

He points to the coffee. "Waiting on you, McGrath."

We pack up our things. I call Steph and fill her in while Max shares the plan with my parents and Teddy. We make a few calls, invite a few people, and the pieces begin to fall into place.

For the first time since I've been home, this feels more than just my job. I don't even care if I get the promotion anymore—I really don't—and I have a chance to do something meaningful here. To share some Christmas magic.

And I'm going to relish every single second of it.

As we're loading things up into the car, I stop.

This is what I've been missing.

Heart.

My stories have been missing *heart*.

And it's time to make it right.

When evening rolls around, we're ready to go. My parents have brought a whole spread of our favorite Christmas dishes, desserts, and cookies, over to Max's house, which looks like Christmas perfection.

Teddy shows up with a woman I don't recognize—leave it to my brother to have a first date on Christmas Eve. My parents have invited a few close friends, and Max invited Henry and Joy and Henry's little sister, Ruby, so now all of the key people that would be running the foundation, or working at the foundation, were here.

As people mingle, Steph finds her way over to me. "Look at this place! Look at the faces of these people—you two really are an excellent team, you know?"

I scan the crowd until I find Max. He's standing with Joy and Teddy and my dad, and when he notices me watching him, he smiles.

"Yeah. We are."

"Are you ready for this?" Steph asks.

"Ready as I'll ever be," I say.

"Great, because we're on in five." Steph rushes off to get everyone in their spots, and I get mic'd up. I sit on a tall stool near the Christmas tree and pull a small stack of notecards from my pocket.

I've written out a whole script, in case words fail me, and as I glance over it all, my heart squeezes with the knowledge that I get to be a part of something really, really special.

I scan the room and the squeeze grows tighter. This is my home. These are my people. This is exactly what Christmas is supposed to be, and I vow to never miss a Christmas here again.

My eyes well with fresh tears, and I blink them away. I can't cry now—I'll ruin my makeup.

As if sensing I need a distraction, Max appears at my side. "You're not getting sappy on me now, are you?"

I laugh. "It's just so good to be home."

He points toward the camera. "Share that with your audience. They deserve to see what I see."

"It's time!" Steph calls out.

My stomach turns a nervous somersault, and I remind myself that I can do this.

The room goes quiet as Danny switches on the light above his camera, and everyone turns their attention toward me.

I don't flip a switch. No more pretend, no more masks. No more presentation, no more fake smiles.

And for the first time I think ever, my shoulders relax when I hear Roger back in Denver, setting up the scene. I get the nod. We're live.

"Merry Christmas from Pleasant Valley, Illinois, where I am situated in a very special place with some very special people. It's a beautifully decorated house, and I'm with my friends and family—I've missed them a lot, and I'm just really, *really* happy to be home."

I look at Max. He gives me a thumbs-up.

"You've all come with me on this journey home for the holidays, and tonight, we get to celebrate with a little extra Christmas magic of our own."

I glance down at my notecards. I know what I'm supposed to say. Max and I agreed to gloss over our fake romance—it didn't matter what the world thought of us. But as I watch the blinking red light on Danny's camera, I'm not so sure.

Steph's eyes widen, but I ignore her and tuck the notecards back in my pocket.

"I think it's time for me to speak from the heart," I say. "I came here after being away for too many years. There were memories I was afraid to remember and people here I'd tried to forget. But being home has made me realize what a huge mistake it was to keep myself from the people I love the most. And staying angry all this time really only hurt me."

I look at the people in the room, all watching me intently. I see pride in my parents' eyes, confusion in Teddy's, and admiration in Max's.

I want to take it all in. I never want to forget a single moment of it.

"You all took great interest in my relationship with Max, and I used our history to try and make my time here at home more interesting. It was wrong, and I'm sorry. To all of you, but most of all, to Max."

He gives me a soft smile.

"But a funny thing happened in all that pretending," I say. "I realized that I am still very much in love with that man, and while I won't be broadcasting our relationship anymore, I'm thrilled that he's willing to give us a second chance." I draw in a breath. "We're standing here in his childhood home, surrounded by the most wonderful memories made by the very best people, and I want to invite Max out now to chat a little about this place and what it means to him."

Max steps into the frame and kisses me on the cheek. It's a *you're doing great* kiss, and it's all I need to keep going.

I ask Max about the house, about the pastel colored lights, the dodgy tree. I ask why this house is so special and how he feels being back here after all this time.

And he answers every single question honestly.

"It's not easy for you to talk about this, is it?" I ask him with a soft smile.

"No, but I want to remember them," he says. "They deserve to be remembered."

"So, a lot of people might think you're going to move back in here," I say. "You own this house, after all."

"True, but I have plans to relocate to Denver," Max says with a grin. "There's a girl that I'm crazy about, and she lives there."

I resist the urge to kiss him right there on television, but I have big plans for when we stop filming. I smile at him. "So, what about this house?"

"It's a special place, and it deserves to be full of special people," Max says. "I met someone recently who gave me an idea." He looks over at Henry. "Henry, can you come over here for a second?"

Henry thinks for about half a second then vaults himself onto Max's lap and waves at the camera.

"Buddy, you were *born* to be on camera."

He's still waving. "My friends are going to *freak out* when they see this!"

We laugh, and Max asks him, "Hey, Henry, do you remember talking to Santa about your mom?"

"Yep."

"And how you wish she had a job and a house so that you didn't have to move?"

"Yep."

"Well, Santa and I talked about that."

"You *did*?" Henry's eyes widen.

"Yep. He and I were thinking that maybe you might want to live here?"

"By myself?" Henry asks, face scrunched.

Max laughs. "No, buddy. With your mom and your sister."

Joy gasps, covering her mouth with her hand. Ruby clings to her mother's side.

"This house is *pretty* special. I had lots of amazing Christmases in it. Santa told me that you and your mom and Ruby needed your own rooms. So. . .what do you think?"

Henry looks at his mom, expectantly bouncing on Max's lap.

Joy buries her face in her hands, and cries. Max stands and walks over to the little family, drawing them all together in a hug.

"Why would you do this for us?" Joy's voice breaks.

"Because everyone deserves a second chance," Max says.

They embrace, and Henry tears out of the room and runs up the stairs shouting, "I get a new room!" and then after a few thumps and thuds, he shouts from upstairs, "Can I have this one?"

Danny holds the shot on Max, Joy, and Ruby for several seconds, and then Steph motions to me to close it out.

"Friends, I've learned a lot being home for the holidays. I've let go of a few grudges. I've opened my heart up for the first time in a long time. And I've been reminded that Christmas magic is ours to make. And I want to make a lot of it. I hope this Christmas that you do too." I smile at the camera. "This is Marin McGrath, signing off and saying Merry Christmas to all of you."

I hold my pose until Steph gives me a thumbs-up. "Clear!"

I eye her for a few long seconds. "Steph, are you. . .?"

She turns away and shakes her head, but I can tell she's trying to discreetly wipe her cheeks dry. "Where's the eggnog?" She walks off toward the kitchen.

Huh. So, the Grinch *does* have a heart.

Max gives Joy and her kids a tour of the house, sharing all of our old memories as he does. It feels nice to relive them, to share them. We eat. We laugh. We open presents. And my heart basks in the glow of the Christmas magic.

As the evening winds down, I stand off to the side, taking in the scene in front of me. I'm overcome with gratitude that I am here in this place with these people.

"What are you thinking?" Max is at my side.

"You did a good thing," I say.

"*We* did a good thing." He turns toward me.

"Thank you for letting me be a part of it," I say.

"I want you to be a part of all of it from here on out, Marin," he tells me.

I grin. "Oh, all right, if you insist."

"Hey!" Henry points at us. "Mistletoe!"

Max and I both look up, and sure enough, there's a small cluster of mistletoe hanging from the doorway overhead.

"Did you stand here on purpose?" Max asks with a grin.

I shrug. "I might've."

"I was hoping you'd say that."

"Are you going to kiss her?" Henry whispers loudly, cupping his mouth with both hands.

Max kisses me softly, sweetly, and with the promise of many more kisses to come.

"Ew." I hear Henry say, taking off down the hallway.

When Max pulls away, I don't open my eyes right away. Instead, I mark the moment in my mind because I never want to forget how it feels to be in his arms.

Like I was born to fit in this exact space. It just took me a little while to get back here.

Max leans closer and whispers, "Merry Christmas, Marin."

"Merry Christmas, Max." I kiss him again through a smile I can't keep away. "Is this the part where we live happily ever after?"

"I think it is." Another kiss. "For as long we both shall live."

Epilogue

Close-up on Sophie Soto:

"What started out as a romance for ratings has turned into a real-life relationship for *Good Day Denver* host, Marin McGrath and her childhood sweetheart, Max Weber."

The camera pans back out, taking in the screen showing clips from the *Home for the Holidays* finale over Sophie's right shoulder.

"Weber, creative business owner and President of The Weber Foundation, relocated to Denver after his childhood sweetheart and high school girlfriend convinced him to take part in a little charade to earn her extra views from fans."

Cutaway close-up on Max:

"I don't know about Marin, but for me, there was never anything fake about my flirtation with her. I'd always regretted letting her go."

Close-up on Sophie:

"So, she was the 'one that got away.'"

Close-up on Max:

"Yep, she was. I'm just glad I got to catch her again."

B-Roll of M + M Creative, Max & Marin walking by a row of taco trucks, and Max behind the camera.

"Often seen out and about in the mile-high city, M + M, as their fans call them, have begun to make their mark as two of Colorado's most promising young professionals. The company they founded, M + M Creative, is a documentary film company they always dreamed of starting, before life took them in opposite directions. Their goal? To make the world a little smaller, one story at a time."

Close-up on Marin:

"We always said we'd travel the world, listening to people, looking for stories, so we figured now was as good a time as any. After all, dreams are meant to be chased."

Close-up on Sophie:

"But you've got your own television show now, so how do you balance the two things?"

Close-up on Marin, who smiles:

"I have a great co-host and a lot of vacation days."

Close-up on Sophie:

"It's a story of second chances, starting over, and chasing your dreams. And it's one we can all be inspired by."

B-roll of Max and Marin, gazing longingly at each other. Max makes a face and Marin laughs.

Sophie, voiceover:

"And let's not forget, it's a story of fake romances, first loves, and Christmas wishes that really do come true. For *Good Day Denver*, I'm Sophie Soto, wishing you and my co-host, Marin McGrath, a very Merry Christmas."

THE END

A Note From the Author

Dear Reader,

Something happened to me over the past couple of years.

I started to realize the importance of joy. I suppose I've always known that happiness is important, but I guess I finally realized it was okay to love the things I love. Even if they seem frivolous.

For instance, light, fun, uplifting romance novels set at Christmas.

I've always loved Christmas. As the daughter of The actual Queen of Christmas, how could I not? So, I shouldn't be surprised that writing sweet Christmas romance stories has been nothing but pure joy.

I especially loved being able to share some of my favorite holiday traditions with you, the same way Marin does in this book. Many of these traditions come from my own life—my grandpa's hand carved Santas, the Christmas Stroll, the Christmas-themed 5K that my boys run every year, the ornaments that all tell a story of their own. . .

Thank you for letting me share these traditions and this

story with you. I know you have many reading options, so the fact that you've chosen to read *Merry Ex-Mas* is truly a gift, and I am grateful. **You** have made my holidays so much sweeter, and my hope is that Marin & Max's story does the same for you.

As always, I LOVE to connect with my readers, so I invite you to find and follow me through my newsletter, on social media or in my Facebook Reader Room. I would absolutely love to see you there!

Drop me a line anytime—I love making new friends.

Courtney Walsh

courtney@courtneywalshwrites.com

Acknowledgments

Adam—For all the things. I love dreaming big with you. What else can I say...you're my favorite.

Me + You.

Mom & Dad—Thank you for always leaving room for Jesus... at least when I was around.

Sophia—Thank you for reading this book even though "it's not really your thing." And for turning out to be one of my best friends.

Ethan—Thank you for always reminding me that my phone camera is dirty. And for being a genuinely good human. I see so much good in you.

Sam—Thank you for making me laugh. And for being one of the most authentic souls I know.

Becky Wade & Katie Ganshert—Thank you for being a constant source of inspiration, wisdom and humor. I would be lost without you guys.

Melissa Tagg—Thank you for sharing this wild two-career life with me. And for the long conversations about all the things. I'm so grateful for you.

Our Studio Kids & Families—Do you have any idea how special you are? You make my "day job" nothing but pure joy. I'm so thankful for each one of you!

About the Author

Courtney Walsh is the Carol award-winning author of seventeen novels and two novellas. Her debut novel, *A Sweethaven Summer*, was a *New York Times* and *USA Today* e-book best-seller and a Carol Award finalist in the debut author category. In addition, she has written two craft books and several full-length musicals. Courtney lives with her husband and three children in Illinois, where she co-owns a performing arts studio and youth theatre with her business partner and best friend—her husband.

Visit her online at www.courtneywalshwrites.com

Made in the USA
Middletown, DE
05 November 2022

14217140R00179